The Rape of Paul Stark

To order additional copies, please contact us.
BookSurge, LLC
www.booksurge.com
1-866-308-6235
orders@booksurge.com

HOLLY
ASHTON

THE RAPE
OF PAUL STARK

A NOVEL

BookSurge, LLC
2004

The Rape of Paul Stark

A novel about greed, pollution, organized crime, rape, and a hero, Paul Stark.

Paul Stark petitions the government to stop the rampant pollution that is threatening his livelihood. What begins as an attempt to preserve the waters he loves turns into a desperate battle to stay alive. Bonaparte, home of Paul, lies nestled beside the vast, untamed beauty of salt marshes and the uninhabited islands struggling to emerge as solid ground. New Orleans, only ninety miles north, is a world away. The quiet and easy life of Bonaparte changes one night in April, as fear and murder rip through her very heart.

ACKNOWLEDGEMENTS

EARLE ASHTON
Thank you for your never-ending love and support.

MILLARD WILSON
Thank you for your unwavering confidence.

MAGGIE GAMBLE
Thank you for your encouragement.

JEAN MULLER
Thank you for giving so freely, all of the above.

Dedicated
To
Jack Hice

PROLOGUE

On the road map, Highway 90 hangs like a sagging grapevine between Lafayette and New Orleans.

From either end, it dangles crookedly southward, through the bayou parishes of Louisiana and traversing a region of sugarcane fields and small towns. Near the bottom of the sag, the highway reaches a saltwater river and follows its north bank for a mile through the township of Bonaparte. A grass median divides the east-west lane. Three lights control the flow of River Street traffic.

The business section lies on the north side of the street, and a row of antiquated brick and frame buildings are separated from the highway by a sidewalk. The most imposing building is the Bonaparte National Bank. Behind these establishments is a scattering of shabby houses. This residential area is served by a crosshatch of streets, paved and unpaved. Homes sitting farther off the road are larger than the rest, and have well-maintained exteriors with fenced lawns.

South, across the river, lies a vast expanse of salt marsh that stretches like a green plain to the horizon. This area is veined with tidal streams and pockmarked with small islands overgrown with scrub vegetation.

Until numerous wells were punched through its muck to the crude oil below, the watery moors south of Bonaparte were the exclusive habitats of birds and small animals. The estuarine plain was also a prolific spawning ground for large mouth bass, snapper, and shellfish.

A quarter mile past the eastern edge of town, an isolated box-like building fronts the river at a point where highway and stream part company. From either end of the building, like out-stretched arms embracing the river, are weathered docks supported on barnacle-encrusted pilings.

Shrimp boats working the Gulf of Mexico once brought their catches to be unloaded here. During most of the year, two or more trawlers were tied up at the dock. The building sags where its supports have settled deeper into the unstable soil. The outer walls are covered with heavy boards, battened at the joints. Faded yellow paint is still imbedded in the wood grain, giving a soft patina to the weathered sheen of the old building.

On the highway side is a parking area, its surface made from oyster shells. A roadbed of the same material extends to River Street through a hundred yards of marsh. This narrow access is wide enough for one vehicle. Just east of the access, River Street loses its identity in the continuation of Highway 90, stretching like an arrow along the first two miles toward Beaver City.

A sign in the marsh identifies the building as the home of Bonaparte Seafoods - Wholesale Only.

On Friday, April thirteenth, at 2:40 in the morning, a ball of flame swept up from Bonaparte, gushing bright orange in the night sky and followed by a mighty thunderclap. Dwellings behind River Street were buffeted by shock waves, as windows were blown in and plaster shards fell from ceilings.

A dog bayed, as if hit by a car; a baby began screaming. People sat upright in their beds muttering questions and windows flared into rectangles of light. Soon, hastily clothed Bonaparte residents were on porches and in yards, turning sleep-dazed faces toward the red glow pulsing above the stores on River Street. They watched open-mouthed as flames rolled up, inside mushrooming pillars of black smoke. They called out to one another in voices edged with fear. A siren came to life, honking coarse glissandos and building to ear-splitting shrieks. The sound blasted across the dark fields like some huge animal in mortal pain. This official trumpet of disaster summoned people to look toward the bloody sky, their faces working with fearful expectancy. Boys darted past those closer to the fire, ignoring the shrill cries of their elders.

Pouring out from the spaces between store buildings, the townspeople huddled together in groups and moved toward the fire. They formed circles around scattered parts of a human body, staring in horror as each grisly mass was discovered and probed with flashlight beams.

"No need to call the ambulance for that," a man was saying to those crowding closest. A boy pushed a stick at a bloody leg and a woman jerked him back. "Don't touch it!" she screamed, slapping his face. This caused a ripple of panic until explanations were passed along.

Later, someone would say that the human chunks were still quivering; implying that sudden disintegration had not released all life at the moment of death. Others would try to describe the severed parts and many stocked their recollections with such details. The night would be described for those who had not been there and whose secondhand information might be flawed. " I c'n tell exactly what took place. I was about the first one there, after she blowed sky high!"

Within the hour, dawn having sent purple fingers of light over the flat landscape, the townspeople knew what happened, knew the exact reasons for the pre-dawn fire and explosions. While the fire was still smoldering, information had been passed along and digested. Conclusions were reached. It was clear to everyone that murder had happened. All possibilities of accident were ruled out. Bonaparte had been given a warning.

CHAPTER 1

It was a Sunday afternoon, the first day of April, when Paul Stark hauled the last drag of his fishing trip aboard his shrimp trawler, the *Helen S.*

He studied the slimy opalescent mass on the afterdeck. A small shark, slithering free of jellyfish and seaweed, tried to swim across the deck. Crabs sought cover in broken shells. Throughout the pile were globs of brownish gook. Tentacles of the stuff hung from the suspended net. The odor was unpleasant.

The catch was worthless.

Paul felt defeated. It had been the same with dozens of other net loads pulled up from the fouled water. He knew the brown slime had floated on the surface before settling into the plankton life of the water.

Once more, he would return to port empty-handed.

The Gulf's surface was smooth. Small ground swells moved past, causing the vessel's bowsprit to dip gracefully. Massed clouds hung in a cerulean sky, casting shadows on the water. He knew his helper, Catfish, was watching him, waiting for a sign. Paul moved his head slowly from side to side and turned his palms up. The wrinkled deckhand, his face the color of birch stain, looked at the catch and shook his head.

They probed the pile with paddles, spreading the mound as they followed each other in squatting circles around the catch. Catfish held up a shrimp by its threadlike feelers. Paul nodded and Catfish pitched it into the wire basket. When the men finished their inspection, they stood and stretched. Paul handed Catfish a shovel and the little man attacked the pile with quick stabs, flinging the bottom trash overboard. Gulls flew over the settling residue, snatching at the morsels. When their scant meal was over, they hovered and berated the men.

Paul took the single shrimp and threw it high in the air. A dozen gulls wheeled, diving for the prize. One bird flew away with the shrimp crosswise in its beak, the others in flashing pursuit. The shrimp was dropped and the noisy formation dived into the water. A gull with black-tipped wings rose with the shrimp half swallowed and darted away. The rest followed briefly, shrieking at having been cheated.

Paul watched the victor skimming the swells. He lingered a moment longer, studying a heavy cloud buildup. Catfish came to the rail and shook his small fist at the water.

Paul laughed. "Give 'em hell, old man."

Catfish grinned, showing toothless gums. Paul handed him the hose and turned on the seawater pump. A stream foamed across the deck plates and water gushed through the scuppers. Catfish gripped the nozzle like the head of a muscular snake, aiming it where Paul pointed. When the deck was clean, Paul secured the hose and lashed the otter trawl boards to the stay of the starboard mast. A light breeze was pushing up small corrugations on the water as Paul set the trawler on a course for home.

In the wheelhouse, he arranged his tall frame on the high stool used when the vessel was running on automatic pilot. He could no longer put off thinking about affairs on land. Again, he was returning empty-handed, with his ice unused and no shrimp in the holds.

Paul's face was etched with lines of despair. The stoop of his shoulders reflected how discouraged he had become.

Gulls were patrolling alongside. They took turns winging ahead and settling gracefully on the water, where they waited for the trawler to catch up. Paul watched their flawless movements and his spirits lifted. The gulls were old friends.

His thoughts turned to Rita.

She had known he was older when, six months earlier in Baton Rouge, she had felt his muscles and spoke of her low regard for men under thirty. With her breasts firm against him, Paul Stark had spoken of old adventures and new dreams. That first meeting had been at a difficult time in his life, when photographs of him were on the front pages of all the newspapers. He was mentally weary from hours of testimony before the legislative committee. Rita was so young, so fresh, so vibrantly full of life and promise that he had fallen in love during their first hours together. After only a few days they were married and on the way to Bonaparte.

She had been visibly disappointed with the house. It was a small frame dwelling, located some distance from the main settlement and connected to River Street by a dusty lane. After only the first week, she had told him she hated the town. He suspected she also hated the house.

Paul had taken her to the shrimp dock. "Where are the other boats, Paul? Out fishing?"

"Most of them are in Key West or Texas."

Her brunette beauty had sparkled in her smile. "How many shrimp boats do we own, all told?"

He was surprised by her question. "Rita, we have only one trawler. This one. *The Helen S.*"

There was sudden bewilderment on her face. "But Paul, Danny said you had a fleet of big fancy shrimp boats and dozens of boat captains working for you."

"My God, Rita, Danny Lapere was kidding. He's the biggest joker in the Fish and Game Commission." She turned and walked to the end of Lou Fisher's dock. When he tried to get her aboard the trawler, she came closer, looked, then shrugged. "I'm ready to go home now!"

Six months later she still hadn't set foot on the boat. Once, during those first weeks, he had asked her to make a trip with him. He was certain she would understand him and his work if she could just experience the world of the balmy sea and clear blue sky. "The weather's good, Rita. We'll only stay out one night. I know you'll like it."

She had looked at him with that calm, stubborn expression he had grown to know so well. "I wouldn't be caught dead on that smelly boat! And if you think I'd go with that nutty old dummy grinning at me, then you're crazy, too!"

He had tried to explain about his deckhand. "Catfish is as harmless as a baby. He's deaf, and can't speak, but that does not make him crazy. He's a good deckhand. Okay, I won't take him. I won't fish. We'll make it a honeymoon cruise." She was composed and beautiful, as her eyes searched his face. "I've a better idea. Sell the dumb shrimp boat and move us to New Orleans."

The words were a slap in his face. "What the hell do you think I'd do in New Orleans?"

"You could try making some money for a change. You could be home with me at night, instead of being gone on that damn boat of yours." After that, she withdrew into her own private world.

Each trip, Paul hoped to make more than expenses, but could not.

The one time Rita showed surprise and delight was when the red convertible turned up on her birthday. But then she lapsed back into a quiet rejection of everything connected with her husband, Bonaparte, or the waterfront.

Rising above the horizon were the offshore oil well platforms. They grew from the water like skyscraper skeletons. Between the boat and the first platform were discolorations, glinting blue and reddish purple on the water. Paul studied the stains with binoculars. The oil covered a wide area. Globs of sludge floated in the swells and he saw lifeless birds in the slick. He guessed the spill would go ashore around Cameron. The gulls wheeled and headed back toward Mexico.

When the coast was a smudge between sea and sky, Paul changed the heading on the pilot and went into the galley. A gas stove, stainless sink, and a small refrigerator were on the port side of the deckhouse. Across the aisle were four wide bunks, two below and two above, with brown blankets pulled tight around the mattresses. He struck a match and lit the stove. Through the rear door of the deckhouse he could see the denim-clad legs of Catfish stretched out on the sun-warmed afterdeck. Small feet were laced in clean white tennis shoes. The old man would be quietly asleep. For a moment, Paul envied him.

The smell of food awakened Catfish and they ate on the forward deck. The trawler was fast approaching the beacon at Point au Far Island. Late afternoon clouds were massing in front of the sun as the *Helen S.* crossed the bay and entered the wide mouth of the Bonaparte River. Toward Texas, a rain shower veiled the sky beneath a small thundercloud. Paul spun the wheel to hold to the twisting channel. The smooth water came at him, rising as a silver sheet. The bow cut into the sheet, lifting small furrows, which coiled away to both banks, sucking and slapping at the grass and washing up the muddy slopes.

He listened to the gentle sound of water swishing off the broad hull as it pushed against the outgoing tide. The boat always seemed much larger inside the marsh which, except during a hurricane, was a haven where a boat had only the wind to fight. He always enjoyed the passage through the grass, whatever the season.

Three miles out, Paul reached Beau's Island, the only landfall between Bonaparte and the bay. A line of ancient live oaks fronted on the river, while a thick stand of palmetto grew further back. Generations of fishermen and picnickers had come to this beautiful and secluded little paradise. That is, until the oil people arrived with a lease from a New York bank. They promptly ended the island's wonderful isolation by building a four-mile road from Highway 90 to the island, and then they barricaded the road with a high fence and a strong gate. The dock was built, but not until threatening signs had been nailed to trees and along the dock. For a generation now, the marsh island had been withdrawn from any use associated with pleasure.

When the oil wells were installed, the crews and their barges vanished, leaving the island once more to the wash of the river tides and the rhythm of the seasons. Wild things returned and new growth covered the scars where bulldozers had tramped down trees and scraped out sandy clearings. Vines climbed over the piles of rusting junk and, after a few years, the dock began to sag from neglect. Beau's Island remained a very special place to Paul.

In past years he had hoped to buy the island and build a house near the dock. On many a windy day or stormy night he had swung at anchor in the river, hearing the cries of wild birds and the sound of the sea wind in the trees. These experiences had touched something deep inside him and made him one with the sea.

As the trawler neared Beau's Island dock, he saw a woman lying between the live oaks. She seemed to be sleeping, but he could see no one else on the bluff. Instinctively, he sounded the air horn as he slowed the vessel, swinging in closer. He saw that the figure was that of a girl or young woman. She did not move, as he studied her through his binoculars.

CHAPTER 2

A few stars were faintly visible as Rita turned her red convertible onto River Street and drove slowly past Bonaparte Seafoods. The *Helen S.* had not yet come in!

A light on the dock made a corona of yellowish illumination against the blackness of the river. She strained her eyes toward the Gulf, looking along the blue velvet under-edge of the sky, but there was no glimmer of light to be seen.

She decided that Paul was staying out yet another night. Nearing Beaver City, she turned the open car into the neon glare of Bob's Drive-In. The place was jammed with Sunday night customers. A car backed out from one of the covered spaces and she drove into the brightly lit parking slot.

No one would ever guess she had already turned thirty-one, she thought. She was dressed like a sexy teenager, in her tight yellow sweater and suede miniskirt. A filmy white scarf captured her silky brown hair. High-heeled white boots were contoured to her shapely calves. Rita put a cigarette into a long gold holder and casually looked around.

The driver in a sedan on her right was staring, his mouth open, a half eaten hamburger poised in front of his pimply face. Another youth in the back seat was craning his neck, trying to see more of her legs. She challenged them with her eyes; their stares wavered and fell. Rita's gold lighter ignited her long slender cigarette. Her breast rose as she deeply inhaled the smoke. She exhaled and sensuously relaxed her breast, feeling the hostility of the girls in the sedan. The night was getting off to a good start.

A moon-faced carhop was at her elbow, her jaws busy with gum. She was plump all over, dressed in a cowgirl outfit displaying a catsup stain on the fringed tan skirt.

The girl said nothing, looking at Rita blankly, with her pencil and order pad held ready.

"What do you have, Miss?" asked Rita.

"Burgers. Fries. Shakes."

Rita tapped her chin with a manicured finger. "Let me think. Perhaps I'll have a chicken salad sandwich. Plain."

The moon-faced girl seemed startled. "Huh? No ma'am. Just burgers. Barbecue. Stuff like that."

"Then I'll have potato chips and a cup of tea, thank you. Lemon. No sugar."

Rita was hungry. What she really wanted was a double hamburger, French fries and chocolate malt. However, she could sip the tea and toy with the chips like an elegant lady. People were bound to notice.

The carhop finished writing. "That all, ma'am? Bob's got a special on fried pies. Two for a quarter."

Rita shook her head. *Really!*

Country music was pouring from outdoor speakers and she listened with detached amusement to nasal laments of rejected love and other whining ballads of misfortune.

"Well... well...well! Hell-o there!"

Rita had glimpsed him coming from the men's room fumbling with his pants. It was the meat counter man at the Bonaparte super market. A short, hairy individual she knew as Joe. In the bright neon, he looked different. She had never seen him without his bloodstained apron. She presented her hand and he grabbed it eagerly.

"Good evening, Mr. —?" She spoke with a low, throaty voice.

"Joe, Joe Riley. At the Mammoth Market."

"Ah, yes, of course. How are you, Mr. Riley?"

"Call me Joe." He was moving his hand over her arm as if he were stoking a cat. "I'm fine, Miss Rita. I never saw you here before. Cap'n Paul out there fishing?"

She watched from the corner of her eye as his close-set eyes took in her breasts and exposed thighs. As he leaned closer, she exhaled her moist breath into his face, enjoying his sudden confusion.

"I got a friend I'd like you to meet."

"It would be a pleasure," she murmured.

He gave her hand a quick squeeze and hurried off into the shadows at the back fence. The carhop plopped a tray on her door. Joe returned with a tall man who, Rita saw, wore a sardonic look. "I'd like you to meet my wife's cousin," mumbled Joe.

"Baker," said the tall man. "Troy Baker from Chicago."

She held out her hand. "I'm Rita Stark, Mr. Baker."

"Pleased to meet you, Rita Stark." He was looking her over with easy assurance. "Where you from, Rita?"

She knew his question was intended as a compliment. "I'm a Southerner, Mr. Baker." She was proud of her genuine accent.

"Go on, I'm listening."

She rewarded him with a modest frown, then a quick laugh. "There's not much to tell. I was born on a plantation near Lafayette; I went to school in Natchez."

She had been to Natchez, wandering alone among the aristocratic homes while her weekend companion, a talent scout, slept off too much Friday night bourbon. "Most of my career has been in the South."

He clutched her hand excitedly. "I knew you the minute I laid eyes on you! No, don't tell me—I've seen you in pictures!"

She smiled broadly. "That's very sweet of you, Mr. Baker. I'm actually a dancer. My acting has been limited to minor and supporting roles. My big break hasn't happened yet."

He leaned over her, lowering his voice under the country and western music. "Look, kid, I'm not staying with Joe. I'm at the Holiday Lodge, here in Beaver City."

She pretended not to hear. She withdrew her hand from his and selected a potato chip. Troy was just another dumb hick after all.

"Rita, I'm in show business myself," he said. "Not as an actor though. I happen to own a piece of *Customer's Choice.* You know what a big hit that is this season. Hell, I could talk show biz for hours, all night even." He regained her hand, whispering, "Maybe we can get together for a little drink somewhere."

Her eyes were laughing at him. She bit into a potato chip, showing white, even teeth. A horn was blowing at the back wall. Joe pulled at Troy. "Better be getting back to the car, Troy."

Troy was still whispering. "Got it, beautiful? Troy Baker. Room two-twelve. I'll dump Joe."

The horn continued to blow as Joe dragged his wife's cousin away from the red convertible.

She saw them drive out the exit driveway. The woman between the two men was big and ugly. Rita wished she had some way to let the woman know she wouldn't be caught dead with Joe or Troy. Two drinks of cheap booze and Troy would be talking show business all right. Like show me what's under the mini and I'll give you the business! She knew the type. Paul might have his faults, but being a hamburger joint Romeo was not one of them!

Her tea was cold.

She backed her car out from the space just as the carhop appeared and grabbed the tray.

CHAPTER 3

Paul cupped his hand beside his mouth and called. "Hey! You there on the island!" No answer!

As he docked the trawler at the Beau's Island dock, the figure up on the bluff remained motionless. She was dressed in a white skirt and tan sweater, and she was lying on her side with her back toward the river, her face cradled in the crook of one arm. Blonde hair splashed against the gray moss under the trees. She appeared to be about Rita's size, maybe smaller. He could see no evidence of other people, no signs of a picnic, but a car could be hidden in the trees.

In a moment he was bending over the young woman, touching her shoulder. "Wake up! This is no place to sleep after dark."

He dropped to one knee and put his thumb on her wrist. The pulse seemed regular. She was breathing. He saw no outward signs of physical violence. At least she was alive. Carefully he straightened out her legs and turned her on her back. "My God! Mary Beth! Wake up! It's Paul Stark."

Her shoulders shook momentarily and a low moan escaped her parted lips. The odor of whiskey was strong! Relief flooded over him. Mary Beth Claiborne was obviously drunk and passed out. But why here on Beau's Island? Why all alone?

She had easily been the most attractive and popular girl in Bonaparte before going off to an Eastern school. She kept her sailboat at Lou Fisher's packinghouse. For more than a year it had been stored at the fish house, suspended from the rafters, its yellow hull covered with plastic and its aluminum mast wrapped with the blue sails.

Paul walked quickly around the clearing and found an empty whisky bottle. He peered down the road that led to the marsh causeway. No car was hidden among the shadows of the moss-hung trees. Unless Mary Beth had been put ashore from a boat, she must have walked to the island. Paul rubbed his head, trying to come up with answers.

He walked back to the unconscious girl, bent over her, and gathered her up in his arms. She was limp and unresponsive.

"Let's go for a little boat ride, Mary Beth."

He carried her toward the boat, stepping carefully on the good planks of the dock. He knew something was wrong. Mary Beth would be about twenty now, he guessed. He remembered her as being bright and happy, and an expert young sailboat handler. She had written articles for the high school paper about Lou Fisher and the *Helen S.* Then she left Bonaparte after high school graduation and went to some college in New England. Her father, Henry Claiborne, had arranged with Lou to store the sailboat. Now here she was, from out of nowhere, dead drunk on Beau's Island.

Catfish was on deck hopping from one foot to the other, not knowing what was expected of him. Paul sat on the forward rail and swung his legs over. He eased his feet to the deck and carried Mary Beth into the deckhouse, bending to deposit her in the lower bunk. He pulled the mattress from the top bunk and spread it out on the forward deck, arranging a pillow at one end. Then he picked up the girl and stretched her out on the makeshift bed.

"Fresh air and black coffee for you, young lady," Paul said to her.

Back in the deckhouse, he poured a mug of coffee and grabbed a blanket from the bottom bunk, which he spread over her. The boat's diesel was running and the trawler was standing out in the current, hanging from a piling by its bowline. Night was settling over the marsh as Paul slipped an arm under her shoulders and raised her to the coffee mug. Her head rolled against his chest.

"Drink this, Mary Beth," he commanded. She moved slightly and he managed to put the mug to her lips. She choked on the coffee and moaned. "Drink it all," he said.

A few minutes later, after the mug was empty, she opened her eyes and looked at Paul. There was no recognition in them. "Where am I?"

"You're on board the *Helen S.*"

"Captain Stark?" she asked, and then said, "I don't feel so good, I'm going to be sick."

Paul lifted her and held her over the railing. When she stopped retching, he put her back on the mattress and brought a damp cloth from the galley. Sitting on the deck next to her, he wiped her face. When he turned on the deck light, he saw that she was pale and unresponsive. He pulled the blanket up to her chin and she seemed to settle into the mattress. "We'll be at the dock in less than thirty minutes. Then you can sleep in your own bed."

"No! I'm not going home!" She struggled to her elbow and put out her hand. "I don't want to go home, Captain Stark, please. I can't go back there." Her voice had risen and she was looking wildly around at the marsh and the island.

Paul could not mistake the fear and panic he heard in her voice. "You've had too much to drink," he said gently. "What you need is a good night's sleep. Your daddy's probably worried sick by now. We can call him on the radio, or phone him as soon as we get to Mr. Fisher's dock."

Mary Beth sat up and there were tears on her face. "I'll never go back there. I never want to see that mean bastard again!" She grabbed her stomach and he helped her back to the rail. The whiskey came up in retching spasms and poured from her into the river. Her shoulders felt thin to him and she seemed frail and weak.

Several minutes later, she apologized for being sick on the boat. She stretched out onto the temporary bed and Paul returned to the wheelhouse, where he nosed the bow up to the dock piling. He saw Mary Beth race to the railing and grabbed her just as she was going over the side.

"Let me go!" she begged. " I said I wasn't going back! I meant it!" She sobbed as she beat her fists against his chest.

"Calm down, you'll feel differently in the morning."

"Please, just put me back on the island and mind your own business."

"It's going to rain and a storm's coming up," he told her. "Besides, you've had too much to drink and you're acting like a crazy kid."

She looked at him, her face a mask of grief. She struggled to get the words out. "Captain Stark, if you leave this dock with me on your boat I'll jump off. I'll hide in the marsh and you or no one else will ever find me."

"Suppose we sit down and try some more black coffee." He led her to the mattress and sat down on the deck. "You won't be leaving until we've had a spot of coffee, now will you?"

His humor was lost on her. "I guess not. Not if you'll promise not to leave right away."

"I promise. Now stay put." He returned in a moment with mugs and she drank a few swallows. "How did you get here on the island in the first place?"

"I drove a friend's car to the gate. The lock was rusted. I couldn't get it loose."

"So you left the car at the gate and walked all the way out here, just to get drunk?"

"Cap'n Stark, I just want to die. Now. Tonight. Will you please just leave me alone?"

He decided she was dramatizing for his benefit. "When I was younger and had too much to drink, I wanted to sing and dance. Except when one of my love affairs blew up. A couple of times I wanted to kill myself, but I sobered up in time. A week from now you'll be laughing at all this."

" I wish my problem was as simple as being dumped, or even being pregnant."

He felt annoyance rising in him. Her father was president of the bank that held the mortgage on his boat. Four payments were already past due. "I know what your trouble is, Mary Beth. You're acting like a spoiled brat who wants some new toy and will pull some crazy stunt like this to get it. You're too smart for this kind of kid stuff, so cut it out!"

He didn't know what else to say.

She was crying quietly as she leaned forward, making sniffing sounds and clasping her hands together. "I'm not the same Mary Beth you and Mr. Fisher knew. I'm a twenty-one year old lousy addict and I can't help myself."

"Dope *and* booze?"

"I didn't want to feel anything when I got in the water, and all I could get my hands on was a bottle of bourbon."

"You need to get home and to a doctor."

"Home! This morning, when I asked daddy to help me get a fix, he began to shout and told me I was scum, that I was nothing more than an embarrassment to him."

Paul could believe her. Henry Claiborne was, in Paul's judgment, a real prick on all counts. The bank was his mistress. He had shown no emotion at his wife's funeral, and had acted as if he wanted to be finished with the public spectacle and get back to his desk. When Mary Beth graduated at the head of her senior class, his face had shown no pride, just impatience. Years ago, Paul had dismissed the banker as a juiceless, sour, and irreversible sonofabitch.

"I heard you were doing real well at school," he told her. "What are you doing back here?"

"They threw me out after I started putting out for fixes."

"Who got you started on drugs?"

"One of my professors. I was in love with him. I thought he was going to get a divorce and marry me. Instead, he got fired. I don't know where he is now." Her words were spaced with sobs. "I came back here to get the money my mother left me."

"You told your daddy about all this?"

"No, but he had a letter from the Dean of Women."

Paul could imagine the girl's homecoming. "He may be mad now, but I know he'll help you, once he cools down."

"He wants me out of his life and away from Bonaparte forever," she said. "Like in some insane place, or somewhere. That's like being in hell without being dead."

Paul got to his feet and secured a stern line to the dock, and then he shut down the engine. Rain clouds were pressing in from the southwest and the wind was rising. When he returned to the forward deck, the girl was holding her arms around her knees and looking toward the marsh. Under the deck light her blonde hair swept back from her face like a golden cape.

Lightning began to streak the smoke-colored sky.

"When did you eat last?" Paul asked.

"I'm not hungry," she said. "I feel awful. I need a drink!"

"Hot soup will do the trick. He helped her stand and then picked up the mattress and pillow. "It'll be pouring in a few minutes."

With the blanket around her shoulders, the girl followed him into the deckhouse, obediently sitting on the bunk while he busied himself in the galley. Paul turned on the lights and she saw Catfish squatting in a corner, a grin on his brown face.

Paul closed all the doors as a quick hail of rain pattered on the vessel. There was a lull, more rain, and then another few minutes when only a few drops were heard. After that the rain became a hard downpour, drumming against the boat and streaming down the windows of the wheelhouse. The wind gusted, tugging at the trawler. The dock responded to the surge of the heavy vessel and began creaking. Rain-dimmed lighting glowed in the darkened wheelhouse and played like blue fire in the round ports of the deckhouse.

"Here, drink this." He handed Mary Beth the soup.

Without looking up, she cupped her hands around the warm bowl and raised it to her lips. Her hands trembled.

The rain continued to beat down and Paul scrambled eggs and cooked slices of ham. While bread was toasting, he opened a can of peaches. Mary Beth shook her head when he offered her a plate, so he passed it to Catfish, who took it eagerly. Paul filled another plate, placed it on the counter, and prepared his own. He ate, leaning against the sink. When her bowl was empty, he took it from her and handed her the plate from the counter. She began to nibble at the food.

CHAPTER 4

After leaving the drive-in, Rita sent the red car hurtling along the dark highway. She leaned over the wheel so the air blast would miss her hair.

Distant lightning sparked inside threatening clouds. She knew the rain was approaching and she drove faster. Rain would force her to stop long enough to raise the convertible's top.

A strong wind was blowing in from the sea, whipping the trees along the roadside. Shards of Spanish moss pointed at her, waving madly, reaching out like ghostly fingers from the swaying trees. The night was filled with menace, electric with sudden light and darkness, and she was frightened.

"Damn this place!" She muttered between her teeth. The air had become damp and chilled.

As she neared the shrimp docks, a band of lightning lit the fish house. The *Helen* was still not there and she wondered if it had been caught outside. Not likely, she thought. Not Paul Stark. He was too smart to be offshore when a storm came along. She would be alone another night! Crazy damn fisherman!

Rita braked at the last moment and turned onto the dirt road leading to the house. Just as she drove into the carport, the first drops of rain arrived. She laughed, glad to have outwitted the weather for once, raised the top and locked the car. Let it pour, she thought. Inside the house, she went from room to room, turning on lights. The ride in the open car had left her shivering, so she switched on the bathroom heater.

Later, she would take a nice bubble bath.

"Hungry, cold, and lonely as hell," she complained out loud, as she turned on a stove burner in the kitchen. She would make her own damn burger and fries!

Rita still disliked the house, especially when Paul wasn't there. She hated the thought of doing nothing but getting old within the neat confines of the fence outside, imprisoned by these yellow clapboard walls.

The place still seemed temporary and she could not get interested in redecorating it. She wondered about Paul's first wife. Other than the fact that Helen Stark had died six years earlier, he had never said what she looked like, or how long they were married, or anything about their life together. A careful search of the house had not turned up any old letters or photographs. Rita often thought about Helen Stark when she was alone, which was often!

Probably died of boredom, Rita surmised, as she molded ground meat and dropped the patty into a frying pan. She washed and dried her hands at the sink and put on a pot of water to boil.

One day, she would catch up with Danny Lapere and give him a piece of her mind! Except that Danny might tell Paul she had been a stripper.

There was loud knocking at the front door and she was suddenly afraid again. Who would come this time of night? And why? The kitchen clock showed ten past ten. The knocking started again and a high-pitched voice called above the noise of the rain.

"Rita! Rita, it's us!"

The voice sounded vaguely familiar.

She turned off the stove and went down the hallway to the front door. "Who is it?" she called.

"Joe and Troy. Our car broke down. We need to call a tow truck."

She reluctantly unlocked the door and they crowded past her into the hallway. Both were soaking wet.

Joe was mopping his face and neck with a handkerchief. "We're just off the highway. We tried to make it back to Potter's gas station, but she was conking out on us. So we turned into your lane."

Troy's face was streaked with water. "Joe was taking me back to the Holiday Lodge."

Both reeked of liquor. She looked them over. "The phones in there, in the dining room."

They looked at her and then through the front door. Sheets of water cascaded from the front porch roof. Thunder banged and rumbled after flashes of lightning. She reached past them and closed the door. *Goddamn Joe Riley!* Why had he brought his wife's cousin to her unimpressive house? Troy Baker was a small-timer, but at least he had tried to make a date. It made her feel good to be asked, even though she wouldn't have him off a Christmas tree.

"Joe, why don't you phone while I wait here?" said Troy.

Joe sniffed. "I smell meat cooking. We ain't interrupting your eating, or anything?"

"It's warmer in the kitchen," she said.

Joe went into the dining room and they heard him dialing.

Troy found the frying pan with the partly cooked meat and attempted to turn the burner back on. "Miss Rita, don't pay us no mind. You just go right ahead on with your supper. We ate at the Drive-In." He seemed to be enjoying some private joke as he took off his wet jacket and arranged it on the back of a chair. Rita saw the shoulders of the jacket were very padded. He was a tall man, with a thin face and bushy eyebrows below sandy hair. He wasn't the sort you would look at twice.

She put cups on the table. "You better have some hot coffee before you go back out there." She wondered if this would be any better than spending the evening alone. Probably not!

Troy produced a bottle from his jacket and poised it over a cup. "Say when . . ."

"I don't drink, Mr. Baker. I never acquired the taste."

He filled two cups half full. Joe came in the kitchen in time to see Troy gulp down the whiskey. Then Joe turned up his cup and drank, coughing as he wiped his lips with the back of his hand.

Troy was smacking his lips. "Beats being out there in the rain." He picked up the bottle again. "Just a short one Rita?"

"No thank you."

She felt at a disadvantage. Obviously, Joe had told Troy she was married to a shrimp fisherman and lived in this unimpressive house. It wouldn't do any good to put airs on now. She wanted them to go so she could eat and take her bath.

"I think the rain's about stopped," she said, hoping they would take the hint.

Troy held up his cup. "I'll have some of that coffee now. Joe, you better go check on the storm."

But Joe held out his cup. When it was full, he sat at the table.

Troy took a taste and made a face. "God, you sure make it so it scalds a man's tonsils!" Joe laughed, cradling his cup in both hands. Rita replaced the pot on the burner.

"It's too hot for you, too," Troy said to Joe. "Better look around outside."

Joe put his cup on the table and stared at Troy. When Troy handed him the almost empty whiskey bottle, he left the room. A moment later, Rita heard the front door slam. "Maybe the truck's come," she suggested.

"Joe's gone back to the car." Troy leaned back in the chair, stretching. Then he yawned. "Come right down to it, I'd do the same for him, if it wasn't on a night like this."

Rita was becoming angry. Troy Baker was about ready to make himself a fool. Men tried to get away with murder after they had a few drinks. She motioned toward the hallway. "You better get going now; you couldn't get any wetter than you already are."

Instead of getting up, Troy pushed his legs further under the table and locked his hands behind his head. "Rita, baby, look at me. Take a good look. You seen me before tonight."

She looked, moving closer, and beginning to shake her head. "Maybe I have, but I don't remember having the pleasure. I've met lots of people I didn't recall later. Anyway, you best be leaving before my husband gets home. He was coming up the river when I drove past the shrimp docks."

His cat-like smirk turned into a grin. "God dog it, Rita, I know exactly where Cap'n Paul Stark is this very minute: tied up out there at Beau's Island. Joe and me went out there before we went to Bob's. He sure ain't comin' in tonight."

Rita knew he was lying. Paul wouldn't stop at the island for hell or high water when he was headed in. "You better leave now," she said.

"You ain't heard the rest of it. The Cap'ns got a mattress out on the front deck, and on that mattress is a little yeller-haired cutie. About your size, but younger."

"You're lying!" she hissed at him. "Now take your filthy mouth and get out of here."

"Your old man's found better ass than he's got at home. What disappoints me about you is how you don't remember your old friend Troy Baker."

"I never laid eyes on you until tonight."

"Well, I sure as hell laid eyes on you. And I laid two hundred bucks on the fat man at Frenchy's after I caught your strip act. He said you'd put out after the show was over and for me to give you another fifty after breakfast. He even told me what to order from room service!"

Rita was feeling sick. "I don't know what the hell you're talking about. The only time I was ever in New Orleans was with my husband."

"Bullshit!" he exploded. "I never said Frenchy's was in New Orleans. I'm talking about my two hundred clams and I'm here to collect. And I damn well intend to get it, one way or another."

She began to panic. The fat man had tried to force her into prostitution. Danny Lapere had been another one of the victims. It was after Danny had told her about the fat man that she fled Frenchy's and agreed to go with him to Baton Rouge and put on the show for his club. Stag Night. She had convinced Danny she wasn't a whore. Not even a high priced hooker. The next day, she met Paul.

"Mr. Baker, you have me mixed up with somebody else. That has happened lots of times."

Troy's face was ugly and filled with contempt. "You and him were in the deal together. That night I went back to my hotel and waited. After you didn't show up I went back to Frenchy's. The fat man was closing up. He said your six-foot-three boyfriend took you away on a trip. I said fine, I gotta plane to make anyway. Just give me back my money and I'll be on my way. No hard feelings. Ya' know what he did?"

Troy was her worst nightmare come true. She shook her head.

"He looked at me like I crawled out from under a rock. He said, "what two hundred dollars, Buddy? You must be drunk!" Then I took a swing at him and somebody clipped me from behind. I woke up after daylight in a back alley, lying between some garbage cans. My wallet, my watch, and my ring were gone. I suppose you got the ring."

"I'm very sorry anything like that happened, Mr. Baker. I hope you called the police."

He snarled at her. "I thought of that, I sure as hell did. I could say I paid out two hundred bucks in advance to get laid by some strip-joint whore. But instead of getting a simple piece of ass, I got knocked on my can and rolled for everything I had on me. Bitch, you must be nuts if you think I would ever forget you!"

She was feeling braver. "Okay, Mr. Baker, now I've heard your life history. And I've said I was sorry you had that bad experience with someone in a nightclub, wherever it was. Now you better go on out there with Joe before my husband gets home and gives you some more trouble."

He sprang at her and she jumped back to the stove, grabbing the simmering coffee pot. "Get away from me, Mr. Baker, or my husband will break every bone in your body!"

He was reaching for her as she shrank back between the refrigerator and the wall. She tried to empty the hot coffee on his head and some of it splashed down his cheek.

He screamed and pressed his hand to his face. "You whoring bitch!" He grabbed the empty pot and hurled it behind him. As she raised her arms, he struck out savagely, the flat of his hand catching her on the left breast.

Rita tried to run past him, but he grabbed her hair and dragged her to the linoleum floor. She collapsed under him, his foul breath in her face. Her hand found his face and she raked it with her nails.

He grabbed her wrists and held them, forcing her arms against the floor as he straddled her thighs. "Go ahead! Yell your goddamn head off! Nobody's gonna hear ya!"

Rain was drumming against the house and lightning was being followed by thunderclaps. She began to sob convulsively.

He held her firmly, panting from his exertions. "We'll see how good my memory is! You got a little tattoo on your leg. High up. Looks like a butterfly. If it ain't there, I'll get up right now and leave."

Before she could stop him he jerked up her miniskirt and was twisting around to look. "Sonofabitch! There it is, all right, where I said it was."

She freed one of her wrists and tried to scratch him again, but he slapped her hard on both sides of her face until her ears were ringing. "Please let me up, Mr. Baker," she begged, wondering if he was going to kill her. She closed her eyes and stopped struggling.

"You got my two hundred bucks?" he hissed.

"I don't know," she wailed. "I'll have to look in my purse." She remembered the hundred dollars she had hidden away. Maybe that would satisfy him.

He scrambled to his feet and pulled her to hers, twisting her arm behind her back. "Okay, lying whore, let's find out. Where's your purse?"

"In the bedroom. I'll get it."

"We'll get it!" Still holding her arm, he pushed her down the hallway. "Which room?" he growled twisting her arm until she cried out.

"In here." She knew her mistake the minute she made it. She tried to stay in the hall, but he thrust her ahead. Her large suede shoulder bag was on the bed, where she had put it when she came in. He pulled her down on the bed with him as he reached for the bag. She was on her stomach, his weight against her back.

"You can have the money, Mr. Baker," she managed to gasp. "Whatever's there, and I have a little more hidden in the house. If it isn't two hundred dollars, I'll send you the rest, honest!" She heard him emptying the bag, remembered that there was a five and three one-dollar bills.

"You cheap two-bit whore! You knew all along you didn't even have ten bucks. But I know how to get my money's worth." She tried to scream as he crawled over her, but he put a pillow over her head. She fought to get her breath, convulsed with terror at being smothered. She went limp and his hands released her arms and began pulling at the zipper of her skirt. She turned her head under the pillow and sucked air into her lungs. He gave up on the skirt and started tearing off her panty hose and then her lace thongs.

She was sobbing, but no longer resisting as he lifted her legs and arranged her lengthwise on the bed, still face down. She heard his shoes dropping onto the floor and the rasp of his belt buckle. Then he was astride her hips and forcing a hard erection between her clenched legs.

She tried to crawl out from under him but he struck her on the back of her head. "Lie still. When I finish with you, you'll be glad you were conscious for it."

Then he was turning her over roughly and spreading her legs. She tried to hide her face under the pillow. He thrust at her savagely with his erection. When he put his hands under her buttocks, she began to struggle again. He slapped her hand and grabbed a breast through her sweater. She became limp, pretending to have fainted. He pulled up her knees and shoved them apart; she felt him forcing his way inside her. Moments later, he became frenzied with desire and his hot orgasm boiled deep inside her vagina.

It was over. Rita Stark had been raped. What had never happened in all those years as a stripper finally happened in this God-awful hick town. She cried softly as he sighed and collapsed on top of her.

Rita pushed against his chest. "I can't breathe."

He rolled off, but left his arm across her stomach. Neither of them moved for several minutes, Rita desperately hoping he would leave. Troy finally rose up on one elbow. "Counting the money I had left on me, and the watch, and my ring, you're into me more'n a half grand. You listening, bitch?"

"My husband's going to come in and kill you, like you're some wild animal," she told him. "But first, he'll beat the hell out of you."

His hand found her breast and gripped it. "I said you owe me over five hundred clams. You want me to give the bill to your big-shot shrimp captain?"

He jerked her head up and she saw the red blotch where the hot coffee had splashed. On the other side of his face were red welts where her fingernails had dragged against his pale skin. "I ain't told Joe a damn thing. All I said was you told me at the drive-in to meet you here. He thought you was putting on all that high and mighty act for his benefit."

"You told him those lies about New Orleans!"

"You think I'd own up to Joe about Frenchy's? I wouldn't give that prick cousin-in-law the satisfaction."

"Mr. Baker, Troy, listen to me, you have to believe this. I was a dancer, a good dancer. I never in my life was a prostitute. Stripping pays three times as much as dancing in a stage play. I didn't know what that fat s.o.b. was pulling. When I found out, I left and never went back. That's the God's honest truth."

"Yeah? So we kiss the money so long? Bye-bye, five hundred bucks?" He put his hand over her pubic hair. "Hell no! I want my money's worth." She tried gently to push his hand away. "No Troy, not again, it's the wrong time of the month."

He pushed her legs apart. "You ain't bleeding none, so stop lying."

She was too tired to object as he mounted her again and yanked her yellow sweater off. His hand closed over her breast and she tried to resist, in spite of her weariness. He drew his arm back. "You keep asking for it, Rita. Either we take this nice and friendly like, or you're gonna get it after you're black and blue."

He tore off her bra. "God, what knockers!"

His grip was firm but no longer hurting as he possessed her again.

She became limp and indifferent to him as he bent his head to slobber on her nipples, nor did she react in any way when his erection was stabbing at her crotch. She concentrated on the ceiling as he forced her legs apart and once again pushed his way inside.

Afterwards, without touching her, he rolled onto his back.

She heard the sound of a car stopping out front and then steps on the porch. She tried to pull up the spread but Troy was lying on it.

"Don't get uptight, that's only old Joe coming back."

She tried to slide from the bed. "Don't let him see me like this. Turn off the light, please!"

He held onto her elbow. "Why not? He knows you went for me in a big way."

Joe came into the bedroom and stared at them. She was trying to cover herself as she bit her lip, not looking at Joe.

"You want me to leave and come back later, Troy?"

"Hell no, we're just lying here listening to that storm out there."

"I've been thinking about Rita ever since I seen her at the drive-in. You sure can pick 'em, Troy."

"You better start peeling off them wet clothes Joe."

She whirled on them. "Don't you dare undress in here!"

Troy laughed. "Go on, Joe. Don't pay any attention to her. She's still putting on an act for you."

Joe hesitated, then took off his coat and began to pull his wet sports shirt off over his hairy chest.

"Don't you listen to him, Joe Riley. You get him out of here!" She was crying hysterically, realizing Troy had promised her to Joe.

"Rita, you listen to me. Old Joe here is a good old country boy. He might have one good fuck left. My cousin keeps him plumb wore out." Troy laughed and Joe snickered, a sickly grin beginning to show.

"Joe, Troy raped me! My husband will kill you both when he comes in!" As Joe lowered his trousers, she began cowering on the bed.

"Joe, did you check on the good shrimp captain?"

"Sure did, Troy. His boat's still tied up at Beau's Island. I drove out to Sandy Point and I could see his anchor light. I guess he's still balling that blonde." Joe came closer and stared at Troy. "It looks like your face got caught in the meat grinder!"

Troy slid from the bed and went to the mirror. Joe stood on one foot and slipped one leg of his trousers over a muddy shoe. Troy jerked a thumb toward the bed. "You better get your ass in high gear," he growled. "Unless you want ice cold cunt."

A cold fury gripped Rita as she planned her escape. She was not afraid of Joe Riley, a chunky little butcher who was a whining nobody. She watched him as he sat on the floor and unlaced his wet shoes.

"Troy, I have to go to the bathroom and I can't wait. Please, I'll be back before Joe's ready."

Troy glanced at her and seemed satisfied. "Sure honey, take all the time you need. He ain't going nowheres."

Rita dropped to the floor on her knees, on the far side of the bed. "My bedroom slippers are here somewhere." Her hand slid under the mattress and found the gun Paul left there. She was thankful he had taught her to shoot. Troy had his back to her, watching Joe remove his red and white-striped underwear. "What's that thing, Joe, one of your little breakfast sausages?" He laughed, as Joe's face became a mask of horror.

Troy whirled around just as Rita waved the gun at him. She was crawling on her knees across the bed, "I'm going to kill both of you dirty, you lousy, stinking bastards. I'll get a medal for it!"

Troy turned ashen and he edged along the wall. "Take it easy, Rita. Put that thing down before it hurts somebody. We didn't mean no harm." His voice had risen. "Don't do it, Rita! You don't kill a man over a little pussy."

She turned the gun slightly and squeezed the trigger. The shot blasted in the room and the bullet splintered the baseboard near Joe's feet. He jumped toward Troy, his face working with fear. "Don't kill me Rita! I got all them kids to take care of. I don't know what's going on here." He looked accusingly at his wife's cousin. "Troy said you wanted to pay me back for all that extra meat I been weighing up for you. Nobody said anything about—!"

"About rape?" she supplied. Troy was trying to get between the chest of drawers and the wall. His teeth were chattering from fright.

"On second thought, I won't kill you." She pointed the gun at Joe's groin. "I'll just shoot your balls off."

Joe and Troy both grabbed their genitals and sank to the floor. Troy scrambled under the bed. Joe slid around the room and crawled after Troy.

From a bureau drawer she took out a ballpoint pen and a sheet of paper. She held these under the bed. "Troy, you start writing what I tell you."

"We'll write anything you say," promised Joe. "Just put that damn gun away!"

"Troy, you're going to write how you and Joe broke into my home and raped me. After both of you sign, you can get dressed and take your sorry asses out of my life. If you ever come back here, either one of you, I'll shoot you dead! That's a promise." She was reviving, becoming stronger with each passing minute.

Troy wrote as she dictated. Once he objected, "They could hang us for this. It's like writing my own death warrant."

"Just keep writing, Mr. Troy Sorry-Ass Fucker Baker. Joe, get out from under that bed and put your clothes on."

Joe inched into view and crawled over to the pile of soggy clothes.

"Now you come out, Mr. Show Biz from Chicago." Troy crawled out on his elbows and Rita took the paper and pen from him. "Stand up." She pointed the pistol at his shrunken penis and laughed contemptuously.

When they were dressed, she read the confession, put the paper on the chest of drawers, and made them sign it.

"Tomorrow, this goes in a sealed envelope to my lawyer. If something bad happens, like some dirty-mouth gossip, this goes to the law. Do you hamburger-stand Romeos understand that?"

They nodded as her eyes bored into theirs.

She watched them hurrying through the rain to Joe's car. After they had driven off, she locked the door and returned to the kitchen.

Rita was bruised and weary; she was no longer hungry.

The clock showed a few minutes past midnight. Before she slept, she took that long, hot bath.

CHAPTER 5

The wind blew harder as they ate, whipping sheets of rain against the trawler and roaring through the live oaks on the island bluff.

Paul guessed the direction of the storm's movement. As he had expected, the wind suddenly slackened and backed around to the northwest, putting the dock under the lee of the island.

By low tide, the rain had become a steady downpour, a cloudburst. Thunder muttered occasionally, but it was echoing, more muffled and far off.

In the warm deckhouse, Mary Beth bent over the plate on her lap, the food barely touched. Paul tapped her shoulder and pointed to the plate.

She handed it over without looking up. "I just couldn't eat anything else."

He wanted to argue with her, explain that a full stomach was somehow critical. No wonder she was so thin.

Paul hoped she was getting drowsy. It was obvious that Mary Beth Claiborne needed professional treatment: she seemed beaten by forces beyond her control. He recalled a pretty girl waving to him as she sailed past in the bay or the river. How long ago? It must be less then two years. She had hardly left her childhood, he thought, remembering a pretty teen-age visitor. Lou Fisher had been her dear friend and they would spend hours talking together.

Lou had been a medical student and Paul wanted to call him through the marine operator. Only Lou no longer had a telephone at his place.

"Mary Beth, we'll go and see Mr. Fisher tonight."

"No, I don't want him to see me like this."

"At least you're warm and dry. By now you would've been soaking wet. It's a good thing I happened to come along when I did."

Her face was full of pain. "Everything would be over by now. When

I finished the bottle I was going to walk out on the dock and fall over and sink to the bottom of the river." She began to shiver and harsh lines of pain contorted her features. "Captain Stark, I've got to have a fix. Right now! My insides are burning up. I can't hold out any longer. Please help me. You must have something. Please, please, I'm begging you." Her voice trailed away and she was shaking violently. While he watched, the spasm seemed to pass.

Paul felt trapped, wanting desperately to help, yet not knowing what to do. That she was seriously ill and genuinely suicidal was no longer in doubt. Some positive and immediate action was necessary. He decided to call the Coast Guard and have an ambulance waiting at the dock in Bonaparte.

He put his hand on her shoulder. "Of course I'm going to help you. We'll get Mr. Fisher and we'll go with you to the hospital in Beaver City. They'll know what to do for you there."

Her eyes opened wide as she shrank back in terror. "No! I couldn't go through that again." Tears flooded her face. "Let me stay on your boat with you and Catfish."

"We'll all help you get well. All your friends will help, your daddy too. He loves you and doesn't want you to hurt anymore."

"I know how little he loves me. He's selfish and a cold-hearted Bible-pounding hypocrite. You just can't imagine how he treated my mother!" Her teeth began chattering and she was hugging her shoulders, making little sniffing sounds, her face twisted with misery. "I gotta have something right now! You must have something here on your boat!"

He stocked a small quantity of morphine, in case of an accident, but it wouldn't do for her to know about the opiate.

Mary Beth stood up and threw herself against him, arms circling his neck. She began pulling his face towards hers until he could smell the liquor on her rasping breath. Her voice was tense with emotion. "You must have something you can give me. I'll make it worth your while." Her hips were pressing hard against him, moving with a pathetic jerky rhythm.

Lacking for words, he simply picked her up in his arms and looked into her sad little face. "Just try to hang on, it won't be long." He leaned forward and placed her gently on the bunk, pulling a blanket over her. She curled up, her shoulders still shaking. Paul knew he had to get her to a doctor. Taking his rain cape from the locker, he began to pull it over his head.

"Don't leave me!" She clutched at him. He moved back, smoothing the cape and putting on a wide-brimmed oilskin hat. "I'm not leaving you. Try to get some rest, I'll be right back." He gently pushed her down and covered her again, and then he stepped into the wheelhouse and started the engine.

The sound of the rain was drowning out the noise of the diesel, but he could feel the slight vibration made by the engine; the instruments told him the trawler was throbbing with life. Paul turned on the running lights and slid open the port door. As he stepped out onto the deck, rain pelted him and flooded from the brim of his hat. In the glimmer of the anchor light he saw thousands of little water stalks dancing on the surface of the afterdeck.

The stern line was water-soaked and heavy. He released it and the tide swung the stern away from the dock. Paul went forward and leaned over the railing, the rain pouring down his back. When the bow line went slack, he flipped it free of its piling and the *Helen S.* drifted toward the middle of the river.

Head bent against the downpour, Paul returned to the wheelhouse and put the clutch in forward. Heavy rain was slanting through the red and green arcs of the running lights. He pressed a button and a tunnel of blue-white light punched out into the glistening rain, finding the edge of the marsh. The trawler moved upstream as he directed the light and peered through the sweeps of the windshield wipers.

There was a crash behind him.

He turned and found Mary Beth on the floor of the deckhouse, her hands frantically going through the spilled contents of the trawler's medicine chest. Immediately, he reversed the wheel and stopped the momentum of the boat. With the control in idle, he picked up the girl as if she were a kitten. She was still clutching vials and packets as he backed into the wheelhouse and sat her down on the couch. He pried her fingers loose from the medical supplies.

"Let me alone!" she screamed. "I'm looking for something to help me sleep."

"We'll be at the dock in twenty minutes."

The trawler, its great light ablaze, was nosing into the marsh when he reversed against the tide and regained the channel. Then she was on the floor, almost under his feet. He grabbed her in his right arm, pulling her to her feet.

"Let me go!" she cried. "Leave me alone!"

He was almost shouting. "You want us to go aground?" Her nails were digging into his arm. Between the rain, the twisting river, and the hysterical girl on his hands, Paul decided against trying to make the run to Bonaparte. Instead, he turned, backed, and curved the boat downriver to Beau's Island. Mary Beth was still struggling, but he held her firmly and eased the boat into the dock. At the last instant, he kicked open the side door and swung her up into his arms, turning around to back into the driving rain. He carried her with him to the bow, holding her on one knee as he located the bowline. His one-arm toss of the noose sailed over the piling and he secured the line to a deck cleat. Cradling her, he hurried back to the wheelhouse and put the girl on the couch. Then he closed the rain out and switched on the overhead light.

Sloppy wet and with her hair plastered against her cheeks and hanging in strands over her tan sweater, she was no longer hysterical. Her blue eyes were filled with tears.

"I'm sorry I had to get you wet like that," he said.

She nodded.

He studied her face for a moment and then directed the searchlight along the riverbank. The bowline was stretched tight and the current was keeping the vessel a few feet from the dock. Good, he thought, there will be no need to get another line out from the stern. He decided to leave the diesel running. He switched off the mile-ray and the running lights. Something crunched under his shoe.

Mary Beth gave a little agonized cry and sprang to the floor.

"Oh, look what you've done!"

He moved his foot and found a smear of powered glass from the broken vial.

Mary Beth was trying to grab the broken glass, but Paul lifted her back onto the couch and holding her there as he scattered the smear with his foot. She leaned back, moaning, and buried her face in a cushion.

The couch was wet from her dripping clothing. He took a blanket from the locker and wrapped it around her shoulders. Then he lifted her to a sitting position and began removing her shoes. "You have to get out of these wet clothes."

She nodded mechanically. He unfolded the blanket and awkwardly began pulling the wet, clinging sweater over her head. After it had been peeled off, he fumbled with the snaps of her bra. Her breasts were young and firm, but not as large as Rita's. She stood up and dropped her skirt to her ankles.

As she casually kicked off her panties, he turned his head and found a beach towel in the locker, handing it back to her.

Paul turned back and Mary Beth was standing there naked. Without a word, he took one of her arms and studied the needle marks. Her skin was damp and cold to his touch. While she stood there unmoving, he took the towel and rubbed her briskly all over, until she was dry and no longer clammy. He removed the water-spotted blanket from the bunk and felt the sheet. It was dry. He arranged a pillow and helped her stretch out on the sheet. He was spreading another sheet over her when she grabbed one of his hands. He sat down next to her.

"Get close to me and keep me warm," she implored, moving his hand to her breast. It was round and smooth to his touch and he allowed her to spread his fingers around it. Little tremors were flowing through her body. Her eyes were open and questioning.

A sad loveliness showed in her sensitive face and Paul realized the casual and innocent prettiness of two years earlier had matured into a tragic beauty. He wondered what deadly forces had used her so savagely. Before the rain, she had told him about it so naturally and without shame. "After I started putting out," she had said.

Almost impatiently, Mary Beth moved his hand to her other breast, rubbing his palm over the soft pink nipple.

It was no surprise to Paul that he felt no desire, even if he closed his mind to her addiction. That she was using her thin body in a desperate attempt to gain his cooperation struck him as pathetic. His entire being recoiled from any thought of making love to her, of taking advantage of her helplessness, even as she was urging him.

Her hands rested lightly on his. For a few moments he allowed the rhythmic noise of the rain to occupy his attention and to remind him that his shrimp trawler was swinging from a deserted marsh island dock, while he caressed a nude and sick girl. His mind turned to Rita. Her growing indifference to his advances had cooled his own desire, so that their sex had dwindled to those occasions when she merely submitted. The last time had been several weeks ago.

Mary Beth was resuming her project, moving his hand along her belly into the edge of her pubic mound. He withdrew his hand. "Captain Stark, you know I'm not a virgin. It would be all right if you made love to me." She struggled up onto one elbow. "You can kiss me, if you want to."

His lips brushed her forehead.

Her arms circled his neck and she was straining against him, her opened mouth against his.

Instinctively his arms went around her, but he quickly disengaged himself.

There was a hint of defiance in her eyes and a sadness on her face, as if she knew she had failed. After a few more sensuous movements of her hips under the sheet, she gave up.

"Mary Beth, close your eyes and tell me the color of your sailboat."

"It's blue."

"That's right. Now, your sail is filled with a good breeze and you're going along through the marsh, sailing down Bonaparte River. Tell me, what do you see?"

"Snowy egrets, blue herons."

"And what color is the sky? How does it look?"

"It looks like snowy white clouds in a feather bed of blue are hurrying along with the wind."

"And you know you belong here, with the wind and the river. You really came out here to be with the birds and listen to the wind in the trees."

A shadow crossed her face. A frown. "I came here to die, I told you that." ●

Her words left Paul feeling old and defeated. "You won't feel that way in a few weeks. It won't be long before you'll have Mr. Fisher putting your boat back in the water and you'll be laughing and having fun with your old friends again."

A wistful smile tugged at her lips.

She was suddenly tossing under the sheet and her eyes were shining with terror. He pressed her hands in his. Her teeth were grinding. Her back stiffened and she seemed to lapse into a coma. Her forehead was hot but he placed a blanket over her sheet and pulled it up to her chin, tucking it under her relaxing body.

In the wheelhouse, Paul picked up the radio microphone, speaking carefully into it.

"Calling the New Orleans Coast Guard. Calling the New Orleans Coast Guard. This is the trawler *Helen S.*"

She regained consciousness in the ambulance.

"I'm here, Mary Beth. You're going to be all right."

The girl clutched his hand. "I was having awful dreams. Where am I? Where are you taking me?"

"We're on our way to Beaver City. We tied up at Mr. Fisher's dock a few minutes ago."

"I'm cold, I need my clothes."

"I brought them with me, but they're too wet for you to put on."

The ambulance moved swiftly, without using its siren, reaching the hospital in less than ten minutes. White-coated attendants rolled Mary Beth through the doors of emergency receiving, where she was transferred to a wheeled bed. Paul smiled and waved as she rolled from his sight. She held up her little hand.

A middle-aged woman with a clipboard came and asked him questions, writing down the answers.

"Mr. Stark, we are not equipped to handle narcotics cases. I hope you understand that."

"No, I don't understand."

"The treatment for addiction requires special equipment, facilities we do not have here. A small hospital like this doesn't have a psychiatric ward, either."

"Are you saying you can't help her?"

"No, of course not. I just wanted you to understand our limitations."

He looked down at Mary Beth's damp clothing in his hand, wrapped in the same towel as her shoes. The woman was speaking to him.

"... however, a new doctor is on our staff, Dr. Washburne... a lot of experience with drug-related illnesses."

"When will this Dr. Washburne be able to see her?"

"By ten or ten-thirty this morning."

"I don't mind staying. I promised —"

"You would only be in the way. Don't worry; she's being given a sedative right now. Enough to make her sleep the rest of the night."

"These are her clothes. They got wet in the rain."

"I'll give them to Mrs. Potter to hang in Miss Claiborne's closet."

Paul rose to go. "When will we know how she's getting along?"

"Probably in twelve to twenty-four hours. You might try telephoning the switchboard in the late afternoon."

"What about visitors?"

"That's for Dr. Washburne to say. You probably will not see her before Tuesday, or Wednesday morning at the earliest. She shouldn't be disturbed for the next two or three days. It's for her own good."

"This Dr. Washburne, is he really good with this sort of thing?"

"Yes, he's one of the best. Will you be responsible for the hospital charges, Mr. Stark?"

He nodded. "Yes, yes of course." He signed the form on the clipboard.

The lights were dimmed in the lobby as he dialed the Henry Claiborne residence. A recording informed him that the line was out of order. He dialed the number a second time and got the same recording. Then he called a taxi.

An all-night talk program was coming over the taxi radio and people were calling in with passionate opinions on gun control. Mercifully, the program went off the air at two-thirty, a few minutes before Paul was let out at his house.

He unlocked the front door and turned on the hall light, so Rita would not be frightened if she awoke. He went quietly to the spare bedroom and undressed. After he turned out the lamp on the night table and stretched out in the bed, he saw her standing in the doorway. Her figure was outlined under a filmy nightgown.

"Paul, is that you?"

"Yes, Honey. I didn't want to wake you when I came in."

She got into bed. "Can I stay in here with you?" Her arms were around his neck and she wriggled close. "I'm glad you're home. I've been awfully scared."

"The lightning?"

"That and other things. Why did you get in so late?"

"It's a long story. You want to hear it tonight?"

"No, just hold me."

They made love in silence, she with her thoughts and he with his. It felt to him as though she were more responsive than usual, maybe even sufficiently involved to reach orgasm. Maybe.

Then he fell into a heavy sleep, cupping one of her breasts in his hand.

CHAPTER 6

Monday morning, Paul awakened before daylight. Rita was facing him, breathing quietly, her knees drawn up to her stomach. He lay still a few minutes to enjoy the warmth, which always seemed to radiate from her body. There was a soft and silky feel to her skin. His homecoming three hours earlier had been surprisingly enjoyable. He remembered their lovemaking: she had been almost passionate, certainly not quarrelsome. Reaching out, he explored the smooth mound of her hip, moved his hand slowly along her thigh. Not until he tried to press his fingers between her knees did she move, twisting impatiently away and rolling to the far side of the bed.

Her departure pulled most of the covers off him.

Paul was only mildly disappointed, as he knew she valued sleep more than romance or sex, a point she had made on many occasions. More than likely, he thought, she would still be in bed when he returned from the dock.

Outside, after he had silently closed the front door, he saw that the wet earth was still disposing of the rain. The damp night carried the scent of honeysuckle, a land smell, reminding him of summer evenings and kissing girls under magnolia trees. The stillness of the dark landscape was like the silence of the ocean, when it was quiet and unruffled by any breeze, flat calm with pre-dawn serenity.

He wished Rita would share such times with him. He walked down the narrow road and a rooster crowed, announcing the approach of dawn. Other cocks answered, their hoarse, multi-noted calls breaking the spell of sleep. The crowing of the roosters had always marked that entrancing time between the end of night and the beginning of day.

The sky's color faded as he neared the dock; trees and telephone poles changed from shadows into trees and poles and the river was a flat sheet of silver. Beyond it, a ground fog lay like a blanket over the marsh, creating the illusion of a snowfield.

Alongside the pier, the *Helen S.* rode motionless. Paul's experienced eye examined the powerful superstructure, approving the sturdy lines of the hull, the upsweep of the bow. She was a fine vessel and he felt a very private belief that his boat was an extension of himself. He had respect for the trawler's competence. A boat could have integrity, just like a person.

There would be a time when other hands would grip the spokes of the mahogany wheel and his ship would go to sea without Paul Stark aboard. Rita had been justified when she had accused him of having a shrimp boat for a mistress. "Other men drive trucks and fly planes, without slobbering all over them, but you boat people have a love affair with your damn boats!"

Paul entered the deckhouse and Catfish stirred, sat up in his bunk, his small face wrinkling with pleasure. Paul held up a hand in greeting and the little man returned the salute. With his back to the deck hand, Paul lit the stove and started their breakfast. There was no need to look behind him to know that Catfish was inspecting and then lacing up his white tennis shoes.

Catfish ate on the dock, squatting next to a piling, as Paul sipped coffee. A half-grown black cat appeared and sidled past, arching its back indifferently. Catfish pretended not to notice, until the animal leaned against his arm. Then the cat was in his lap, sharing his plate. Paul smiled, shaking his head, and the old man's face rippled with pleasure.

It was after seven when Paul unlocked Lou's office and dialed the Claiborne residence. The line was still not working. A note was propped on Lou's desk:

> Paul,
> In case you come in Sunday night, I'm in New Orleans. Your compressor got here Thurs. and is run in, ready to put on board. Mel has the Honey L. in dry dock. I will be back Mon. afternoon to help with the compressor.
> Lou

Paul let out a sigh of relief. The elusive compressor had finally arrived, after being lost by the truck line for six weeks. With Lou helping, he estimated six or seven hours would be needed to complete the installation. After that, his showdown with the ocean would begin.

The letter from the bank had put his appointment at noon. There was no alternative, nothing acknowledging his need to be fishing or installing a compressor at twelve o'clock. Mr. Claiborne would expect him at noon on Monday, April 2nd. Paul wondered what Claiborne would say when he knew his daughter had spent most of the night on his trawler and had ended up in a hospital bed.

He called the hospital. Miss Claiborne was sleeping after a restless night. The switchboard had no further information.

Catfish was still stroking the cat when Paul boarded the trawler and descended into the spotless engine room. For the next hour he busied himself checking the big yellow power plant and the other vital organs of the vessel. He added oil to the diesel generator, checked the batteries, and pumped a small accumulation of water from the bilges. Then he started the generator and inspected the electrical system.

After a final look around, he was satisfied.

Before leaving the boat, he hung up the damp blanket from the wheelhouse couch and put the pillow out in the sunlight. Rita was still in bed when he returned to the house and, for the second time that morning, he began to prepare breakfast.

Sooner or later, most visitors to Bonaparte ask about the Cameron mansion. It was impressive, very colonial, and very white. A mile west of town, it was set far back from Highway 90, in a wide expanse of trees and landscaping. Natives would explain:

The Camerons were big in oil, cattle, farming; you just name it. The old man was dead and his widow spent most of her time in Europe. Places like that. There was only one boy, twenty maybe, and he lived out there now, all by his lonesome. The house was big enough for ten families of plain ordinary folks.

Pressing for more information, one might learn that the son had no head at all for making money. "Not like old Cal Cameron." The banks in New Orleans took care of the investments, while old Barley Johnson, the caretaker, lived at the back of the estate and ran the place. "The boy drove around in one of them foreign sports cars. They say he didn't like school too much."

"Did he work at anything?"

"Hell no! With all that money, he didn't have to hit a lick at a snake!"

It was after daylight on Monday when Jonathon Cameron, scion of oil, cattle, farming, and other empires, stirred in his bed. His tongue explored the bad taste in his mouth. He sat up and rubbed his eyes. Every artery and vein inside his body was twitching. He unlocked a closet and prepared a syringe, the contents soon squirting through a needle into his arm. He began to feel better, much better. Remembering his car, he rushed to the front windows and pushed aside the drapes. It was not down below in the curving driveway, a reality that made him angry. Goddamn Mary Beth! Tell you one thing and do something else. "I'll be back soon, Johnny," she had said in front of the house, then she had driven off and he had stretched out in his room to think about his project. And had slept all night. Damn!

The laziest of all maids, Joselyn was nowhere in sight as he went down the stairs and out the back way.

He backed his mother's sedan from the garage, glad his old lady was still screwing around in France. For his big deal, he needed swinging room and a bundle of cash. He would sell his car, but the title was in his mother's name and her jewelry was stashed in safety deposit boxes.

The allowance from the bank was peanuts, barely enough to buy gas and beer, and his mother had canceled his credit cards.

He had to find Mary Beth; she was his ticket out of this piss-hole town of Bonaparte.

Henry Jefferson Claiborne was in a bad mood as he drank his prune juice and opened the New Orleans paper. He wondered what he had done to deserve a prostitute for a daughter.

A picture of Letty Cameron smiled up from the paper. Letty was outdoors on snow skies, in some Austrian town. The caption explained she was the widow of the late Calvin Lagare Cameron of Bonaparte, Louisiana, and New York City, and that she was enjoying the early spring skiing at a new resort high in the Alps.

The society writer had said nothing about the plans of Cameron's widow to return to Louisiana.

When, Letty, when?

She should already be back. He put down the paper and buttered a slice of toast.

"Hannah! Hannah! Where are you?"

A worn-out old woman shuffled into the breakfast room.

"Is Miss Mary Beth upstairs?"

"I don't rightly know, Mista Cleybun."

"Haven't you looked?"

"Nawsuh."

He knew she was lying. "Then go look, damn it!"

"Yassah." She tramped heavily from the room. He hadn't heard Mary Beth come in during the evening, but he could have missed her. He had fallen asleep in the library during the storm and had not gone upstairs to check on her before going to bed.

Hannah was back in the room, a serious look on her wrinkled face. "Well...?"

"Miss Mary Beth isn't here jes' now. Mebbe she left to go in huh boat."

"Has her bed been slept in?"

"It sho' looks like it."

He checked the impulse to go upstairs and make his own survey of his daughter's room. Hannah would have already arranged the evidence. "Hannah, you listen to me. Miss Mary Beth is sick, she's got to spend a good long time in a hospital."

"Mista Cleybun, I c'n take care of huh right here."

"She's not sick that way, Hannah."

"I heah she takin' dope. I'd keep it outta huh reach."

"It's not that simple. She's a grown woman now. We have to put her somewhere so she can't get anything, except what the doctors say she can have. Miss Mary Beth is going to a place in Dallas. Pack up all of her things."

The old woman looked at him with frowning suspicion. "That place like a 'sane asylum? Does it have bars on the windows?"

"How the hell do I know?"

"Asylum's no place for Miss Mary Beth. Wild birds die, penned in a cage."

His temper rose. Hannah had always sided with the women of the household. "She's going to die, damn it, if something isn't done. Who knows where she is right now? Her boat's not in the water, but call the docks and make sure."

Hannah left and returned a minute later. "The phone's not working. A tree limb fell on the line."

He fixed her with his eyes, squinting over his glasses. "How much money is missing from your household box?"

"Nothing that I know of."

"Bring me the box, Hannah."

She brought a cigar box to the table and sat it down, unopened.

"Open it up and count your money, Hannah."

"She looked at the unopened box and said, "I s'pect it's all there."

"Count it, Hannah."

Hannah was painfully slow in opening the box.

The box was empty.

"Hannah, we both know she took the money so she could get more drugs." He rose from the table. "You call me the minute she shows up. We have to send her to Dallas."

"Yessah."

Then he remembered the downed telephone wire, a circumstance that could be used by Hannah and Mary Beth to outwit him. "I'll have the telephone people out here first thing."

"Yessah."

He looked at her in exasperation before putting on his coat and picking up his hat. Hannah was getting even more difficult, in her old age.

His mood did not improve, as he drove through the bright April morning. His daughter, a Claiborne, taking money and selling her body like a common whore! He had wanted her to settle down, to marry some nice young man with a good family background. Like Letty's boy, that would be a good pair. Johnny was a little wild now, but that was to be expected. He came from hot-blooded ancestors who had wrung fortunes from the cotton and cane fields of Louisiana. Later, they captured the banking, oil, and insurance markets. Claiborne estimated the Cameron fortune at seventy to seventy-five million. As Johnny grew older, he would need sound and prudent management of his wealth.

Letty had not responded to his suggestions, or to his offers to end her lonely widowhood. She preferred her spendthrift friends, but Claiborne was sure she would get over that. Sooner or later she would come back and settle down, then she and Johnny would need someone who could keep the Cameron portfolio from getting into the wrong hands.

Mary Beth could wreck all these carefully laid plans.

Jenny, his secretary, followed him into his office. "Mr. Claiborne, a Mr. Paul Stark has called several times. Say's it's urgent."

Claiborne's attention focused on the affairs of the bank. "Do I have an appointment with him?"

"Yes, at noon. Shall I call him back for you?"

"No. I want him here in person."

"He sounded mighty anxious to talk with you. He said it was very urgent."

He stared at Jenny. She reminded him of a chicken, the way she fluttered around him. The only favorable thing about her was that she was a good secretary, in spite of being the ugliest woman in the bank. At least with Jenny there would be no gossip.

"Jenny, when someone is about to be foreclosed, their calls are always urgent."

She nodded, leaving. Then she was back. "That Mr. Stark is on the line again and won't take no for an answer."

"Tell him I'm tied up all morning in a meeting, but I'll expect him at twelve sharp."

After the third futile attempt to reach Henry Claiborne by phone, Paul went into the bedroom and began the ordeal of getting his wife out of bed. He put his hand on her shoulder. "Rita—"

She burrowed deeper under the covers. "Go 'way."

"Breakfast is ready, it's almost ten-thirty."

"I'm not hungry."

"Here's your robe."

Her head emerged and she looked sleepily at him. Then she sat up, clutching the covers to her chin, and slowly slipped back onto the pillow.

He dropped the robe on the bed. "Wake up." They began a tug of war with the bedclothes.

"Damn you, Paul, I'm not ready to get up, and I'm not ready for breakfast."

Without replying, he scooped her up from the bed and carried her to the kitchen.

While Rita picked at her breakfast, Paul reviewed the day ahead. He resisted the impulse to tell Claiborne's horse-faced secretary that his call concerned her boss's daughter. That was something he would tell Claiborne in person.

The letter left little doubt that the bank would not extend his payments or refinance his boat mortgage. Paul was certain that Claiborne wanted to give him the bad news in person.

"I don't like grapefruit," Rita said crossly. "You should know by now that I never eat grapefruit."

Here comes the argument, the first shot across his bow, he thought. "Then don't eat the grapefruit," he said mildly, taking it from her plate. "Have some bacon and eggs."

She took a slice of bacon and a small helping of eggs, as he poured the coffee.

"Toast?"

"No. I said I don't want breakfast."

"Are you feeling all right?"

"I feel lonely, depressed, bored and sleepy. I feel awful! Are you going out on your precious boat today?"

"That lost compressor came and Lou's going to help me get everything finished. Maybe I'll be ready to leave tonight."

"So you won't be here tonight, or tomorrow night, or God knows how many nights after that?" Her look was accusing.

"Right now, Rita, I'm trying to make every day count. The spring run—"

She cut him short. "The spring run! What is it now—two, three weeks late? I think that something is running in your head."

His temper was rising. She showed no concern about anybody but herself.

"I suppose you came in this time with a big load of shrimp?"

"No."

"Well now, isn't that just amazing? Those lil'ol' shrimp jes' a-hidin' out there from the great Cap'n Stark. And he's the one that told all them government people how to catch shrimp. "

"That's enough. Fishing is like anything else: It has its ups and downs."

"I'm not going to shut up until you get that boat off your hands and find a job that pays something."

The bank might take care of that, he thought. No use telling her that, however. Foolishly perhaps, he had taken two of the boat payments to buy her car.

He tried to change the subject. "If the invention proves out, I'll have to stay on the hill and turn them out for other boats. Then I would be underfoot all the time."

"Provided the invention works!" There was heavy sarcasm in her voice. "And after it does and we make a mint, we buy up Beau's Island and build us a great big house where we can see all the shrimp boats floating past our doorstep, while we sit in our rocking chairs and rock and rock!" She pretended the kitchen chair was a rocker.

"Lou thinks it will work. He says I might get a patent."

"Is that so? Mr. Lou Fisher thinks your wonderful gadget just might catch us a mess of shrimp? What other experts have the same nutty idea?"

"You know I can't tell anyone, if I'm going to apply for a patent. I haven't even mentioned it to Mel Wilson, as close as we are."

"Paul, what about me? Do you expect me to stay out here forever in this God-awful place, while you waste time out in that stinking boat of yours?" Her voice was becoming shrill.

He rose from the table, his breakfast only half-eaten. "Rita, you better get this through your head: You married a fisherman; that's what I know how to do. Our boat isn't a fleet, but it represents ninety thousand dollars and I am not going to sell it and try to live your way. If you had gone with me to Key West, we'd have money now."

"That isn't true!"

"Yes it is, Rita. You wanted me to fail."

Her face was set, frozen. "Paul, you're a liar. You wanted to leave me on the beach at Key West with a bunch of conks, while you went merrily off to sea. That's why I wasn't willing to go. And for no other reason."

He lowered his voice to a conversational level. "I have to take a shower and get to the bank by twelve. Will you be using the car?"

"If you'll have it back here by one. I have an appointment at the beauty salon."

"In that case, I'll walk."

"Suit yourself."

After he shaved and bathed, he put on his dark suit and knotted a tie. Rita had locked herself in the bedroom and he tapped on the door. "I'm leaving now."

There was no answer.

He tried again. "Why don't you come by Lou's after you get finished in Beaver City? We could go to a good restaurant tonight, before I shove off."

There was no sound from inside. Paul hoped she would calm down during the afternoon and come to the dock. She had never seen the invention.

He arrived at the bank at noon and was kept waiting an hour.

Claiborne's secretary motioned to him.

The banker was seated behind his desk and remained there as Paul walked into the paneled office. "Good morning, Paul," said Claiborne. "Have a seat."

"I've been trying all morning to get you on the phone."

Claiborne shut him off. "Your loan has been taken out of my hands. The bank directors—"

Paul saw red. "I wasn't calling about the damn loan, I was calling about Mary Beth."

Claiborne seemed startled. He leaned forward, his face hardening. "What about Mary Beth? Do you know where she is?"

"She's in the hospital at Beaver City. She's being treated by a Dr. Washburne, for drugs and whatever."

The banker frowned and pressed a button. His secretary's voice answered over the intercom. "Get me the hospital in Beaver City. I want to speak to Dr. Washburne. Tell them it's very important." He looked at Paul. "How did you know about all this?"

"I took her there in an ambulance about one-thirty this morning."

"You took her? Why wasn't I notified? What right—?"

"I tried to call you during the night, but your phone was out of order. When I called the bank this morning, you decided my business with you could wait until noon. Then you let me sit out there another hour."

Claiborne was swelling up, his face growing red. "You should have sent the police to my house, or come yourself in a taxi. I would have paid for the taxi."

"Oh, shut up, Hank. There's no way you can ever be anything but what you've always been and that's a white shirt stuffed above the ears with goat shit. If you'll keep your goddamn fat mouth shut a few minutes, I'll tell you what I can about Mary Beth."

Claiborne settled back in his chair as the intercom buzzed. Dr. Washburne would call him back.

"I'm listening, Stark."

Paul told of Claiborne's daughter lying on the bluff, and of him tying up at the old dock and bringing the unconscious girl on deck.

The banker interrupted. "You should have called me. Your boat has a radio, I presume."

"I was alone, except for Catfish."

"Who's he?"

"My deck hand. He can't hear or speak. My first thought was to get Mary Beth out of the weather and try to revive her."

"What had caused her to be unconscious?"

"I don't know what else, but plenty of bourbon. She threw it up after I got her to drink some black coffee."

"Stark, I don't know if I believe that. She never drank, not to my knowledge."

"Mary Beth intended to drown herself last night. She tried to numb herself with the bourbon. At least, she convinced me."

"And I suppose you fell for that?"

Paul wanted to lean over the desk and hit the banker. "No, I didn't believe her at first. Not until she told me what you had said to her, what you had called her."

Claiborne flushed. "It's none of your affair as to what might have transpired between a daughter and her father."

"Hank, I tried to get her to go home, where her daddy could see that she got the best treatment available. That made her try to jump overboard! By then I was certain the last place on earth she wanted to be was under your control."

Claiborne's look was ugly. "My daughter's a drug addict. A whore. She has brought disgrace on my house, on my name."

Paul listened in amazement. "You can save that crap, Hank. You're talking to Paul Stark. I've known you from way back when. We both know how much ass you had to kiss to get ahead. Right now, I feel like kicking yours from one end of River Street to the other."

The phone chimed. It was Dr. Washburne. Paul only heard one side of the conversation, but he gathered that Mary Beth had been given something to lessen her agony. Claiborne was breaking off the conversation: "I've already checked into that, doctor. I mean no reflection on your qualifications, but my daughter is being sent to Dallas as soon as she can be put in an ambulance. I've already made my decision. All I want from you is her release from the hospital." A pause. "No, tomorrow morning at the latest."

The banker hung up and looked at Paul. "Is there anything else you need to tell me about my daughter before we close the subject?"

"Just this, Hank. Mary Beth is pretty desperate just now. Unstable. She needs understanding and affection. Also, a very special type of medical attention." Paul remembered the woman at the hospital.

"You mean she's temporarily insane, don't you, Stark? All that talk about suicide goes to prove it. I should have had her committed long ago."

Paul leaned across the desk, pointing his finger at Claiborne, breathing hard. "You do that, Hank, you put that young girl in a place like that, and I'll..."

"Stark, you mind your own business or you'll find yourself in jail! You must think you're talking to one of your waterfront bums."

"You can't do it. She's over twenty-one."

The banker looked smug. "That won't make any difference in her condition."

Paul rose to go. "I've known some pricks in my time, but none of them are in your class. You make me want to puke!"

Claiborne handed Paul an envelope, a mean little smile showing. "Here, Stark, take this with you. A registered original is being mailed. The law requires it. You have thirty days."

Paul turned without a word and left the bank. He was disgusted with himself for losing his temper. Maybe Lou would have some answers.

CHAPTER 7

Monday morning in New Orleans, Lou Fisher walked down the carpeted hallway of the Harris Clinic and entered the third door on the right. A youngish man in white was standing behind a plain table. Lou was surprised; he expected to see the doctor who had examined him two weeks earlier.

"Mr. Fisher? I'm Dr. Ben Thompson. Please sit here." He motioned towards a chair. The telephone rang and the doctor answered, his voice strong and decisive. Lou avoided the folder on the table. His eyes were drawn to a spot of color in the antiseptic room, a framed photograph of an attractive young woman with three children. They seemed to be saying that the doctor, in spite of his youth, was a family man, a good provider, dependable, competent.

Dr. Thompson ended the call and sat down across the table, his gaze level. "Mr. Fisher, you asked us to give you all the facts about your condition."

What's he getting at? "Yes, that's correct."

Thompson was tapping the table slowly with a gold ballpoint pen. "In most cases, we prefer to discuss this type diagnosis with a member of the family, rather than the patient."

This type diagnosis! "Yes I understand," said the patient, not even wanting to understand. "I have no family. I wanted to know as much as possible about my condition." Under the table, Lou's hands were gripping his knees. The face of the doctor had become disembodied, as if submerged in water. The lips were moving, but Lou's mind was moving counterpoint to the doctor's words, to the pronouncement he knew was coming.

" ... all concur that your tumor is malignant. Quite advanced, in fact. We do not recommend surgery."

Lou had wondered all his life what dying would be like; the answer would soon be revealed. The doctor's face remained suspended in front of him.

"…not infallible, if you would like to check our findings with others
. . ."

"No," said Lou, caught up in a haze of unreality. "I'm sure the
verdict would be the same as yours."

Harris Clinic had investigated his organs, his cells, and his juices.
They had probed with instruments and measured with machines. Traces
of him had been studied under microscopes. They had delved for the
truth about Mr. Louis M. Fisher.

Doctor Thompson was now routinely summarizing with no
outward sign of compassion, no change in the even cadence of his voice,
except that it had sped up, as if the man wanted to get the confrontation
over and done with so that he, too, could be alone with his thoughts. Lou
heard fragments. Something had exploded in his consciousness and he
was hearing the pieces drop.

"…others in your condition…various periods without severe pain…
new drugs…frontiers of discovery…breakthroughs every year…therapy…
don't ever give up hope for remission…"

Lou suspected this carefully worded speech had been learned from
cue cards. At least there was simple clarity in the first statement: *Your
tumor is malignant.*

The doctor rose and extended his hand, and only then did his eyes
flicker, showing his concern. "The receptionist has a detailed report. I
suggest you go over it very carefully."

Lou stood up. "Thank you, Doctor."

Thank you, Doctor? Thank you, doctor, for starting the final
countdown of my life? Lou understood his mind had been stretched
and hammered, that thanking the doctor was a mere amenity, without
any relationship to gratitude. He turned to go. No, he would not ask
the doctor how much time is left. The clinic couldn't tell him, so why
press for an educated guess? Some held on longer than others. Became
vegetables.

". . . avoid any undue physical effort. No alcohol. Take time to rest
each day. Take medication… all there in your report."

Lou wrote a check and the receptionist handed him a thick envelope.
Her face, sparkling with good health, was an expressionless mask. Lou
wondered if she knew about him.

Driving west in the pickup, he circled the wagons of reason around his emotions. The clinic had made official what his body had been suggesting for some time. He scouted his mind for apathy or panic and found neither.

He did not feel any sense of fear. Damn strange! Maybe he was in a state of shock, like a person feeling no pain after being severely wounded.

He envied those without a blueprint of their dying. People who suddenly deceased without prior knowledge, were lucky people indeed. His reason assured him there was nothing more natural in the great arc from birth to death than the termination of life. So why should he, one obscure mortal, be the least bit agitated by an event set in motion from the first moments of his own infancy? He would need these empirical understandings to see himself through, until he would have no further need for such awareness.

Lou wondered what chemical and cellular processes were taking place inside his body. Some of the answers would be in the formidable envelope riding beside him. Louis Fisher was fifty-five, one hundred eighty pounds, six feet tall. When stricken, he was keeper of a fish house. The report would be laced with impressive words to confuse and intimidate laymen. This he knew was the prerogative of the professions. If he had continued in medical school, instead of joining the Air Force, he might better understand his beast in residence.

Death . . .?

Impersonally, he considered the word: death. Death he decided, is a condition of repose; a non-being or a happening to others.

He had survived the war, when many close to him had not. Young men, full of life and the expectancy of continued living, were suddenly gone without ceremony, while he had gone on living.

How does one behave while waiting around to die? There must be steadfast discipline. He would need to consider a code of conduct. He would allocate to death only a part of each day; he would concentrate on the process of being alive. He would enjoy the brilliance of nature, including the sun setting and slowly disappearing into the sea. He would make the most of what was left for him.

This resolve made him feel in charge of his life, thus stronger. He gripped the wheel of the pickup.

He would not write the book he planned, even though that was the goal that brought him to sleepy Bonaparte after the war.

He would not build the freezing plant at the bend of the river, nor would he be around to marry Maggie. A man needed time to realize his dreams.

But Lou Fisher was almost out of time to do anything except prepare for dying.

Ahead, in the midday sunlight, was the packinghouse of Bonaparte Seafoods, with the *Helen S.* at the dock. Paul would need another pair of hands.

With the warm sun on his back, Lou was pleased that he was being helpful to Paul. Several hours would be required to install the new compressor. By tomorrow, the octopus, as they had named it, would be finished, ready to be turned loose on the sea bottom. The weather forecast was favorable.

Lou's body was cooperating by only registering the familiar low-level pain. He was determined this would not interfere with the work. There was a risk, of course, that severe, uncontrollable spasms might batter him and betray his condition, but he had to chance this. He watched his hands making electrical connections, seeing them as if they belonged to someone else. They were not old hands; they were graceful, performing skillfully. They were capable and unimpaired, like the hands of a fine surgeon. The clinic had given him no points, however, for admirable hands.

His eyes turned seaward, sweeping the marsh. For a moment. the green wetlands seemed like a place he had seen in a dream, insulated from him, tantalizingly near yet no longer possessed by him. It would all be there long after... he felt a great sadness. As a youngster, he had known the same feeling as he stood on the rear platforms of trains and watched familiar places grow smaller, until they were no longer there; when the beginning of a journey meant leaving places he loved and felt a part of.

The black cat danced stiff-legged along the planks, with Catfish ambling in pursuit. He and Paul watched as the cat vanished at the end of the dock and Catfish scrambled down the ladder.

"Moonbeam's got a hiding place under there," said Lou. "Catfish can't get to it without getting his shoes muddy."

Paul laughed. "I wish we could keep her on the boat."

"Moonbeam's mighty welcome here, Paul. You suppose she'll ever get her sea legs?"

"Not very likely. Whenever the engine starts, she takes off."

"What happens, Paul, if Moonbeam gets careless crossing the road? Or finds a tomcat with more sex appeal than your deck hand?"

"It would be pretty rough on the little guy."

Lou finished the last connection. "I might look around for a stand-in. Moonbeam the Second, so Catfish will always have a female waiting in port."

Paul told of finding Mary Beth on Beau's Island and taking her to the hospital. He described the meeting with Henry Claiborne. "Lou, could that pompous ass have her committed?"

"I don't know, he is her father and she may be dangerously ill."

"Mary Beth is no longer the high school kid we knew. But even sick people have rights."

What does age have to do with being sick? Lou wondered. He looked across the compressor housing, at Paul's worried face.

"Hank draws a lot of water around here, it's a fact of life. I suppose he could get papers signed. He would buy off whoever he had to."

Paul pulled on the big wrench, making a face as he strained. "Mary Beth is scared silly. She thinks he's putting her into some quick cure-or-kill place. Wouldn't that about finish her off, considering her present state of mind?"

"A doctor might be able to say. Hank wouldn't put her in a state institution. Couldn't keep that quiet. My guess is he'll try to buy her a cure the same way he buys another piece of property."

"Away from here?"

"That's for certain. Meanwhile, he'll hang on to her money as long as he can keep her out of sight."

"What did the hospital mean, Lou, when they told me she was doing as well as could be expected?"

Lou had also wondered. "Hard to tell Paul. Depends on who's doing the expecting."

"Didn't you get those answers when you were studying to be a doctor?"

"Never got that far. Chances are, Mary Beth is still under heavy sedation."

As Paul worked the dock hoist, Lou positioned the compressor over the deck anchor bolts. The heavy machine was lowered to rest solidly on the base plate. Working silently, they tightened the galvanized nuts against the lock washers. Paul looked up. "Is Hank still making a play for Letty Cameron?"

Lou laughed. "If he is, he's got about as much chance with Letty as a marsh weasel has of catching a butterfly on the wing. She knew Hank before she ever met Cal Cameron, and wouldn't give him the time of day then."

"But there was something in the New Orleans paper about Hank and Letty. Some social gossip."

"I read that. I also remember reading about your testimony in Baton Rouge. Were those accurate accounts?"

"Hell no! You read the transcripts. I said some of the things, but the words were all twisted around. They meant something else when the papers got through with me. But what's that got to do with Hank and Letty?"

"Hank planted the gossip so he could trade on the Cameron name. When Letty hears about it, she won't bother to get a retraction. If she did, it would only help fan the rumors. So Hank wins either way."

"How could Hank swing a deal like that with the New Orleans papers?"

"No problem, he has friends now. Oil people are playing on his team these days, and he on theirs."

"Oil people—"

"About ten months ago, twenty-five million dollars came into Claiborne's bank from oil and paper companies. My contact said the money was being put back here where it was earned, to help the local economy."

Lou saw the look of surprise on his friend's face.

"The local owners sold out? To the oil people?"

"No, it is not that simple. The old stockholders still control the stock. The bank gets to keep the fat new accounts; as long as it knows which side its bread is buttered on. Nothing's in writing, doesn't have to be: It's understood."

"Well, I'll be damned!"

Lou wondered how much he should tell Paul. "The truth is that anyone who bucks for ecology, or agitates for new legislation or certain types of enforcement, is the customer of some bank."

"—and the bank can scrag ass?"

"I'm not saying there's a connection, but new money landed here right after you went to Baton Rouge."

"Right after I spilled my guts!"

"Paul, it could still be just a coincidence. Hell, who knows anymore who pulls what strings?"

Paul tightened a copper fitting. "Lou, we both know if the laws we already have don't get more respect, it's just going to get worse every year. It will get worse not only for fishing, but also for the whole human and animal populations. We no longer have any alternatives."

"I know what you said, and what you meant, but the word was that you were trying to stop progress. Throw people out of work."

"Which is pure crap. When we succeed in wrecking the natural order of things, no one will have a job. Why can't the papers ever get things right?"

"Good question. Chances are, the reporters did an honest job. Maybe someone higher up saw the chance to make some points."

"It'll be a sorry day for Louisiana when ass-kissers like Hank Claiborne take over. He's stupid and ambitious, and that's a bad combination."

"Just don't let our friendly banker lower the boom on you, Paul."

Paul wiped his hands on a rag. "He already has. I got thirty days to pay up, or this trawler goes on the auction block. Hank gave me the letter as I was leaving his office."

Lou was astonished. "You must be kidding! Hank knows shrimp fishing has been off. How much are you behind?"

"Four payments."

Lou whistled. "You couldn't owe but a few more notes on the trawler. Why didn't you let me know?"

"No sense both of us losing sleep. A fisherman keeps thinking he'll hit it big. I'm no exception. I should have gone to Key West last November. At least they made expenses."

Lou waved at the new equipment. "None of this would have gotten done if you had been in Key West." He studied Paul's face. "So Hank thinks he's putting you on the hill, for four lousy payments!"

"That's what he planned to tell me about today, when he gave me the letter, but we were busy in a yelling match about Mary Beth."

"Why didn't you phone Hank to tell him about his girl?"

"I tried to, but couldn't get through. Anyway, I got the letter ten days ago to show up at noon today."

"I think I know the reason. Hank wanted to offer you a deal. You stop shooting your mouth off and the bank might be willing to work out something on your payments."

"Hell, Lou, I never thought of that. I called him a no-good prick and told him he was full of shit. Plus a few other things."

Lou chuckled. "Now Hank's looking forward to whacking off the good captain's balls a month from now." Paul didn't answer. Lou stood up, glad the pain was still bearable. "If she's not ready now, Paul, she never will be."

"Okay, Lou, let's fire her off."

Lou pressed the manual start button and the big compressor roared, gulping air into its cylinders and pressing it into the tanks below deck. "When the pressure gage shows two hundred and fifty pounds, the compressor shuts itself off," Paul explained.

"Your answer to Hank Claiborne is right here." Lou spread his hands over the silent machine. Paul smiled and led Lou into the wheelhouse.

"What the hell's that?" Lou pointed to a nozzle mounted to the right of the helm.

"An extra air line. Its main use is to experiment with sea water and bottom silt."

Lou was acutely conscious of feeling good and of joking with Paul. A light breeze in from the gulf pushed back the smell of the paper mill. For the moment, he forgot about the envelope.

"Paul, you may be the first shrimper in history to find the one foolproof way to catch shrimp. Can't miss. You'll be blowing sand in their eyes and up their asses at the same time!"

Paul laughed. "Good! They'll weigh more." He started the generator, then the main engine, as he studied the instrument panel. Lou realized it was time for Paul to go; a feeling of loneliness spread over him.

Paul turned off the diesel, but left the generator running. "I'm not casting off yet. Rita might come by and take me out to eat. Anyway, I have to pick up some groceries."

"We can go in the truck."

Paul called the hospital and found that Mary Beth was responding to treatment.

The men made a run to the market and Paul bought supplies for the boat. At the meat counter, Lou saw that Joe Riley was pale and shaking. "You having a chill, Joe?"

"I ain't feelin' so good. Got spring fever, I guess. Ralph, git out here and wait on these customers!" Joe left hurriedly through the swinging doors.

It was dark outside when they stopped by Paul's house. Rita's car was gone.

"I suppose she's still in Beaver City," said Paul. "Probably went to a movie."

Lou nodded and turned the pickup around and headed back to the dock. Paul's wife wouldn't be seeing him off. But then, she never did.

Paul stared ahead. "It's no picnic for Rita, with me gone all the time."

When the provisions were stored, the men went into the office. Lou took a bottle from the filing cabinet and poured drinks. "Here's to a safe trip, and success with the invention!"

They swallowed the bourbon.

"Does Rita know about the bank?"

Paul paused for a moment before answering and contemplated his future. "No. If I lose the boat, she'll have me working on the hill. She'd like that."

Lou studied his empty glass, glad of the forbidden drink in his system. "Don't worry, something's going to turn up. Take my word, you will not lose your boat."

"Thanks for the confidence," said Paul, dialing his home number. There was no answer; he looked at his watch. "I'm keeping you here, Lou. If you see Rita, tell her I waited until after ten."

Lou lifted the lines from cleats and pilings and handed them to Catfish, who carefully coiled them on deck. The *Helen S.* was soon gliding downstream and Paul waved from the wheelhouse door.

Lou stood under the light and held up his hand. In a few minutes, the trawler was around the first bend, then doubling back in the marsh as it threaded the channel of the river. When he had lost sight of the ghostly superstructure, Lou waved in farewell to the mast light that was hovering over the night marsh like a lonely star. A chill was beginning at the base of his spine.

CHAPTER 8

Inside the locked bedroom, Rita listened to Paul's footsteps crunching down the road. The sounds slowly faded until finally, he was gone. Let him walk to the bank. Who cares? *Damn him,* she thought, stretching on the soft bed. If he had been with her, instead of cruising around on that lousy shrimp boat, she wouldn't have been raped. It was as simple as that! She had been tempted to tell him about it, after he had come in and taken his pleasure. If Paul only knew, he would rise up and explode. Rape or no rape! He was particular when it came to his wife's virtue. There hadn't been anyone besides Paul since she became his wife; he had no worry in that department. He didn't know it, of course, but she never really liked sex all that much. Some people really took on about it, especially men.

Troy was probably on his way back to Chicago and Joe wasn't all that guilty. Better let sleeping dogs lie. With their signed confession, they wouldn't be bothering her again.

She should have let Paul take the car. Her appointment wasn't until two-thirty. She decided that after her hair was done; she would stop by the fish house and look at his invention. And she might get all dressed up and go to the Holiday Lodge in Beaver City. Paul was handsome, tall and strong, but he was broke and in debt.

No, there was no future for her and Paul. He would never find those damn shrimp, but would never give up looking. Everyone except Paul knew shrimp couldn't live on an oil diet. He would keep on and on, leaving her alone to be insulted and raped by any Tom, Dick, or Harry, or Troy and Joe, who came along, until she got to be an old lady and lost her good looks.

Someday, maybe someday soon, she would have to leave Paul and strike out on her own again. Before she left, she hoped he could start catching something again. Anything. So he wouldn't miss her as much.

The phone rang. It would be Paul, asking her to come by the fish house. No, thank you, Captain Stark. She let it ring and then slept until the bright midday sun was reaching warm fingers into her bed.

The clock showed it was past one.

Rita put on a robe and went to the mirror to study her face. The first tiny wrinkles wouldn't show for a few more years. Makeup would cover them at first; her skin was still flawless. She practiced smiling. Even without cosmetics, no one could guess her right age. With the routine of a stripper, she removed the robe and turned until she had studied every part of herself. She had put on a little weight, but in the right places. Most men liked a girl to be filled out. With her face and figure, she could still drive them right up the wall!

No one could tell she had been raped. No black and blue marks on her creamy skin. Troy's face sure would need some explaining. She laughed as she remembered her victory. On top of having his face scratched and being scared shitless, she hadn't cooperated in bed, so he had to feel downright rejected.

Again, she thought of Paul and decided she would go to dinner with him before he left.

Rita's stomach knotted with a quick sensation of fear when she saw the big woman come through the side entrance of the beauty salon. She looked closer; satisfied she had never seen that coarse, ugly face before. The woman was tall and big-boned. She wore a soiled white uniform, sweat stained at the armpits. It stretched tightly across wide hips and smoothed her breasts into flattened melons. Oversized legs were stuffed into white stockings. When she walked, she rolled from side to side.

Rita watched the woman tramp heavily into an alcove, heard her loud voice cut through the buzz of other talk.

"She died, ol' lady Hopkins—that's Daisy Hopkins—about four this morning. None of her folks were there when she went. Guess they's glad she won't be yellin' her head off at them no more."

Rita tried harder to concentrate on her magazine as the voice in the alcove got louder.

"Busy night. Got a call about a bad accident. The ambulance went out and got 'um. He was maybe twenty-five. Bleedin' like a stuck hawg. They said his head was hung up in the windshield. When I first saw 'im, I sez to Nelly Sutton—she has the night shift duty with me—I sez Nelly, that 'un ain't gonna last till daylight. They kept a-workin' on 'im anyways, but he died about the same time as ol' Daisy Hopkins. I had to clean up the mess he left. They say the woman with him might pull through. She was hurt bad. Face like it's been in a meat grinder. The Highway Patrol found her man drunk as a skunk down in Grand Isle. They brought him to the hospital and he was a-sayin' he hopes she dies fer messin' around on 'im. After somebody tolt 'im about the man she was out with, the one kilt. It was his half brother."

The voice died out and the sound of spraying water was heard in the alcove.

A short time later, an operator brought the woman out; her faded yellow hair in curlers, and seated her near Rita.

"Ye's be Paul Stark's woman, ain't 'cha?"

Rita didn't look up. "Yes, I'm Mrs. Paul Stark."

"My name's Isobel Potter. Most folks call me Belle. We live in Bonaparte, on t'other side of town from y'all."

Rita nodded.

"My man's Horace Potter. He has the Texaco station."

Again Rita nodded, trying to read.

"My sister Emma's married to Joe Riley, the butcher."

Rita tensed. "Riley? I don't know them, but I've only been here a short time." Rita glanced at the heavy features, and turned a page of the magazine. Inside, she was trembling.

"Yore man gittin' any prawns?"

"He doesn't tell me if he does or not."

"Ya like livin' in Bonaparte?"

"It's not so bad." Rita tried to signal her operator.

"I seen ya at Bob's last night."

"Bob's?"

"Bob's Drive-In. I seen ya aholdin' Joe Riley's hand and cozyin' up to him like you's hopin' to bust up him and Emma."

Rita looked up then, anger building. "I spoke to several people, but I don't place the name Riley." The close-set eyes and the mustache opened a crack in her memory.

The Juvenile Home! The bull-dyke matron!

"When I seen ye's at Bob's, I was a'wonderin iffen yore man got hisself fixed up at the bank?"

Rita was caught off guard. "Fixed up at the bank?"

"I thought ya knowed tha bank was takin' ya shrimp boat. Like they take ya car or teevee if ya don't keep up your payments."

The operator put Belle under a dryer just as Rita stood up, boiling mad. She leaned over the plastic dome covering the big woman's hair and shouted, "I'm glad you mentioned the bank, because we've just found out something you and Horace ought to know!"

Rita went for her comb-out. Paul hadn't said a damn thing about losing the boat. *Goddamn him again!* The operator was unrolling her hair. "Don't pay no mind to old Belle."

Rita was furious. "I'll fix her fat can, you just watch!"

Belle was still under the dryer as Rita paid the cashier. The salon had filled with customers. Rita walked to Belle and switched off her dryer, leaning her weight on it as Belle tried to lift it off. "Belle, has your Horace seen the doctor yet?"

"Horace? See a doctor? Why? He ain't sick."

"That's what the other bank customers thought, Belle."

"The others? Ye's ain't makin' no sense." Belle pushed Rita away from the dryer and got her head out. "The bank ain't said nuthin' to Horace."

Rita's voice knifed in. "It's that *woman* over there."

"What woman?"

"You know the one I mean Belle. I'm talking about that hot ass bitch at the bank, who has been screwing all the hen-pecked husbands and spreading syphilis." Rita felt a savage joy as she watched the words bite into Belle. There was a titter of laughter, like a puff of wind in dry leaves. Belle's face mottled with rage.

Rita walked to the door, angry but pleased. There would be plenty of hell around the bank. The wives of Bonaparte wouldn't know which one of the bank women to suspect, so they would suspect them all. With her hand on the doorknob she turned to Belle. "Like I say, Belle, Horace and you better see a doctor."

As Rita went through the door, Belle was screaming. "Ye's better ast yore man about that yella-haired gal on his shrimp boat!"

Rita closed the door and listened. Belle's voice was high-pitched. "The ambulance brung 'um straight from the fish dock. 'Bout time Nelly and me a havin' a bite tuh eat. At two-thirty break. She's was nekkid as a jaybird, ain't got a stich on 'er, and the Cap'n a totin' her things in a rolled up towel."

There was a sudden drone of conversation.

"Ain't all. Her man's a payin' the bill at the hospital."

Halfway to the car, Rita's knees buckled as she remembered what Troy and Joe had said. Something about Beau's Island and a blonde on a mattress out on deck. She hadn't paid any attention to them.

But Paul did come in way past midnight, getting undressed and getting in the other bed. Without saying why he was so late.

Everyone knew about his girlfriend except his wife!

When Rita reached Highway 90 she hesitated, then turned east towards New Orleans, picking up speed as she kissed off Paul, the bank, Belle Potter, and the whole lousy Bonaparte setup. Including his boat!

Fuck 'em all!

She drove recklessly. So the high and mighty Captain Stark had found someone to go fishing with him! It wasn't so hard to guess how they did it. Pick her up at Beau's Island on the way out and drop her off on the way back. Paul wouldn't want Lou to know and old Catfish could never talk!

If they had to get to the hospital before she had time to get dressed, it must have been an emergency. Maybe the blonde was already sick when she was outside on the mattress. And why hadn't they used the girlfriend's car when he took her to the hospital?

Rita's mind was spinning with questions. She hadn't believed Troy and Joe, but they had come to the house without any hesitation; they must have known Paul wasn't coming in.

After Troy had finished raping her, Joe had told Troy that he had seen the boat at Beau's Island when he drove out to Sandy Point. If Joe's car was broken like he said, then how could he drive to Sandy Point?

They had lied about the whole thing, except about Paul! Men, goddamn men!

When Rita calmed down, she realized that she felt no jealousy, except that Paul was her property. He was hers to keep until she decided to leave him. His blonde bimbo ought to at least have the decency to wait until his wife had decided to dump him!

But who could the blonde be?

Rita made a mental check of people they knew. The only blonde she could think of was Lois, Mel Wilson's wife. But Lois wasn't Paul's type. She had two kids and seemed very much in love with Mel. No it couldn't be Lois.

Maybe it was someone Paul took in like a stray cat. Stray pussy was more like it!

Paul was so stupid about women. Like all men.

She was glad the car was paid for and in her name. It was little enough to show for the ten long months of being buried in Bonaparte. The car and some clothes were all she had gained. Of course, Paul had given her the diamond wedding band she loved to flash at the local markets.

Since Paul hadn't mentioned taking someone to the hospital, he had to be guilty. He had strolled in long after midnight, after his wife was just raped, and helped himself to seconds, with barely more than a Hi, Rita, wham bam, thank you ma'am. Before daylight he was off again, probably to check on his other bedmate. Of all the nerve, asking her to go out to dinner, to show up in some public place with everybody knowing about his hot romance on the shrimp boat. That's reason for divorce. With a smart lawyer on her side, she might get a settlement. Except that Paul would need all he could rake and scrape together to pay off the bank. He had always put the shrimp boat ahead of his own wife!

She hoped to see Danny Lapere again and give him a piece of her mind. All those lies about the famous Captain Stark and his fleet of boats!

It was dark when she stopped for a slice of pizza at Pizzarrelli's. By now, Paul would know she wasn't coming to the fish dock and would be heading back out. Maybe his blonde was out of the hospital and he could pick her up on Beau's Island. Rita wondered where they hid the car while they went fishing and the blonde made love to him. What must Catfish be thinking? Even if he couldn't hear or say anything, he could see!

She realized by the flashing road sign "vacant rooms" that she was in New Orleans. She had to put Bonaparte and Belle Potter behind her. Paul had left five twenty-dollar bills on the kitchen table, so she wasn't broke. She wasn't exactly flush, either. One thing for certain, there was no point in rushing back. Paul would be out for three or four days, maybe more, depending on the weather, the shrimp, and of course, his blonde slut.

Then she remembered Sam and his place on Bourbon Street. Sam's Hideout. Sam wouldn't have customers this early at night.

She parked inside a garage near his place. The lounge was empty when she walked in and climbed on a stool. Sam moved in front of her.

"I must be dreaming! Rita's back in town!"

"Hello, Sam."

"Damn good to see you again. Rye on the rocks, with a twist?"

"You remember right, Sam."

He prepared the drink and served it with a flourish. "How's the world treating my girl?"

"Can't complain, just bored stiff sometimes. Living on a plantation out in the boonies is sure not like New Orleans." She knew Bourbon Street wasn't for hard luck stories.

"Yeah, I wondered what you were up to. Hadn't seen you around lately." He milked her hands between his soft white palms and she noticed he was still wearing the good luck ring with the embracing snakes. She studied the four tiny ruby eyes. His hands smelled of lime.

"How long you in town, Rita?"

"Oh, just overnight, I guess." She realized the decision to stay was made at that moment. Until Sam asked, she hadn't thought about her next move.

"What's the big rush? Where're you staying?"

"I just now drove in, and haven't had time to find a hotel. I wanted a drink first and thought you might know what's happening."

"Hell, pretty much the same old routine. If you're looking for action, Monday night's dead in the quarter. But you know that. What'd you have in mind?"

She didn't have anything in mind. She was restless, angry, bottled up. This wasn't something she could mention to Sam. He would have to pretend he cared, but he would be bored. Bartenders hate to listen to everybody. "I thought about some Dixieland for a change. I haven't heard any good jazz since I left here."

"I don't know, Rita, Monday night—" He polished the bar. "I have a friend that might like to have a sharp date to take to dinner, if he's in town."

She laughed. "Maybe he's planning on opening up a big fancy cabaret, starring a well-known dancer."

He hid his face behind the bar towel. "Cut it out, Rita! How was I to know that bastard would screw us both?"

She was feeling better as he took her empty glass. "Sam, your friends have a habit of crawling back into the woodwork."

"Okay, okay, so I made an honest mistake, but this guy's for real. The one I'm telling you about." He put his hand on hers.

"All right, Sam, let me guess: Your friend's a horny hick in town for the horse doctors' convention?"

"No, Rita, he's in investments. At least that's what's on his fancy card. Lives in a suite at the Royal Orleans. Thirty-five-ish, sharp dresser, big tipper. He won't touch the local pros with a ten-foot pole." Sam pushed another drink across the bar.

She knew that was meant as a compliment. She propped an elbow on the bar and rested her chin in her hand. "Where's his wife?"

"I don't think he has one. At least not that I know of."

That's sporting of Sam, she thought. He could have said his friend wasn't married. She smiled at him. "So he's asked the friendly French Quarter bartender to find him a date?"

"He can find his own around this town. He'll go for you in a big way. The reason I say that is, he's in here three, four times, with the big star in a stage play. Her picture was in all the papers. I forget the name of the show. She does some of the tunes over there at the piano bar. This guy, he just sits against that wall like he's cornered the best piece of ass this side of Broadway. The show just left for Dallas or somewhere."

"After that, he comes in here and cries all night?"

"He comes in here, all right, but without anybody, and looking like he's down on the world." Sam leaned over the bar. "Yeah, she was about your size, but not half as good-looking."

She moved her finger in circles on the dark varnish. "Investments? What's that exactly?"

"He never said. His card just says Tony Milano, Investments. He looks more like a movie star than some big business dude."

She smiled as she finished her drink.

Sam went to the telephone. Two minutes later he was back. "You're in luck. Tony's in town."

She was inclined to be glad. It could lead to a good meal, a night on the town, some laughs. *God, do I need a few laughs!* She leaned over and patted his cheek, slipping a five-dollar bill under her glass. "Thanks anyway, for thinking about me, Sam. Maybe Tony will be around some other night."

He grabbed her arm. "Tony's waiting for you in front of the Royal Orleans. He said take a taxi. He's got on a red shirt and white tie. I told him what you looked like."

She slid from the stool and adjusted the strap of her shoulder bag. "Sam, you should find your red-breasted woodpecker a nice pro. You know that I'm no pickup!" What Sam didn't know he couldn't broadcast. She had always been careful about her reputation. That, plus her talent and good looks, were her stock in trade.

"I told him you was a big star before you married some rich old guy and went to live on a big spread out west. He knows you're no hundred-dollar lay."

"Thanks, Sam, that's mighty decent of you. Some other time, maybe." She gave him her best smile with plenty of teeth.

Then she walked offstage, her shapely hips waving a farewell to Sam and his Hideout.

CHAPTER 9

By nightfall Monday night, Johnny was convinced that Mary Beth had split in his car. All day Monday he had driven his mother's sedan up and down Highway 90, and through Beaver City's paved and unpaved streets. Whenever he saw a green car, he sped up, but it was always someone else. Several times during the day he had returned to the mansion to ask Joselyn if anyone had called or come by. The maid had been no help. When he had left again, he had driven past the Claiborne's house, only to see that the drapes were still closed in Mary Beth's upstairs room.

One time, he saw Hannah on the porch sweeping, and the downstairs windows were open. A breeze was blowing the curtains. The Claiborne housekeeper wouldn't be out there on the porch sweeping, he reasoned, if some big crisis were happening. He would have liked to stop and question Hannah, but he gave up that idea, knowing that he couldn't stiff-arm the fat old hag. Blacks had raised him; they understood him. Hannah wouldn't give Johnny Cameron the time of day.

By afternoon, Johnny was hurting from anger. He drove aimlessly to places already covered and became more certain that Mary Beth had grabbed his car and gone to New Orleans.

It would be more than twenty-four hours for her by now, and he knew she'd be racked up sure, ready to do anything for a fix. He felt like kicking himself for letting her have the stuff on credit, and for not yelling for her to stop when she was driving off. By now his car would be out of gas and left somewhere, and she'd be floating around dead broke and owing him four hundred bucks! So what if he had charged her double. Nobody but a jerk would do business on the cuff without lagniappe, a little something extra, for his trouble. He had believed her promises to come up with the bread. Only now she had skipped out on him.

He was almost out of money himself, with a source in New Orleans who wouldn't even talk unless the cash was spread out in advance. You'd never catch those boys opening up a charge account for you. Once Johnny had tried to fly some on the Cameron name. His supplier had eyes like a card shark; you couldn't tell whether he was looking at you or not. "Listen, kid," the man had said. "You ain't got the fucking cash on you, fuck off!"

He put himself in Mary Beth's place. She'd have to go to the city. Her best bet would be to get in with the college crowd and find a campus pusher. Someone who'd give her a quick fix for a quick screw. Johnny knew that it was the advantage bitches had when they were broke.

And she could damn well drop out of sight for weeks, being passed from one fraternity to another. While she was screwing around, time was running out for Johnny. Any day now his mother would be phoning from New York and he'd have to meet her at the New Orleans airport. That's when the shit would hit the fan. She'd get on him first about his car, then she'd call the school. Joselyn was probably her paid spy.

Even if his mother did manage to find his car, she'd lock it up or sell it. This time he would get his ass kicked out for good. Without a dime!!

He had to move fast! But first, he had to find Mary Beth, or he wasn't going anywhere.

When Johnny finally gave up looking, he was lopsided with anger. Again he tried to figure out her course of action. If she ran out of gas in New Orleans, she wouldn't think to lock the doors or even take the keys. Maybe he could accuse *her* of stealing his heap!

Old man Claiborne wouldn't like that. Johnny laughed. It would serve the old bastard right to have his kid thrown in jail. For a few moments the plan bloomed in Johnny's head, and then it popped like a soap bubble. Her daddy wouldn't pay off to have Johnny drop the charges; he'd let her go to jail.

Mary Beth had said her old man was planning on having her locked up, just because of her habit. Jesus, what a father!

If that happened before Johnny left Bonaparte for good, they'd find out from Mary Beth where she was getting the junk. Then Claiborne would rat to his mother; his wheels would take wings; and his chances of cutting out and making any deals would be a fat zero. Shit!

Joselyn had left his dinner in a covered dish. As he ate, he told himself to cool it.

In the morning he would start looking again. Maybe go to New Orleans and hang around the campuses.

Rita spotted the white tie against the maroon shirt, as the taxi rolled under the brightly lit marquee of the Royal Orleans.

Sam had not exaggerated.

Tony was tall, good-looking, with Big City written all over him. He was wearing a gray sports jacket and wine colored slacks that matched his shirt. White teeth showed as he smiled, opening the taxi door. "Hello, Rita."

"Tony! It's good to see you again."

"Glad you could make it on such short notice."

"The pleasure's all mine. But I can only stay for one short drink." She was delighted. The chitchat was for the taxi driver and the doorman wearing the general's uniform. No hooker would carry on a conversation like that. Tony had picked up on cue like a pro.

"A dollar eighty, Mister."

Tony spread three-dollar bills in the driver's face. "Keep the change, Mac."

Then her handsome escort had her by the arm, steering her into the splendor of the hotel.

She had always been awed by the Royal Orleans. She thought it elegant and luxurious, a place where only the wealthiest or most important people were permitted to stay. Tony took her up in the elevator and down a corridor, which had fancy wallpaper and a thick carpet.

He unlocked a heavy door that opened into a world of gold-burnished white furniture and champagne carpeting. Delicate white curtains crossed over tall windows. A creamy leather bar filled a corner of the large room. Through a doorway, she saw a wide bed with a satiny canopy overhead, and more white and gold furniture.

Tony lifted her purse strap from her shoulder and held up the bag, looking at the suede patchwork design. "I've seen one of these before, only it didn't have initials. I take it the *R* stands for Rita?"

She was pleased that he had noticed. The bag was expensive and had contained the keys to the new car. Paul had pretended the purse was her only birthday present. When she opened it, she found the car keys.

"This sure is a nice place, Tony."

She watched him as he hung his jacket behind the bar, his gold cufflinks flashing.

"You name it, Rita."

"Rye on the rocks, with a twist."

While Tony made the drinks, Rita crossed to one of the tall windows and looked down on the French Quarter. Night people were already moving along the streets. She knew there would be tourists and convention groups on the prowl, people being hustled into joints by sidewalk barkers. There would be pimps trying to find johns, and college kids roaming around. It made her realize how much she missed the city.

Rita felt secure here, high above the crowd. Sam's whiskey had given her a feeling of being alive and aloof. The night was young. The sound of drums beat through the noise of traffic, reaching for her, and she tried to decide what they would be playing to that rhythm.

Tony brought drinks. "Cheers!" He raised his glass and she knew he was looking her over and approving.

"Cheers," she said.

"I'm expecting some phone calls. You like prime rib?"

She nodded, wearing her best half smile. "End cut, well done. French dressing." If he wanted to have dinner in the suite, she wasn't going to object. She was hungry; they could do the town later.

Tony picked up the ivory telephone and ordered, then took her empty glass to the bar. She saw him drop what looked to be a cube of sugar into her glass, but she checked the impulse to protest. If he wanted her flying, he could damn well put on his own traveling shoes! With Paul out there making it with a skinny blonde, she reasoned, why shouldn't she kick up her own heels?

Her drink had a slight sting and was sweeter than she liked it. She was feeling reckless as she sipped. *I can take this town apart, she thought.*

Tony was exploring her with his eyes. The breasts were real. "Sam said you live down on the bayou?"

"About ninety miles out." She reached her arm toward the city. "It's good to be here, if only for a few hours." She was floating on clouds. "Have you ever been on the stage, Tony?"

"Naw, it's outta my line." He raised his glass to her. "Sam says you were in the big time in the old days, before you bugged off."

"I've not been gone even a whole year!" Sam must have laid it on good, she thought. "Do you spend much time here in New Orleans?"

"Not too much. I move around a lot."

She pressed the attack. "I mean, is your main business around here somewhere?"

"Mostly I'm at the other places."

Other places! The Royal Orleans would be like a motel room to him. "Let me guess. You have something to do with oil?"

"Well, I burn a lot of it. I ain't got no wells, if that's what you mean."

"Then it must be you're in real estate?"

He frowned. "Yeah. Shopping centers, high-rises, a few restaurants, and nightspots. Wherever I can turn a buck."

"Do any of your night clubs have shows? One of my best acts was a monologue, with me dancing all the time. Real funny. Always got laughs and encores."

He stepped back and looked at her figure. "You sure got the body for it, Baby."

She whirled gracefully around the room. Her skirt flared, revealing smooth thighs. Unlike most dancers, she didn't have heavy leg muscles.

"Hey, Rita, that's great!" He went to the bar and she floated past, putting down her empty glass.

He clapped his hands. "Maybe I get my own private show, huh?"

She became a Spanish dancer, snapping her fingers, moving to her inner music. "Could be," she teased. "Depends on whatever I feel like doing."

A waiter rolled in a dinner cart, set it up, and withdrew with a big cash tip. A bottle of champagne was in a frosty silver bucket. Rita resumed her dance and Tony popped the cork from the bottle.

She was high, but she didn't care. This was *her* night, for a change, her answer to Paul, to Bonaparte, and the shrimp boat. And to the damn blonde! Tony would know by now that she was no pick-up. No whore in Louisiana could dance like that. Men couldn't resist when she was doing her act, when she felt like she was in a world of her own, unattainable. This was maddening to them, although she didn't quite understand why.

Tony pursued and captured her, waltzing her to the table.

They ate without speaking.

Afterwards, Tony pushed the cart into the hall and chained the door. He turned some dials and music flooded the room. Rita knew he was already important to her, which made whatever he did important. They could make the French Quarter spots some other night. She felt drowsy, yet strangely elated.

The music began to sway and twist her and she floated around the room, past the bar where he had another drink ready. She stood on tiptoe to pour it down her throat, a swan, graceful, gliding alone in a royal lake.

Almost like a football tackle, Tony rushed her back into the broad sofa, with her toes still pointing. Then he was kissing her hungrily, his breath smelling of garlic. The music increased her mastery over him and she began to return his kisses. And then she was all over him, hands moving like two butterflies, her mouth showering quick, moist kisses as she pressed her hips and legs against his lean, hard body. She imprisoned his hand between her thighs and clamped it there for just a moment, before slowly spreading her legs and revealing to him the source of her power.

She felt her panties tearing.

They struggled on the sofa with mad abandon and then slid to the floor, grasping each other in the fury of desire. They flung their clothing aside. Rita was wild with desire and tried to smother his handsome face with her belly. Startled when he pushed her down and entered her with a savage thrust, she cried out, but quickly joined his rhythm.

Afterwards, when she had cradled him against her breasts, the music stopped and he rolled onto the soft carpet.

When the music started again Rita struggled to her feet and resumed her dance.

CHAPTER 10

The *Helen S.* rode down river on the falling tide Monday night and Paul wished that Rita had come to the docks to see him off. Or, at the least, had joined him for dinner.

He liked to go places with her, to be seen. When she was happy, she sparkled like a child finding toys under a Christmas tree. And when she was like that, beautiful and full of life, she was always the center of attention.

Catfish came into the darkened wheelhouse. He would have the lines coiled flawlessly. The knack of whipping a noose over a piling had somehow eluded him, but he knew to turn the rope into a circular arrangement, once he had it on deck. The windows were open to the night air, heavy with the muddy smell left behind by an outgoing tide. The only sound, like a heartbeat, was the throbbing of the engine.

Catfish stood to the right of the wheel, peering ahead, looking frequently at Paul for approval. Paul wondered what words they would need if the old man were suddenly able to talk and hear.

In front of the Beau's Island dock, the live oaks were blotting out some of the moon's pale track on the water. A green glow from the running light flickered along the edge of the dock. The events of the night before crowded Paul's mind. He remembered Mary Beth's wet blue eyes, the lightness of her body when he finally put her to bed in the wheelhouse. His thoughts turned to his invention, the octopus. Would it work? He would soon find out!

He spun the wheel and the trawler heeled over slightly, as it rounded a hairpin bend in the river.

Before midnight, they dropped anchor in the cove off Point La Croix. Catfish was sleeping when Paul closed the windows and lowered the mahogany shelf from the bulkhead. He weighted down the curling edges of a chart, smoothing the sea flat with his hand. Working from the compass rose on the map, he drew a line from North Point light 195 degrees toward Mexico. For the next thirty minutes he consulted the notebook, placing bearing marks on the line.

Far out in the gulf he drew a tiny oval. In less than three hours he would follow the line, allowing for a thirteen-degree compass error. There was a chance that it would be a wild goose chase.

When the *Helen S.* finally faded into the marsh, Lou felt an overwhelming sense of sorrow. He stood on the dock, watching the lighted circle in the waters. He heard the familiar sound of unseen birds calling and the river's outgoing voice, as the water gurgled and sighed below him. He wondered if his grip on reality were already weakening, in some merciful dimming of awareness, preparing him for the end. But no, his mind was moving along in its normal pattern of thoughts and ideas, as if the doctor had never told him his fate.

He knew that there would be times when he would be jerked back into the present to face the harsh reality of his approaching death. With Paul gone, Lou wondered about the night ahead. Sleep would be out of the question. Tomorrow, there would be things to do, final errands to keep him occupied. It was important that no one suspect why he was suddenly wrapping up the loose ends. Catfish would need another guardian.

Moonbeam was purring and rubbing against his leg. He would have to find another black cat, a stand-in for Moonbeam, as he had promised Paul. He would need to take the papers on Paul's invention to Earle Black, his long-time friend who knew about patents.

Earle could draw up a will leaving his estate to Paul. There would be more than enough left after expenses to pay off Paul's boat.

What about Maggie? He had put off thinking about her until last. Should he go to her and tell her that he no longer wanted to marry her? She would not accept that, not Maggie! Instead, she would probe until she found out the reason, and then there would be specialists rushed in from all over the world, investigations of miracle cures and witch doctors. When all these efforts failed, his death would be horrible for her and she would blame herself for not having done more. It would be best for her not to know.

Lou thought of the assets of his life, how he had always considered good health a person's ultimate wealth. It would no longer be on the proper side of the ledger. There was the house and business, a little money saved, insurance, not much else. Bonaparte Seafoods was almost worthless, as a result of the decline in shrimping. The building and dock would revert to the township, after the lease ran out, when there was no longer a tenant to open the place and go through the motions of waiting for boats that came no more.

He would not die in Bonaparte!

Paul and Maggie knew he had relatives in the mountains of North Carolina. For years, he had threatened to visit them. The lull in shrimping would be the best time for him to be away. He would see one more time the mountains that, from a distance, looked like blue smoke. Soon the laurel, rhododendron, and flame azalea would be in bloom and there would be the moist earth smell of secret places and the sound of rain under the trees.

Yes, he could find his people in the hills, but it was too late. Kissing kin were not dying kin; there would be no point in spending his last days bringing pain to their lives, just to recall lost and forgotten days of youth. Nevertheless, Carolina kin would provide him with the excuse to leave Bonaparte for an extended time.

He locked the fish house and stopped by Mike's for coffee, determined to put aside until Tuesday any further thoughts of dying. His pain was still manageable and the medicine was in the truck.

The restaurant was warm, smelling of fried fish and hickory smoke. Lou looked around at the familiar tables, the scenic calendar on the wall, the clock, and Mike behind the counter. Everything was in place, just as expected. Mike's hadn't changed, just because Lou Fisher was entering the final stage of his life.

He had read something in the New Orleans paper about the latest oil spill off the coast. Experts claimed there would be no real damage. Lou thought of Paul and his invention, the octopus.

When he finished his coffee and a few words with Mike, he drove northwest on Highway 90 to his turnoff, and then through the woods to his house on the edge of the marsh.

CHAPTER 11

Tuesday morning, when the *Helen S.* neared the oval on the chart, the sun was an easterly ball of flame above a quiet horizon. For a few moments, the sea was the color of blood. Long ground swells journeyed past, on their way to distant beaches. Paul took frequent bearings with the direction finder, locating small *x* signs on the chart line.

He was feeling foolish. It had been years since the trip to the Mexican coast, when he found that undersea plateau, a flat mesa fifteen or twenty feet higher than the surrounding bottom. He had been far off course, skirting a big storm on his way back to Louisiana. The depth had suddenly changed, becoming shallower for several miles, and then dropping back to the depth shown on the chart. There was no indication on the chart of this mysterious rise, and he had always wanted to come back to it. It was a pinpoint in space; lost somewhere below the waves, and finding it might take days of searching.

Months earlier, he had determined to take the octopus beyond the polluted inshore waters. It was his belief that the shrimp population still existed, but in cleaner waters, withdrawn to areas less contaminated by the march of progress. The thought of the plateau had always intrigued him; but he doubted that any shrimp boat had ever put a net down that deep, or so far from land. According to his calculations, he should have reached the place on the chart. He looked around at the empty reaches of the sea, wondering if the plateau really existed. The flasher on the fathometer was moving! He switched on the recorder and watched the numbers print out on paper. His heart began to pound.

The ocean bottom had tilted upward!

The instrument steadied, once more registering level bottom. As he wrote down the arrival time, his hand shook. Set on automatic pilot, the trawler continued on course for fifty-nine minutes before the bottom fell away again to the chart depth. Paul took three radio fixes and, as the vessel drifted, pinpointed the far edge of the plateau. Beneath its hull, he knew that there was a wide hill with a flattened top, and it was at least ten miles across!

Paul came about and retraced his track, returning through the bubble slick of his own wake, back across the edge of the undersea formation. It took thirty minutes to reach the center of the plateau. He stepped onto the side deck and waved at Catfish, who threw a bamboo marker off the stern. Paul watched the cane drift for a few minutes and then snap upright, indicating that the sash weight had plunged to the mesa's surface. This would hold the marker in position, tethered to the end of a monofilament line.

Paul reduced the engine rpm's to the slow crawl best suited for dragging shrimp nets. By then, the trawler was a half-mile from the marker and west of the original track.

Catfish came forward, anticipation on his face.

"We found it, Catfish!" Paul went outside and swept his arm at the water. "Here's where we turn the octopus loose!"

The marker was bearing ten points off the starboard bow when he switched on the autopilot; this heading would result in a slight roll, rather than forward pitching, meaning the net would pull well.

Catfish followed him to the stern, where a large reel of air hose was housed inside a cage of iron rods.

The air gauge under the gunwale was registering the correct pressure. Paul turned a small handle, until a loud shriek told him the valve was in good condition.

They threw the net overboard, cod end first, until it was pursuing the boat, a long brown stain below the black silver water. Paul ran his hand over the tiny metallic mouths of the larger hose, which would be dragged just ahead of the lead line. These were in the tentacles of the octopus.

The net wings pulled slowly over the stern rail, until they were tugging at the large 5x10- foot trawl boards that had been swung out over the water. The cable drum of the winch backed off slowly, until the boards were swimming upright, pulling away from each other. Paul stopped the winch, to check the valve device at the point where the trawl board cables were shackled to the big winch cable. This was the head of the octopus; a series of carefully machined ports and valves, which would feed bursts of air to the tentacles. He connected the air line from the deck reel to the air-metering device, let out more cable, and then watched as the boards pulled under the surface. The red air hose ran smoothly from its reel and swung below the black cable. *So far, so good!* Now, hold it there.

Again, Paul locked the winch and moved to the stern, where he connected a metal-wound hose from the air tanks to the core end of the hose on the reel. He turned the valve that supplied the octopus with life-giving air.

The hose extending into the water writhed with a sudden life of its own, twitching at heartbeat intervals. The needle on the gauge began to snap in quarter-circles, in unison with the pulsing hose. Under its housing, behind the deckhouse, the compressor started.

Paul stood up, looked over the stern, and saw exactly what his mind had imagined a thousand times. Well astern, between the underwater comets tails dashing behind the shadowy trawl boards were streaming curtains of lights rising and glistening inside the translucent swells on both sides of the boat's wake. Millions of air bubbles were flashing into walls of diamonds, reaching up from the depths in sequined tapestries, laddering the boat's trail with a crosshatch of frothy bubbles.

"Take a look at that," Paul breathed, fascinated. He couldn't take his eyes away from the upright sheets of underwater light. And then he saw the majestic rhythm and a lump rose in his throat.

Satisfied with the under-surface performance, Paul turned off the air, disconnected the tank line from the reel hose, and resumed his position at the winch. He allowed the cable to run smoothly through the heavy block on the boom. The trawler was moving slightly faster than the speed of the turning winch drum, so there was sufficient pressure on the boards to keep the wings of the net spread.

Paul knew that the otter trawl was dropping toward the ocean floor like some giant bird of prey, its wing span sixty feet and its body more than a hundred feet long.

He watched the depth markers on this cable, finally locking the winch at three hundred fathoms. Moments later, the drum creaked from the strain on the cable and he knew that the arms of the net would be angling against the bottom of the sea, behind the sliding upright trawl doors. As the hose stiffened and began to snap with energy, he connected the hose from the tank and opened the valve. *This is it!* This was the moment of truth!

The boat was pulling evenly, swaying gently.

Paul tried to imagine what was happening on the surface of the plateau, deep below the trawler's keel. The octopus should be spitting its hard breath into the bottom of the ocean's floor, blasting tiny holes. Clouds of silt should be blowing upward to startle the burrowed shrimp, forcing them behind the silt explosions and into the forward V of the air walls, until the lead line of the net slid under them.

All he could do was wait and pray. Paul looked at his watch. He had decided on hour-long drags, less than half the usual time, and with half the drags made without air. Only then would he know if, by using his octopus-like invention, he could actually catch more shrimp.

He both anticipated and dreaded the answer.

While the *Helen S.* worked slowly past the yellow pennant, Paul made coffee. The ocean's surface was still placid, with occasional clouds of flying fish that erupted and then skimmed over the swells, until they lost speed and plunged back into the water.

Paul looked at his watch every few minutes. He went to the hose, put his hand on it to check the number of pulsations per minute. He studied the cable, while trying to calculate the added weight of the octopus. As the marker moved astern, he sat on the gunwale and waited.

A thin contrail was being drawn high in the cloudless sky and he strained his eyes to see the jet. Nothing. Then he caught the flash of sunlight on metal and knew that the vapor path was resulting from hot turbines. This caused him to think of the trail left by the octopus, until he was struck by the absurdity of his conceit.

In moments of self-examination, Paul knew the law of averages was stacked on the side of failure. Any idea with real promise would have already been put into practice long ago. Marine biologists, or perhaps big business, or even the government, any one of them would have developed the octopus. Each year, millions of dollars were poured into finding better ways of catching fish.

Therefore, he reasoned, and in spite of Lou's confidence in his idea, the octopus was preposterous from the beginning. Whatever the outcome, he was glad that Lou had encouraged him, especially when he was about to give up and junk the project. He respected Lou's judgment and intelligence. As for Mel Wilson, he would still be his friend, whether the jets worked or not, and even if the *Helen S.* had to go on the auction block.

Paul wished that Rita had more faith in what he was doing. But why should she? His world was strange to her. He looked at his watch: ten more minutes!

He remembered when he and Mel had gone to the Texas shipyard to supervise the outfitting of the *Helen S.* and the *Honey L.* They had sailed them back and tied them up at Lou's dock, their new generation of steel shrimpers and the last word in seaworthiness and brute power. He had wondered at the time if the outmoded bottom trawl might be improved, which had led him to the original concept of the octopus.

Five more minutes!

Now there was no time left for hope or worry. When the net reached the surface, it would bring the answer with it. Paul allowed himself one deviation: If there were no shrimp at all in both the air and the non-air attempts, he would conclude that the plateau was barren of any shrimp and the test wouldn't count.

The hour was up. Paul disconnected the reel hose from the air tank hose. Before the big drum of the winch was turning, he reduced the engine rpm's. The net felt heavy, but this could mean anything. He had pulled in big loads of bottom trash before.

As the weight swung loose from the sea floor, Paul knew the trawl boards had come together, clasped hands reaching up through the green water, closing the wings on the pregnancy of the cod end. The red hose was threading itself back on its reel, an umbilical cord no longer needed.

The cable shackle, holding the eye splices of the board cables, raised dripping, the octopus tentacles shooting out from the apex. He stopped the winch and disconnected the hose from the octopus brain, allowing the hose to snake onto its turning reel.

The boards were lifted into the boom and it seemed an eternity before the bag of the net was at last in the grip of the hoist line and moving toward the surface. His body was filled with emotion and anxiety, as if, at this moment, his life had reached its final apogee. The net lifted, spilling water as it rose into the sunlight. He saw it was filled with large shrimp. The great mass was swung inboard and Paul began yelling, trumpeting like some beast triumphant over its prey. The sea had bowed to his will!

"Catfish, we've done it! We've really by God done it!"

Catfish was dancing with excitement as Paul pulled the drawstring and the harvest spilled onto the deck, a silvery cascade of light raining on them. Tears slid down the sea-weathered face of Paul Stark. For a brief moment, all that existed on earth stood still.

CHAPTER 12

J ohnny dreamed that his car was smashed and Mary Beth was lying beside the road.

At daylight, he phoned the Beaver City hospital. A girl answered and he made his voice husky. "Louisiana Times here."

"Oh... a newspaper?"

He could see some girl preening at the switchboard. "I'm checking on your accident cases."

"Oh, yes. Sunday night was pretty bad."

A cold chill swept over him. His car would be twisted junk. "Names, please."

The names meant nothing to him. "Miss... uh?"

"Stacy. I'm Miss Judy Stacy."

"Let me get this right. S-t-a-c-e-y?"

"No. Just c-y."

"Thanks, Miss Stacy. Do you have a patient by the name of Claiborne? She's about twenty-two."

There was a moment of silence. "Yes, here it is. Mary Beth Claiborne. They brought her here in the ambulance."

Johnny felt he had been hit with a hammer. He tried to keep his voice from squeaking. "I need to know about her condition. What are her chances, et cetera?"

More silence. "I don't have that information yet. If you'll call back a little later—"

"Thanks."

He hung up, a cold sweat popping out. So the dream had been true and she was in the lousy hospital! *Goddamn her!* He smashed his fist against the desk in his mother's room. No telling what shape his car was in. All that time wasted on Mary Beth, hoping she'd get her hands on some cash, and she'd played him for a sucker. Everybody knew her old man was the tightest skinflint in Louisiana. Now, the police had her in the hospital.

The police! Hell, it had to be the police. No dopehead would go in the hospital of their own free will, even if they were in a wreck. Maybe she had already squealed on him; maybe the narcs were waiting outside the mansion now!

He tiptoed to the top of the stairs and heard the phone ring. Joselyn was talking. "I doan know, ma'am, if Mistah Johnny come home las' night. His caah ain't heah."

Silence, then, "Let me write that numbah down. Duh hospital in Beavah City? Hit's about his caah?" Johnny raced back to his mother's room and heard Mary Beth on the line. "Joselyn, I got it upstairs."

Joselyn hung up.

"Mary Beth, where the hell are you?" He saw no point in saying he already knew. At least she was able to manage a phone call.

"In the hospital in Beaver City."

"Did you wreck my car?"

"No, nothing like that. I just wanted to tell you where I left it."

"You mean it ain't totaled?"

There was a sarcastic laugh. "Thanks for the concern. I just couldn't get it back to you. I was too busy dying."

She's outta her mind! "Where is it at?"

"Beau's Island."

So his car was still in one piece. His mind turned to more pressing business. "When can I see you?"

"Maybe we had better not see each other for awhile." Her voice was hesitant. "I've got, you know, other plans right now."

"Plans? What plans?"

"I'm going away on a boat, whenever I get out of here."

He could see the Claiborne money growing wings. He was trying to think fast.

"Johnny?"

"Yeah, I'm still here, trying to get some fuckin' sense outta you. Have you talked to anyone? The police, for instance?"

"No Johnny, your ass is safe."

"Where you calling from?"

"There's a phone in the hall near my room."

"I better not come up there." He had to be careful. The last thing he wanted was for people to spot them together.

"Johnny, I have your car keys."

"I know. Meet me at the corner of Oskam and Champagne."

"Are you crazy? I can't leave here yet. I'm in an ugly green hospital gown that's open all the way down the back."

"Where are your clothes?"

"In the closet, I guess. They got soaking wet last night; they must be a mess."

"Leave! Meet me at the corner."

"How can I leave Johnny? Get real."

God, how stupid could she be! "Just get dressed and walk out. You ain't crippled or anything, are you?"

"No. I just got drunk last night and I landed here."

"Remember, Mary Beth, Oskam and Champagne. I gotta have my car right away. You can make it."

"Oh, alright. My head is in twenty pieces, but I know you don't care. Give me thirty minutes."

Johnny hung up and went to his room, where he unlocked the bedroom closet and took the things he would need. Right now, he told himself, he needed Mary Beth Claiborne. He laughed about the keys. There was an extra set in his bureau drawer and another hidden underneath the car, in a magnetic box. He knew he'd have to come up with some way for Mary Beth to get money for him. What the hell! Her old man was head honcho at the bank. Mary Beth could cash some checks around Beaver City, after the banks closed. They wouldn't bounce checks signed by the president's daughter. Or she could grab whatever cash or jewelry she could find around her house. He would convince her the stuff was hers anyway, so it wasn't like stealing.

The first move was to get her out of the fucking hospital and high again. She sure as hell wouldn't get away from him a second time. He knew he had to work fast.

Mary Beth dressed quietly in her room. She heard footsteps and got back under the covers, until they passed her door. A few minutes later, she strolled out the front door and through a lobby crowded with people. She didn't see anyone she knew.

She walked from the grounds, feeling dizzy, and wondered how bad the day would be. She wished she could be like the spring morning, all fresh and clear. Her aching body pushed aside her drowsiness and panic began to rise inside her. Johnny would be yelling for his money, using that squeaky voice he got when he was mad.

He was waiting in his mother's car, wearing wrap-around sunglasses and a cap pulled forward. He swung the door open. "Get in." When she was inside, he reached across, pulled the door closed, and drove off.

"Johnny, we don't have to leave here." Mary Beth handed him the keys.

His voice was heavy with sarcasm. "How the hell do you expect me to drive two cars back to my place?"

Her head was spinning. Up ahead was Bonaparte Seafoods. The *Helen S.* was at the dock. She touched his arm. "Please turn in up there, Johnny. I have to ask about my boat." She knew she would be safe if she could find Captain Stark or Mr. Fisher. "I'll ask them to sell my boat and give you the money."

He slowed momentarily, and then sped up. "Hell, they wouldn't give me any of your money!"

As they passed the mansion and turned into the faint tracks of the Beau's Island road, her withdrawal spasms worsened. In the woods, near the gate, they found the car where she had left it.

Mary Beth climbed out of the car. Her body was screaming for relief and she fell on her hands and knees. Johnny had a syringe in his hand. She rolled up her sweater sleeve, anticipating the rush. As the narcotic took effect, she began to cry.

"Cut out that crap!" said Johnny.

Mary Beth managed to drive his car and park it in the garage behind the mansion. She climbed into the sedan with Johnny and they drove through the gate, turning right.

"Johnny, please, I have to go back to the hospital. I promised I'd give his treatment a try."

There was suspicion in his face. "You promised? You promised who?"

She knew there was no use answering. She also knew that they were speeding toward Lafayette.

CHAPTER 13

Tony awakened, burning with thirst, and feeling warm flesh against his back.

His mind retreated from a waterless desert, searched its memory, and put a name to the body pressed against his: Rita. Rita something-or-other.

Then he realized it was still dark outside.

He slipped from the bed and went into the other room, finding the ice bucket on the bar. He turned the bucket up to his lips and drank. Most of the ice had melted.

"I'm thirsty, Tony."

He spun around, startled. Rita had come up behind him and was standing against the dim light of the window, her nude body a pale statue. She took the bucket from him and tilted it clumsily to her mouth. Water and ice spilled down her stomach and fell onto the carpet. Cold fingers touched his when she handed him the emptied container.

She moved toward him, pressing him against the bar, her arms around his neck. He pulled at her elbows but she only tightened her hold. They struggled until he lifted her up and stretched her out on the sofa

"Rita, snap out of it!" Tony freed his neck and gripped her wrists. He tried to remember how many cubes he had put in her drinks. *The damn broad is strung out!* She was tripping out and might start screaming. Damn! He debated slapping her hard, as he put his knee on her thrashing legs.

Her voice was becoming shrill as she talked about the shrimp boat.

He ran back and put his hand over her mouth. "Shut up, you crazy bitch! You wanna wake up the whole damn hotel?" She bit into the fleshy part of his palm and he sucked his wounded hand, and wondered how to shut her up. He considered dragging her into the shower and turning the cold water on her naked body, but dropped that idea. Why get his own ass wet?

She stopped yelling and began talking a mile a minute. He made no effort to stop her. If he let her rattle on, she would have to run out of steam. Tony was only half listening when he started hearing her words.

"Oughta give up shrimping... bank's gonna take the damn boat anyway...your high and mighty ass will be on the beach. Where will you hide your blonde girlfriend then?" She laughed hysterically.

Tony began fitting a picture together in his mind. A shrimp captain not catching any shrimp? Better still, a hard-up shrimp captain not catching any shrimp, with his girlfriend on board and his wife sacked out in New Orleans.

By daybreak, with very little prompting, Rita had spouted information—like a broken water main sprays water—showering Tony with details, until he knew all about Bonaparte, Paul, Lou Fisher's dock, Beau's Island, and the impending loss of the boat to the bank.

Rita offered no resistance when Tony carried her back to bed. She was fast asleep when he left the bed.

The morning sounds of the city were seeping into the bedroom when Tony picked up his watch and held it in a shaft of light. It was ten fifteen.

His mind was busy as he shaved and dressed. When he walked out of the suite, he left the Do Not Disturb tag hanging on the doorknob. Across from the hotel, in a drugstore telephone booth, he placed a call and dropped coins in the slots. A hoarse voice answered, "Yeah."

"Tony."

"Tony, huh? You sure fucked up good down there."

Tony felt injured. "Hell, I took care of my end. Somebody there musta talked."

"Yeah, we know who tipped the Coast Guard."

"Coulda been worse," said Tony. "It wasn't a complete bust. We didn't lose anything but some grass."

"Sure, Tony, you spending good money telling us what we already know?"

"That ain't what I called for. I got a chance to go fishing for a few days, on a shrimp boat."

"Yeah."

"Shrimping ain't no good around here. My friend thinks we might find some red snappers. Says he knows a real good place, twenty or thirty miles out."

"Maybe, Tony, you catch some fish, huh? When you leaving?"

"That's the trouble, I can't leave right now."

"You want somebody else?"

"Yeah, you don't get many chances like this. No sweat."

"We'll work it out. How's the weather? We're freezing our balls off here."

"Nice and warm, best time of the damn year to go out."

"Call us back, Tony, in a couple of hours."

"Sure thing."

"Hey, Tony."

"I ain't hung up."

"You gotta cut down expenses. Let us know when you call back."

The line went dead. A fat woman elbowed past when he left the booth.

Two hours later, Tony called from a different booth.

"You meet the one-thirty plane from Miami," he was told. "It's National, number seven-sixteen. Name's Delbert Morgan, calls himself Duke. He's a young guy, wearing a black and white polka dot tie. Better rent him a car from our people down there and fix him up with some expense money."

The hoarse voice continued with details and Tony wrote down the information.

"Speaking of expenses, what you done about them, Tony?"

"You check that out tomorrow with Thomas Martin. He'll be at the Crescent City Hotel here. Ya got that?"

"Yeah, I got it." The line went dead.

Tony looked at his watch. He had time for a quick drink before renting the car and fighting traffic to the airport. He also had to pick up the cash. Rita was still in bed and one of the boys was coming to town. Sonofabitch!

CHAPTER 14

Duke Morgan was temporarily alarmed when the hoarse voice on the phone began questioning him.

"Duke, you know anything about fish?"

Fish! Duke thought about the question a moment. "I ain't what you'd call no expert. When I was a kid, I worked in the Fulton Fish Market up there."

"What about restaurants? You know how they buy stuff for the kitchens?"

"Hell, I never worked in no kitchens." Duke thought of the years he worked in the Jersey supper clubs, hustling tables and bouncing drunks. They *knew* all about that.

"Okay, write this down."

"Shoot."

"National flight #716 leaves Miami one-twenty your time. You get off in New Orleans."

Duke wrote on the pad beside the telephone and then looked at his watch. "It's already past twelve," he objected.

"That's your worry. What color tie you got?"

Duke thought about his collection. "Make it a black and white polka dot." He tried to listen and write at the same time. Fish, kitchens, New Orleans. It didn't make any sense. "When do I get back here?"

"Coupla weeks, might take longer. Marty'll cover for you down there. Duke?"

"I'm here."

"Wasn't nobody else we had we could send on such short notice."

Duke thought of a number of questions, but asked only one. "Anything else?"

"Just make sure you don't miss that fucking plane." There was a click and the hoarse voice was gone.

Two years of easy living in Miami had not affected Duke's ability to move fast. At the airport, he bought a one-way, first class ticket, and boarded the flight carrying a valet pack and an under-seat bag.

He was only mildly curious about the sudden trip. No use wearing out his brain, he thought. He'd know the score soon enough.

Miami had been good to him. The routine was smooth, he knew he wouldn't want to move somewhere else, and the city gave him his choice of sexy broads. He ran his business from an unlisted phone that was under a dummy name, and that phone was in a furnished apartment rented under yet another name. The windows of his office apartment overlooked a cluster of phone booths on Biscayne Boulevard and his managers came at different times, hanging around those booths and never knowing which phone would ring. All the while, Duke studied them with high-powered binoculars.

He knew them; they had no idea who he was. He had the location and numbers of most of the pay telephone booths in downtown Miami. It was a good system.

The apartment where he lived was rented to him, Delbert Morgan, a legitimate and respectable businessman. If the heat were ever turned up on his business address, he had a ready-made hideout where he could drop out of sight for weeks.

The money came to his post office box, rented in still another name. When Duke insured outgoing parcels, or signed for incoming packages, the people at the window thought he was a jewelry salesman and joked about free samples.

Duke concluded that whoever thought up the new system was one smart bastard.

It was easy for him to pass himself off as a successful businessman. Gambling at the tracks was legal; so was bingo. His numbers and loan sharking deals were profitable, but for the time being, illegal. He had gotten a kick out of working Dade County. The fix around Miami was in, and most of the cops and lawyers had long forgotten about taxpayers and straight clients. He undressed the stewardess with his eyes, watching as she poised the champagne bottle over his glass.

Duke was walking along the concourse at the airport when a flashy but expensively dressed man fell in step with him.

"How was the trip, Duke?"

"Smooth all the way."

"You got any baggage checks?"

"No, this is it. I travel light."

When they were out of earshot of the other passengers, the man said, "You can call me Tony."

Tony led him through acres of parked cars to a green station wagon and handed him the keys. "You'll be driving, Duke." Tony got in on the passenger side as Duke started the engine and turned on the air conditioning.

"What did they tell you about this action, Duke?"

"All the man said was to get my ass over here and you'd lay it out."

"I hear you know restaurants, how they buy meat and sea food."

Duke laughed. "You hire a good chef and he knocks down like fifteen, twenty percent. Without a good chef, you ain't got nothin'."

"Here's the setup, Duke. You're a seafood buyer for a chain of eateries back east. You got a big chunk of the action. The fish wholesalers are giving your places a screwing, so you're down here putting in your own buying place."

They're turning me into a goddamned fish peddler, thought Duke. "Yeah, to cut out the thieving middleman." Duke laughed at his joke.

Tony remained serious and gave Duke a side glance that took away his smile. "You need some fresh air for a change, you hafta get away from the rat race. Got the pitch?"

Duke made no comment, waiting for Tony to continue.

"Get this straight: You got a lot of dough tied up in this feed chain and now you want to sell out and take it easy. So you're building up the business, World's Best Seafood. Only you're selling fish on your menu below cost. Fatten up the deal, with customers coming out your ears. Then you unload. People will believe it, if you let them know you're out to give somebody the shaft."

Duke filed this away. "Yeah, I got it." He stared at Tony.

Tony lowered his voice. "Our import business is way down, we've lost some big shipments. We need a new place on the coast. Like, you might say, a private seaport."

Comprehension flared like a rocket in Duke's brain. *Big league!* He nodded, licking his lips. "I see what you mean, Tony."

"We're going into the shrimp business. Boats come and go all the time, nobody ever stops them. Your job is setting up the place to bring in the boats."

"You want me to look for some good spot?" asked Duke.

"Got one already. Hick town called Bonaparte. It's a wide place in the road, ninety miles out Highway 90. There's only one fish house. Man named Lou Fisher has it. Fisher is losing his ass. You buy him out cheap and close the place up for remodeling."

Duke remembered the fish piers in New York, people always showing up and rubbernecking when a boat came in. Even in bad weather. "Tony, you plan on bringing the shipments right up to the dock and unloading them, like bales of cotton?"

"I ain't finished, Duke, we have more sense than that. Down the river from this fish house is a dock, out of sight from anything. It's on an island where nobody lives. The oil drillers put the dock there. They call the place Beau's Island and a road goes out to it from the main highway. See about a lease. Get a ninety-day option to buy. You can spread some crap about starting up a private fishing lodge. The place ain't worth a damn for anything else."

"You mentioned something about a shrimp boat."

"It's already fishing there. Guy named Stark. His boat's the *Helen S.*"

"So we take a charter?"

"No, we got an easier way to go. Stark is in hock up to his balls. The bank's putting the snatch on his trawler if he doesn't come up with all the back payments. You talk to him, show him some real dough. Get him to play along with us, say once or twice a month, and he keeps on fishing and helps us out at the same time."

"He might need some help making up his mind," suggested Duke.

"No rough stuff. What we want is a nice smooth operation, no waves. This ain't like your fucking loan payments."

Duke heard the contempt in Tony's voice. "What am I supposed to be using for dough?"

Tony took an envelope from his coat pocket, opened it, and flipped through a stack of bills. "Here's ten grand, that oughta do it. Watch out for Fisher, 'cause he might want you to take the place over as a gift, trying to sucker you into paying his debts. That would mean investigations by creditors and things getting screwed up. You pay him in cash and make him pay whatever he owes. Get a bill of sale and a receipt."

"What if he wants like twenty-five G's? What if I run into trouble like that?"

"He won't. The town owns the land and he leases it from them. There ain't any real estate, just a broke business."

"Why's he losing money?"

"When they drilled all them oil wells, the goddamn shrimp just hauled ass and left. Some day you'll be able to strike a match over there and set the ocean on fire. Fisher is stuck with the tent after the circus left town."

Duke spotted the part that didn't add up. "If there ain't no shrimp, then how come this guy Stark is still out there busting his balls? That seems pretty screwy."

"His wife won't go with him to fish somewhere else, and he won't leave her. He thinks the shrimp are coming back, so he must be a screwball."

Duke wondered how Tony had all the details, until he realized the organization had the best intelligence system in the country. "You think this dumbfuck Stark will be any trouble?"

"Show him the color of your money and he'll be kissing your ass. All he has to do is run the goddamn boat."

"What if there's some foul-up? Like that boat over in Florida I read about?"

Tony looked at him with a hard expression and Duke was sorry he had brought up the subject.

"Just you get over there and stay put," said Tony. "All you want is to buy seafood. Later on, you have a private club started up for your friends. You don't know from shinola."

"You mean, if she blows I'm clean?"

"That's the general plan. Here's your schedule. You got a reservation at the Bonaparte Motel. Go on down there. Look around some before it gets dark, and find out what you can. Every night at eight, I'll phone you, no matter what. When I call tonight at the motel, give me the number of an outside booth. We play it cool until we get everything lined up."

"What about these wheels?"

"Rented. The papers are in the glove compartment. Your name is Richard Anderson and you'll have a Tampa hotel address. If anyone tries to trace you through the car, they'll be looking at a big hotel in Tampa."

"I hear you ain't got a record."

Duke was pleased that Tony knew. "I keep my nose clean. Who am I at the motel in Bonus—"

"Bonaparte, like Napoleon. Sign in as Richard Anderson, but I'll call you *Duke* on the phone."

"How long am I supposed to stay buried in them fucking swamps?"

"Two, three weeks, 'til you get everything set up right. One reason they wanted you is nobody has anything on you. I hear you ain't even been fingerprinted?"

"I play it smart," Duke acknowledged.

Tony took a city map from the glove compartment and showed Duke how to switch over to Highway 90. He cracked the door open. "One more thing: You left the broads in Miami. Bonaparte is a small place and I hear you got hot nuts, so keep your cock outta sight."

Duke felt annoyed. "Sure, Tony, you can count on me."

CHAPTER 15

Lou slept well Monday night, which surprised him. No dark dreams disturbed the placid hours of sleep and his pain had mercifully receded.

It was still early when he showered and dressed. He drove through Bonaparte to the packinghouse, enjoying the beauty of the day. To the right of the highway, the treetops on Sandy Point were sprayed with gold. The marshes stood straight and tall, reaching for the morning sun.

His arrival at the waterfront had been the same for how many springtime mornings? He thought of the seasons, the moods of each: cold winter mornings when gusty winds swept in from the north; nights when summer rain drummed against the building; fall afternoons when the air held the promise of frost to come. There had been other times when the great weather wheels of the mighty storms had reached in from the sea, pushing the water over the marsh, and lashing the building with wind and water.

Paul would be making his first test with the octopus.

Inside the packinghouse, Moonbeam appeared and paced beside him until he poured milk into her bowl. He replaced the bottle in the cooler, and as the cat lapped the milk, he rubbed her arching back.

There was a cool silence inside the packinghouse, the smell of tarred nets and old cork, and he looked around with keen appreciation.

Inside, the office air and light entered through the opened door. Lou breathed carefully, but deeply, enjoying the seaweed smell of the morning.

Papers he was taking to Earle Black were located and slipped into a worn plastic folder.

Judge Earle Black, attorney-at-law, was in his office above the hardware store. When Lou entered, he swung around from his huge roll-top desk.

"Good morning, Earle."

"Lou! Come in, my friend, come in. Sit down. I was just thinking about you."

Lou pointed at a large oak table in the middle of the room. "Is there a paper drive on?" The leaning stacks of books and old files were gone; the surface of the table was shiny.

"Had to get everything put away, Lou." The judge looked at the table. "I haven't seen that wood in years."

"The place doesn't seem right. You taking in a partner, Earle?"

"Nope, going on a trip. Mexico. That's why I've had you on my mind. Flying from New Orleans Friday afternoon. You remember Valerie, don't you? My granddaughter?"

Lou recalled horn-rimmed glasses and a pretty girl in blue jeans. "Yes, I remember Valerie."

"She's down there doing graduate work in archaeology and needs me to show her where to dig." The judge held up his airline ticket. "I'll be gone a few weeks, I guess."

Lou heard the note of indecision in the man's voice. Perhaps old people were never really positive about their plans. He looked at the lawyer's frail shoulders and snowy hair. *I won't see him again after he leaves!* "I'm glad to hear that, Earle. All of us need a change of scenery occasionally."

Judge Black hesitated, as if struggling with his memory. "Didn't you spend some time in the Yucatan before you came here?"

"Two years, right after the war." Lou remembered the ancient ruins and the emerald waters of the Caribbean, his flight to a timeless and lovely land, after the trauma of exploded cities and burned, sometimes buried, populations.

They talked about the fabled Mayas, tourist papers, and pesos. Lou watched the lawyer's rheumy old eyes seeing past Friday.

The judge looked curiously at Lou. "Forgive me for running on so. Was there something you needed before I go?"

"Just some odds and ends. I'm going on a trip myself and these are some things I've been putting off." He opened the folder, amazed at how casual he managed to sound.

The judge reached for a legal pad and sucked blue ink into his outmoded fountain pen. "Never put off until tomorrow ... What's on your mind?"

"You remember Catfish Davis, the little guy who fishes with Paul Stark?"

"Catfish Davis," he repeated. "Wasn't there a court order?"

Lou produced a document. "That's the one. He was declared legally incompetent and I was appointed his guardian. You drew this up at the time." He handed the paper to the lawyer. "Since I might be gone for some time, it would be more appropriate for Paul to be his guardian. Paul's had all the responsibility the past twenty years or more anyway."

"Whatever you say." The man looked over the document. "Did you ever find out his real name, or where he came from?"

"No, never did. At first he wrote 'Davis' in the sand with a stick. Maybe that's his name, maybe not. We started calling him Catfish because I never saw another human who could eat so much of it."

They both laughed.

"He might have come from a river town," said the lawyer. "Somewhere where that fish is the main seafood."

"Most likely, we'll never know," said Lou. "He just showed up that morning and we've had him ever since. That was twenty-five years back. Our best guess is that someone brought him out here and dropped him off, like he was a dog or cat they didn't want. He never would have found Bonaparte without some help. Even now, he won't go as far as the highway, unless it's with someone he knows.

"How old do you think he is, Lou?"

"We have no way of telling, but I figure he must be at least seventy. He never seems to age; looks the same as when he came."

The judge chuckled. "We should find out his secret. Is he still living in your storeroom?"

"Not for years. He moved onto the first shrimp boat Paul captained. Since then, he's lived aboard whatever trawler Paul has. Pays him like a regular deck hand and I've been putting that money into a savings account for him. By now, there's enough to take care of him, even if he became too feeble to go out with Paul."

"What happens to his estate when he dies? Without any known relatives . . ."

Lou was surprised. "Damn, I never thought of that."

"Someone should be named to inherit. Otherwise, whatever's left will go to the sovereign State of Louisiana. Would Catfish want that?"

"I don't think he would. I was mostly thinking about him not being able to work, not dying. He just seems to go on, like the river."

The judge was writing. "I'll draw up a new order and a will. You can sign as his guardian, naming Paul as sole heir to the estate. Thursday, I'll be at the county seat; I'll get it approved by the court."

Lou handed Earle a large envelope. "Paul's been working on an invention which might be a big help to shrimpers. He's trying it out this trip. These are all his notes, drawings, everything. I promised to talk to you about a patent."

The judge put the envelope into a drawer. "I know a good man in Washington. Before I leave, I'll phone and mail everything up there. He's one of the best."

"Fine, Judge," said Lou, hesitating as if trying not to forget anything. "You know, maybe I should have a will, too. I could always fall off the dock, you know."

"There's a regular form, Lou, but you tell me what you want to bequeath to whom and I'll get it drawn up tomorrow."

"Everything would go to Paul."

"Does Paul know about this?" asked the judge.

"No."

They discussed a few more details and Lou rose to go. The judge promised to have the papers ready by noon Friday. "I'll stop by your place," he said. "Sue Ellen is taking me to the airport, so we'll have her notarize everything. Say one-thirty?" They shook hands and wished each other enjoyable and safe trips.

Lou took care of some other details and then returned to the fish house. Settled in, he wrote checks and paid all his debts. When the last envelope was sealed and stamped, he held the small stack in his hand and realized that he was square with the world. Thanks to the will, Paul would have the fish house, if the octopus worked out. Otherwise, it would revert to the town. Then Lou realized that Paul wouldn't be fishing if his invention succeeded, he'd be making octopuses!

In either event, the packinghouse would be a liability for Paul. Like Lou, it had outgrown its usefulness.

Mike called in the late afternoon about someone wanting to talk about seafood. A Mr. Anderson.

After leaving the New Orleans airport, Duke had found Highway 90 and made good time to Bonaparte.

On the outskirts of town, he located Bonaparte Seafoods - Wholesale Only, and drove slowly past the faded yellow building. A side door was open; a pickup truck was parked in front. He thought the place looked run-down.

The day clerk at the motel had his reservation; he checked into a room with a view of the fish house.

Down the street, past a bank, he found Mike's Place.

A heavyset man behind the counter looked him over. "We only got sandwiches this time of day. I could heat up a bowl of gumbo."

Duke sat at the counter and read the menu on the wall. "Make it ham and cheese. On rye."

"All we got is white bread."

Duke nodded and the man turned to the grill.

"They have a lot of seafood around here?"

"Seafood?" The man turned to look at Duke.

"Yeah, you know, shrimp, lobster, fish."

Mike nodded slightly. "Depends on the time of the year."

That's a lot of help, thought Duke. "Look," he said, "I'm in the restaurant business myself, down here looking for a place a man can find good seafood. Fresh. Wholesale loads. Thought you might know."

The man turned the slice of ham on the grill and turned to face Duke. "You might be looking in the wrong place, mister. Fishing isn't like it was before they put up all them oil wells." He lowered his voice and leaned over the counter. "Don't get me wrong. I'm not a saying the wells run the shrimp off, just couldn't say if they do or not."

Duke nodded, pretending to be interested, watching the man put the sandwich together.

"The only person around Bonaparte that could tell you the score is Lou Fisher. He has the shrimp docks."

Play it dumb, Duke reminded himself. He ordered coffee. "Where's he located?"

"The other side of town, just as you come in on the highway. Can't miss it, it's a big old place settin' out there by itself. Looks like she's about to fall down, but don't let that fool you: the hurricanes hardly touched that old fish house."

Duke took a bite of his sandwich and a swallow of coffee. "He sounds like a man I should meet. You have a phone? Maybe you'd call and see if he's there, save me a trip."

The man looked at the pay telephone and back at Duke. Duke handed him two dimes.

"What's your name, mister?"

"Anderson, just say a man named Anderson wants to talk to him about buying seafood for a chain of restaurants. I can go over there now, if he's not already left for the day." Duke finished his sandwich, while Mike made the call.

"He said he'd wait over there for you."

"Thanks. You must be Mike?"

"That's me. I've had this grill almost as long as Lou's had his shrimp house. We're old-timers around here."

"Is that so?" Duke tried to look impressed and paid his check. "Thanks again, Mike."

"Glad to make your acquaintance, Mr. Anderson."

Duke shook hands warmly and left.

Number two. Number one was the motel clerk, the boy with the pimply face. He also knew that Richard Anderson was a seafood buyer, would swear to that if necessary, and had assured Richard Anderson that buyers always stayed at the Bonaparte Motel. "It's quieter here than Beaver City," he had said. "They have the Holiday Lodge, Mr. Anderson, but it's quieter here."

Duke had looked around, wondering when they rolled up the sidewalk. "I can see that."

A man stepped onto the raised walkway as Duke drove up to the fish house. He got out of the station wagon and locked the doors. "You must be Mr. Anderson?" The man had graying hair and a smile.

Duke thought he must be in his late fifties. "And you're Mr. Fisher?"

"Come on in the office." Lou led the way. The office was a room partitioned off from the interior of the large warehouse-like building. Another door opened from the office into the building. Through it, Duke could see the dock and the green fields across the river. He wondered if they grew rice or something over there. On the office walls hung a number of out-of-date girlie calendars.

"Mr. Anderson, would you like some coffee? Or a shot of bourbon?"

"Thanks. But I just had coffee."

For a man who was losing his ass, Duke thought Fisher seemed mighty cheerful. The latter listened attentively as Duke told of his need to buy large quantities of seafood for his restaurant chain, and of his interest in setting up a base of operations. "So we can send buying trucks up and down the coast. We ship whatever we need to our places and sell the rest on the wholesale market in New York."

Lou listened, nodding as the stranger spoke. "You'd be better off buying what you need on the New Orleans market," he said. "That way, you get exactly what you want. In the long, run it'd cost you a lot less than having a place of your own, where you'd have the overhead, whether or not the fishing happened to be good."

Fisher wasn't much of a salesman, thought Duke. "I know it'll take time to build up, just to break even," he explained. "Time's what I got plenty of. I need to get outside more, settle down in a quiet place and do some fishing myself. This country looks mighty good to me." Duke looked out the window and admired the water.

"It's a fine place to live, Mr. Anderson. Do you have a family?"

"No, not yet, but I'm engaged." Duke laughed, pleased at his cleverness. "I won't be footloose and fancy free much longer, so I need to decide on where I'm going to live."

"I hope your bride will like Louisiana. That is, if your business plans work out."

Duke decided to lay it on the line. "Mr. Fisher, you ever think about selling this place?"

Fisher seemed surprised. "Not recently. Sure, I'd sell it if someone wanted a business that's lost money for several years."

"How come you're not making any money?"

"The shrimp schools seemed to have moved away from our part of the coast."

Duke considered this, nodding. "You got coolers, freezers? Maybe I could use them to freeze fish brought in from somewhere else. I'm not worried about losing dough. Fact is, I can afford some losses. I'd sure like to look around, if you don't mind."

Lou took him on a tour of the packinghouse, pointing out where minor repairs were needed and the age of the refrigeration systems. They ended up on the dock, where Duke craned his neck to inspect the building's exterior.

"Maybe you got some idea how much you might want for this place?" Duke realized he was pushing hard on such short notice, but he needed to have a good report for Tony.

"I don't own the land, Mr. Anderson, it belongs to the town. I built everything you see and put in the road out front. I also put in the fuel tanks. All I have to sell is the lease and the equipment, plus a business that isn't making it. I don't suppose you'd be interested in that?"

"Well, I just might be, if the price was right."

Thirty minutes later, Lou came down from his first figure of eight thousand and accepted Duke's counter offer of five thousand.

"Lock, stock, and barrel," said Duke. "Only I don't want to take over any debts."

Fisher said that was understood.

Duke thought that Lou seemed to be in pain and wondered if he was sick.

"Why don't you sleep on it," said Lou. "You might want to change your mind after you've gone over the books."

"No danger of that, sir. They say I'm a man of my word. What about meeting you here in the morning? Say, ten or ten-thirty?"

They agreed, shook hands, and Duke returned to the hotel to wait for Tony's first call.

CHAPTER 16

The second drag of the morning, made without air connected to the octopus, produced a half basket of shrimp. By usual standards, this would have been an acceptable result.

Paul weighed the shrimp and made entries in his notebook. Air was sent down to the octopus on the third drag. While the trawl gear was sliding over the bottom, three hundred fathoms behind and below the *Helen S.,* Paul prepared a meal for himself and Catfish.

Paul was too excited to eat.

When the hour was up, he started pulling in the net and checking on the retrieval of the hose. When the trawl boards broke from the surface, he saw the net wings jerking violently. Soon, the head of a great shark surfaced, its huge gray body rolling and whipping in an effort to free itself.

Paul saw how the upswept tail was looped by the weighted lead line and then drawn tight by a nozzle section of the hose. When the shark's head reached the level of the railing, Paul locked the hoist and went into the wheelhouse for his rifle. Hollow-point bullets tore out chunks of flesh and bone, as the giant creature lashed furiously with its tail. A well-placed shot smashed its nervous system and it sagged, quivering, a bloody froth oozing from its rows of teeth and running down its white belly.

Damn, thought Paul. Look what it did to the net.

With an S-hook caught in the shark's mouth, Paul hoisted the giant beast up higher, working vainly to free the tail. This was not going to happen without cutting both the lead line and the tentacle of the octopus. Paul went into the wheelhouse and returned with a machete.

Catfish watched him chop the shark in two, near the tail. Purplish blood spilled into the water. The severed tail section slipped through the tangle of lines and netting, and then fell into the sea. Paul lowered the mangled carcass back into the water and loosened the S-hooks from the lolling head. For a few moments, the animal was buoyed by the swells, turning and sinking until, finally, its shimmering white belly was no longer visible in the black silver depths.

"That was a big one, Catfish. Twelve feet or more, I'd guess."

At least two hours were required to patch the net damage, but Paul was not concerned: the octopus appeared to be unharmed.

Before lifting the cod end on deck, he washed away the blood and slime. The deck was wet and glistening when the second haul of the octopus poured from the bag.

Paul knew that some of the catch had floated out of the cod end during his ordeal with the shark, but the octopus catch had still been much better than the regular catch.

The sun had rolled far down the afternoon side of the sky, when the net and its trailing red hose were lowered for the fourth time. The webbing had been repaired and the shrimp catch was packed in ice.

A front was moving in from the Caribbean. The forecast was for high winds and heavy rains during the night, followed by clearing skies on Wednesday.

"When we pull in this time, Catfish, we'll head for the cove and wait out the blow." He ruled out the idea of going all the way to Bonaparte; that would cost him at least a day's fishing. He wished he could call Lou, but dared not use the radio. If he did, the whole coast would know about his catch.

He smiled to himself, thinking of Lou's face when the *Helen S.* brought in this unbelievable load of shrimp. Lou had bought many of the components from his own pocket, and had staked him through these lean months. The brilliant success of the octopus would make it all worthwhile.

The patent!

He hadn't even thought about the patent since mentioning it to Rita. Lou would know how to handle that. Paul Stark, inventor. Wow!

And Rita! The octopus would buy Beau's Island. They would build a workshop back in the trees and repair the dock. Boats would tie up there to be outfitted with the invention.

He'd build her a house overlooking the river. A plantation!

There wouldn't be time for him to fish, except for experimental trips. Surely, by then, she'd want to go along, at least part of the time. Maybe she'd be willing to have children. The island was a perfect place to raise them. Maybe now, Rita would be happy.

Paul and Catfish were eating when the trawler suddenly shuddered, stopped, then moved ahead with a cable gone slack. Paul dived for the deck controls and reversed the wheel. It was too late. Something had stopped the rig; the cable no longer had a load. He took a quick bearing on the marker and decided that an uncharted wreck lay on the plateau.

The boards were lifted into the rigging and Paul saw immediately that the net was gone. The wings were in tatters, beyond repair. Anxiously, he inspected the tentacles of the octopus. There was only one break, and he could repair that.

Catfish surveyed the damage, looking over the stern for the lost net, and then shook his head at Paul.

As the trawler moved past the pennant, Paul obtained more radio bearings from land based stations and entered these into his book. He secured the deck and set a course for Point LaCroix. Lightning flared, signaling the approach of the storm.

The sheltered bay behind the island would be needed for the tedious job of hanging in a new net. As soon as the April blow passed over, he could return to the plateau.

With the trawler moving ahead on its autopilot, Paul removed the tattered webbing from the boards and rebuilt the tentacle of the octopus. Before the outlying islands were reached, the wind grew stronger, pushing waves into the stern and whipping spray onto the deck.

It was well after dark when they rounded North Point and dropped anchor in the cove.

They worked until after midnight hanging in the new net, as the main body of the storm moved toward the coast. The western tip of the island sheltered them from the rough waters of the open gulf, but its low marshes and few weather-beaten trees afforded no protection from the rising wind, which had begun to moan through the trawler's super-structure.

On the outer beaches, Paul heard the plangent crashing and pounding of the seas as waves rose and stumbled in the shallows and sucked back, tripping up each oncoming wave until it curled forward and slammed into the boiling sands.

The net was completed, just as torrential rains swept in from the gulf and drove the men inside.

Paul checked the barometer, and was glad to see it had steadied.

The worst of the storm was past, yet he knew he'd have to sleep while the weather had them pinned down in the cove. His mind was still reviewing the events of this first day with the octopus.

Paul went into the wheelhouse. Under the dim anchor light, the foredeck was gray and ghostly. He watched through streaming windows as big drops of rain whirled toward him, like bullets of light, and spattered into the glass.

The trawler was a weather vane in the wind-streaked waters of the cove. It was also a fortress from the elements, a sturdy world in itself.

Inside the cabin, it was warm and dry. Paul looked around with approval and affection. Only hours before, all this had been threatened. The sea had given it back.

The roar outside was diminishing to fitful, unorganized gusts.

After Paul made certain the barometer was rising, he stretched out on the lower bunk and slept.

CHAPTER 17

Johnny thought about smacking Mary Beth in the mouth. He'd been driving around Lafayette all day, burning up gas, trying to talk some sense into the bitch. He told her how to go through the Claiborne house and find money, jewelry, whatever. Her old man had to have some money kicking around. Bankers are bound to keep a fat roll of big bills to flash.

She could also get her checkbook.

The more he argued, the dumber she got. "Mary Beth, all you have to do is look around. Goddamn, it's *your* fucking house!"

"I can't go back there," she told him. "Hannah will catch me."

"Who's running your life, you or that old hag?"

"If I go home, my daddy's going to put me in some awful place."

"He's just feeding you a line of crap."

"He isn't, Johnny! You don't know him like I do." She pulled at his arm. "Please, take me back to the hospital."

He was sick of hearing that. "I sure as hell don't get it, Mary Beth. Your old man's got you freaked out, but you're not worried about getting stuck in that damn hospital."

She was silent.

"Then again, maybe I know why. Maybe you think that shrimp guy'll look out for you, or maybe you're screwing your doctor. Or both."

She was wishing she had never mentioned Captain Stark. "He just happened to come along in his boat," she explained.

"You must think I was born yesterday," said Johnny. He knew his voice was squeaking, but no one could hear him except Mary Beth. "You said it was just getting dark, then you tell me it was two in the morning before he gets you stashed in Beaver City? Tell the truth!"

"I was sick and scared, Johnny. I wanted to jump off the boat. There was a big storm, and he couldn't handle the boat and hold onto me at the same time. He had to head for sheltered water."

He laughed. "Maybe all he wanted was to stay there, at that old dock, with you shoving it right under his nose. I hope you made him happy, you damn slut."

Tears streamed down her face as she gave Johnny a hard push to his shoulder. "You're nothing but a lousy pimp, Johnny, so get out of my face."

Johnny half-heartedly pushed her back. "What time does Hannah go home?"

She shrugged. "But my daddy's there and he must be wondering where I am. He'll be mad as hell."

Johnny was certain that a search would be going on, but old man Claiborne wouldn't raise a stink. He'd probably like it if Mary Beth never came back. Having a drug-whoring daughter wasn't exactly good for someone responsible for everyone's money.

He tried again. "After dark, we can drive back and see if the lights are on. Maybe your old man's working late, or gone to a meeting. Hell, my old man was gone all the time." He knew this was a lie: It was his mother who was never there.

A car was approaching and Johnny pushed Mary Beth down in the bucket seat. "Stay outta sight, you want the cops picking you up?"

"I'll get a taxi to the hospital."

"Goddamnit, don't say that again! I got a better idea. We go by your house. If the lights are on, we keep moving and go on out to Fisher's. Lights off, you dig up something I can have as part payment, then you cash a check or two in Beaver City. After that, I'll drive you right up to the front door of the hospital."

He had to bend his head to hear her say, "All right, who gives a shit anyway?" There was defeat in her voice; he knew he'd won. "We'll kill another half hour, then go back to your house and the hospital." He could make the drive in a little more than an hour, but he wanted the highway to be dark. Even if she got caught, they'd only send her off for her cure. And she would never mention his name, he was sure of that. He had everything to gain, and not much to lose, by feeding her that line about taking her out in the woods at old man Fisher's. Even if her daddy was home, she could still cash the checks. Then he'd have to think of his next move.

Of course, if his old lady came home, his ass was grass, and she was one hell of a lawnmower.

Mary Beth was touching his sleeve. "I have to find a bathroom."

Me too, thought Johnny. "Okay, there's a diner up ahead."

The restrooms were in the back. Mary Beth went into the ladies side, bending over and holding her stomach. .

When Johnny came out, Mary Beth was still inside. He walked around to the screened service window in front, where a boy was reading a comic book.

"Gimme three hot dogs and a big orange," said Johnny. "And step on it!"

Johnny sat in his car and ate, watching the door to the ladies' room. Disgusted, he got out of the car and strode to the door. Knocking, he called out "Mary Beth, what's taking you so long?" He thought he heard crying over the noise of running water. The door was locked. "Come on out, I got you a hot dog."

When she didn't answer, his anger grew. Was she planning to spend the whole fucking night in there? He went back to the service window. "My date needs a key to the ladies room." The boy passed him the key, eyes never leaving his comic book.

Mary Beth was sitting on the wet floor with her head slumped forward. Water was spilling from the basin. Johnny saw his black cloth roll-up case and his skin began to crawl. He grabbed it. Every pill was gone, but the syringes were still inside. He was afraid to turn on the light.

Johnny stepped outside and looked around. There were no houses nearby and only one car on the highway. He ducked until it passed. Either Mary Beth had passed out, or she was trying to scare him. He could drive off and leave her, but the kid inside might remember him.

Johnny got into the car and turned it so the passenger side would be close to the restroom. After another quick look, he lifted Mary Beth and put her on the seat. She was limp, but she was still breathing.

They were halfway to Bonaparte when she stirred against his shoulder and tried to speak. Johnny shook her. "You can't do this to me!" He didn't know how many pills there had been; he didn't want to know. Twenty minutes later, Mary Beth was dead. Johnny knew the exact moment it happened. First, she had stiffened, her head jerked far back, and then she had fallen heavily against him, her raspy breathing stopped. He shoved her back against the seat and began to panic.

It was raining, making it difficult to see, and it forced him to slow down. His hands shook and his teeth chattered. He pulled off the road and, using the map light, prepared a syringe. Rain was everywhere, blue lightning flashing nearby. The engine idled as he waited for the drug to kick in. Mary Beth slipped toward him. Rigid with fright, he pushed her against the passenger door, causing her head to fall forward and her long hair to fall onto her knees.

His mind raced. It was too late to drop her off at the park near the hospital, but she had to be left somewhere near town. If not, people would start asking who did she drive off with?

Johnny had never been closer to a dead person than the door of the room holding his father's casket. The presence of this lifeless body terrified him. He put the car into gear and spun its wheels in the wet ground. The humidity inside the car caused him to break out in a cold sweat.

Johnny felt trapped, and scared as hell.

Ten miles before the turnoff, he hit on a solution. Beau's Island! It was perfect. She had tried to kill herself there on Sunday, so everyone would think she'd left the hospital to finish the job. Hell, she could've gone out there in a taxi, or caught a ride. The shrimp fisherman would have to tell everything. Sure, they'd suspect him first; but then they'd figure she stole the pills at the hospital and overdosed.

Johnny was no longer shaking. If he played his cards right, no one would suspect him!

The gate was unlocked. Johnny drove through to the marsh and turned off the headlights, guided across the narrow causeway by lightning. It lit up a sodden, dismal stretch of the road, each time it glowed behind the curtain of rain.

At the clearing behind the dock, he found the old trail, turned into it, and drove as far as the fallen tree. Johnny was home and in bed before midnight.

An hour later, unable to sleep, he got up and packed a small suitcase, cleaned out his closet, and left it unlocked. Before leaving, he wrote a note for Joselyn: "Visiting friends in Mississippi." No names. No telephone numbers.

Let his mother try to figure that one out!

The rain was only a drizzle when Johnny drove out between the white pillars of the Cameron estate and turned left, away from Beau's Island and Mary Beth. The traffic lights in Bonaparte were flashing yellow as he drove the length of River Street, then sped up again on the dark and rain-washed highway. Bonaparte was as still and silent as a graveyard.

His supplier in New Orleans would know how to unload the car, he felt sure of that.

CHAPTER 18

It was Wednesday morning when Rita decided that the noise she had been hearing was thunder. She sat up and pressed her hands to her temples. She had a splitting headache and her body was sore all over.

Tony!

She held her head in her hands and pressed tightly to try to stop the unrelenting pain. Water. Cold water would make her feel better. Rita dragged herself into the bathroom and held a wet cloth to her face, while leaning against the wall for support. A wave of nausea came over her and she forced herself to be very still. When she knew she wasn't going to throw up, she crept back to bed and buried herself under the covers.

Exploring hands were feeling her and she pushed them away. Someone was calling for her to wake up. The hands were cupping her backsides, pressing her against a man's body. The voice again: "It's Tony, snap out of it." "Rita, it's Tony! Keep those goddamn knees still!"

Her mind began to awaken. "Tony, where've you been? I woke up and couldn't find you."

"You want to carry on a fucking conversation?"

"Wait," she protested. "You're hurting me."

"Relax then, open up your legs."

On Wednesday morning, Paul awakened and showered. The stinging water felt good on his skin. After shaving and dressing in clean work clothes, thick bacon sizzled in the iron skillet and the aroma of fresh-brewed coffee filled the salt air. With breakfast in the works, he went forward to study the weather.

Through misting rain, the beacon flashed off North Point, each five-second rotation forming a halo. He listened to the waves hitting the beach, knew that the gulf was still too rough for fishing. Daylight was another hour and he was anxious to take the octopus back to the distant plateau. His eyebrows heavy with rainy mist, he returned to the deckhouse.

Paul watched, smiling, as Catfish began to stir. The old man responded to food, also to heat and cold, with utter simplicity. Paul often envied him. Undoubtedly, the old man had lived in mysterious infancy since the time when his mind had ceased to grow. Perhaps, Paul reasoned, the gods had taken away the power of speech and the ability to hear in order to insulate Catfish from the indignities of life.

The blackness was dissolving outside when they finished breakfast, and the drizzle had stopped. The cove was smooth, but Paul knew it would be hours before the open sea would forget the muscles of the wind. It was important to be able to drop the net over, when they reached the oval on the chart. However, if the seas were too rough, he'd have to lay to, with the bow into the waves, and patiently wait for the sea to calm.

If, on the other hand, he lingered overlong in the cove, important fishing hours would be lost. In any case, it would be a rough trip out, with the trawler breasting into the seas. All these things were considered, as he planned the day.

Paul started the diesel and descended into the engine room. He placed his hand on the throbbing yellow monster, as a physician feels for a fever. Moving with assurance, and in the protection of the island, he did what was necessary to return to the sea.

On the forward deck, Paul switched on the capstan motor, pulling the vessel toward its anchor, until the large flukes had risen from the water and were locked into the bow. Before the *Helen S.* reached the end of the headland, the surge of the ocean gave the sense that the trawler was climbing marching foothills of water. Her bow rose and fell in a slow cadence, until they rounded the point and reached the unprotected part of the bay.

The trawler reacted to the thrusting power of the waves and reared, like a stallion sensing battle. It surged forward, steel bosom smashing relentlessly into the crowding seas and sending frothing tongues shooting out from the bow. Spray struck the wheelhouse windows.

Paul stood at the wheel, feet apart, riding the bucking and plunging giant, exulting in her power and competence. He knew the *Helen* S. was a strong ship, built to take the full fury of a storm-lashed sea. There was nothing timid about her arrogant mastery of these wild waters. Paul moved with the action of the sea, remaining upright in a constant counterpoint to the trawler's movements. Dawn was bringing clearing weather.

When they were far offshore and clear of the oil platforms, Paul transferred control to the automatic pilot. The wheel began to turn of its own accord and he heard the soft clanking sound of the drive chain turning the rudder sprocket. Below deck, another instrument would remember the course he had selected and would follow it.

Rita opened her eyes.

Tony was standing beside the bed holding a bathrobe. He was dressed and ready to go out.

"I got breakfast coming up," he said. "Take a shower and put this on so we can eat."

She bathed, rubbing her skin to a warm glow with a large bath towel, and then put on the robe and went into the living room. A table was filled with frosty-looking silver bowls and pots. She smelled the food and sat opposite Tony.

"I'm starving, my headache's all gone."

He lowered his newspaper and looked at her. "You sure were dead to the world yesterday."

"Yesterday? What day is this?"

"Wednesday, and it's already after ten-thirty."

She remembered having arrived in New Orleans on Monday. "Something sure knocked me out."

After breakfast and a good laugh, Tony told Rita it had been fun, but it was time to say goodbye. He had urgent business out of town. She would need to vacate the room by noon.

Bewildered by his sudden need to leave town, Rita could hardly sputter out that she was hoping to work in one of his clubs up north.

With great flourish, Tony wrote a message on the back of one of his business cards, told Rita to give it to any club of her choosing in Philly, and she would be hired. He told her to go home and pack, and hit the road for Philly.

Overjoyed, Rita swirled around the room, and soon left for Bonaparte to pack.

She had a lot to think about on her trip back to Bonaparte. Like who was the blonde on Paul's boat? Why was she taken to the hospital? Where was she now?

Outside Beaver City, she stopped at a roadside phone booth and called the hospital. She told the operator that she was passing through and had promised a friend that she'd send flowers for him. "He wrote down his friend's name," she added. "But I lost the piece of paper."

"Is the person a patient at this hospital?"

"Yes, I've seen her picture. She's quite young, at least in the picture. Slender, blonde hair."

"I'm afraid that doesn't help much."

"Oh, yes, and he said she was taken to the hospital about two or two-thirty on Monday morning, in an ambulance." There was a silence at the other end, and then "That would be Miss Claiborne, but she's no longer here. Just a moment, please."

A man's voice came on the line. "Are you a friend of Miss Claiborne?"

Rita repeated her explanation. "But I don't know her at all."

"Please tell me the name of the flower shop," he said. "Could you wait there a few minutes? It's quite important."

Rita hung up and dialed Bonaparte Seafoods. Lou answered. No, he hadn't heard from Paul. The radio was still in for repairs. He was certain that Paul would stay out as long as the weather held, which could be at least two more days. Did she need anything?

"No, Lou, not right now, but thanks."

It was just as well. If Paul came in before she left, there would be a big scene, and it wouldn't be over a stupid shrimp boat. She wondered what the skinny-ass slut looked like, and what she had that Paul found so damn special. She found herself wanting to see the blonde, face-to-face, and tell her off. It wouldn't do for people to think she'd lost out. But if she left, how would they know it was because she was tired of Bonaparte and being poor, not because she gave a damn about some dumb blonde? Rita was not anxious to drive on to Bonaparte, and stopped for a snack.

Why had the Clayborn girl been rushed to the hospital? Did she have a miscarriage? It would take something like that for Paul to take his girlfriend to the hospital in the middle of the night.

For a man who had been married twice, he sure was stupid when it came to women!

If the blonde hadn't stayed in the hospital, she'd be out there with Paul. Rita laughed hollowly. Catfish! The old dummy on the boat must be getting an eyeful.

Lou certainly wouldn't know about Paul's girlfriend, Rita was positive about that, so Lou couldn't be helping them get away with it.

They *had* to be using Beau's Island. And this Clayborn person *had* to have a car to get out there.

As Rita ate, she became convinced that the Clayborn car would be on the island, hidden from sight.

Before leaving this place for good, she'd pay the island a little visit. She knew the road: Paul had taken her there on picnics. A lot could be learned about a woman by looking in her car. Maybe there would be letters or pictures in the glove compartment.

Before leaving Beaver City and heading into Bonaparte, Rita collected her clothes from the laundry and cleaners. She finished most of her packing that night, everything fitting into two large suitcases. She locked them in the car's trunk, along with a fur-trimmed coat and a black rain cape. Everything else, Paul could give to the Salvation Army.

She would have to buy new costumes, since she had given hers to a stripper in Baton Rouge. Before Rita went to bed, she wrote the letter to Paul.

CHAPTER 19

On Wednesday morning, when Lou arrived at the packinghouse, he was surprised to see Anderson's green station wagon already there.

Anderson was inspecting the pilings under the building. Over the years, hundreds of visitors had come to talk about boats and fish, or use some other pretext to walk along the dock and look down at the water. Usually, they spoke of a desire to live on the coast and leave the confusion of the cities behind. Lou understood this human longing and always made such people welcome. He had not expected Anderson to come back.

Before noon, the agreement to end Lou's ownership of Bonaparte Seafoods was completed and he had telephoned Judge Black. The papers would be ready on Friday. They shook hands on the deal and Anderson left for lunch.

After Anderson was gone, a melancholy came over Lou. If Anderson actually went through with the purchase, the money would be an unexpected windfall. He could use it to make a stand in the battle with his runaway cells, as soon as he had reached some distant place.

He was also shocked at the seemingly casual manner in which he was disposing of such an important part of his life. A five-minute call to the judge, a signature on Friday, and it was over. The building and dock seemed to be slipping away, dissolving beyond some dream–like, rain-blotted horizon.

Don't get sentimental, he told himself. After all, he was selling a rundown old place, which, like him, had become obsolete. Perhaps Anderson could bring the place back and make it active and worthwhile again. Especially if Paul's invention succeeded!

While Lou was out on the dock looking toward the sea, Anderson returned. As they spoke, Lou separated the business into segments—the building, dock, refrigeration and electrical systems; fuel installations, workshop, and other components—explaining everything to the new owner. While he talked, his mind ranged back a quarter-century to when he contracted to buy all the cypress, which was much costlier than yellow pine. The cypress had hardened with time, tightening around the nails and bolts, coming to terms with the seasons. Some of the wooden legs had sunk deeper into the marsh, which imparted a warped effect and gave the packinghouse a gnarled and sinewy character.

He hoped Anderson would come to understand these things. There had been a time, preserved in the papers stored above the freezer, when he had dreamed of an empire. Plans had been drawn and long meetings held. An architect's rendering of a steel and concrete factory had been presented and explained. Plans were made for great quantities of shrimp to be brought, cleaned, and frozen. Before anything had been settled, however, the oil drillers had moved in.

After that, the promoters of the big plant had driven off in their Cadillacs.

Lou told Anderson how the packinghouse operated. The house whenever requested provided regular shrimpers fuel, ice, nets—including cash advances. The vessel landed its catches at the packinghouse to be graded, repacked in ice, and sold to the wholesale buyers. Seven cents per pound was charged on fresh shrimp. After deducting the amounts due the house, the balance was paid over to the captain or the owner who, in turn, paid his men. When shrimping was good, four or five boats could make the packinghouse a modest profit.

Anderson listened, nodding from time to time. "Mr. Fisher, now that we've got all this settled, I want to find me a place on the water. Off by myself, where I can have a boat."

Lou thought about Beau's Island. Paul had wanted to buy it for years, so perhaps he and Anderson could go in together.

Lou described the beautiful little island and, at Anderson's request, phoned the real estate agent in Beaver City. The agent assured Lou that a deal could be made with an option to buy, and an appointment was arranged.

Anderson took an envelope from his coat pocket. "I brought along money for a deposit, Mr. Fisher."

"That won't be necessary. Judge Black will have the sales contract and lease assignment here for us at one-thirty on Friday. You can still change your mind, if you don't want to go through with this."

Anderson looked around. "No chance, a deal's a deal. You don't mind if I hang around and get used to the place?"

"Be my guest." Lou handed him a ring of keys and explained the locks each one fitted. "Make yourself at home."

"After I meet that real estate man, I'll come on over," said the new owner. "Spend the day, if that's okay with you."

Lou saw another advantage. "If you're going to be here tomorrow, I could leave by two and take care of some errands." He might also rest some, as the doctor had suggested.

"When's that boat coming in?"

Lou glanced at the sunshine outside the office. "By Friday night, I'd say. There ought to be two more days of this good weather." An electric shock paralyzed his insides and gripped his muscles.

"Mr. Fisher, you alright?"

Lou fought for control. "Just a pain or indigestion."

"You'd better let me take you home."

"Thanks, but I can make it." He rose as the pain reached the threshold of nausea.

"I'll follow along behind you."

Anderson locked up and drove behind the pickup to the turnoff from Highway 90. A half-mile through the trees, Lou parked at his house and Anderson walked to the porch steps. "Sure is a nice place you got here."

The pain was easing, but Lou was exhausted and wanted to lie down.

"You got someone here to look after you?"

"Not anymore," said Lou.

"If you're sure you're going to be okay, I'll be going." He turned to go and then stopped. "I hope you'll call me Duke from now on." The truth was, he couldn't decide which name he hated more, Richard or Anderson. Hell, he thought, what does it matter what these hicks call me?

Lou thanked him again and stood at the steps until his visitor drove away. He had asked Duke to call him Lou, but he, too, wondered what it mattered. Lou went inside and stretched out on the bed. His body relaxed and the pain started to disappear. It seemed odd that he had just withdrawn from the seafood industry. It would take time to get adjusted.

Time.

Trying to recall the flowers of Hawaii, he drifted off.

On Wednesday evening, Duke ate at Mike's.

A few minutes before eight he drove to the closed-up Texaco station and parked at the phone booth. The phone rang inside and his report to Tony was short.

"Duke, tell me exactly when we'll have the dock."

"We're signing the papers at one-thirty on Friday. I have the keys in my pocket. Fisher's sick as hell, but not admitting it."

Duke told Tony about the appointment with the real estate agent and Fisher's plans to visit his folks somewhere back east. He told him about the repairs being made in New Orleans on the radio transmitter and relayed Fisher's opinion that the shrimp boat would be in late Friday.

Tony told him to close up the fish house for remodeling. "Things are moving faster than we thought," he added. "We just might need to have everything ready this weekend."

"Hell, Tony, I just got here yesterday!"

"Keep your shirt on, you're doing fine. Just be sure to get that lease right away, on that place down the river. And Duke," he added. "Don't fuck up that deal."

"No sweat, Tony. Like I said, it's in the bag."

"You better talk to that shrimp guy when he gets in. Look him over real good. Maybe he likes broads."

"I hear different, Tony. What he needs is dough, and lots of it. Leave everything to me." Duke felt good.

"Call you tomorrow night, same time." Tony hung up.

When Rita got up and looked outdoors early Thursday morning, she saw that it was sunny, without any wind. That meant Paul wouldn't be coming in.

This was her last day in Bonaparte, which gave her a strange feeling in the pit of her stomach.

She wondered if Paul would be having breakfast with his Miss Clayborn, who was probably pretending she was riding around in a yacht. Rita smiled to herself as she turned the sausage and began cooking her eggs. If his girlfriend had a miscarriage, it sure would mess up their sex life. Chances were that Paul wouldn't move her into the house. With the bank hounding him, it wasn't exactly the best time to show up with a mistress. Or, she thought, the bank might be willing to take the house in place of the boat.

Whatever! That was his problem now.

Her mind drifted to Tony. He was handsome, smart, and a sharp dresser, just as Sam had said. Men had never really turned her on in a sexual way, although most of them didn't know that. A girl had to flatter the male ego and pretend to be deliriously stimulated in bed, especially if she expected to be successful and make a name for herself. Except with Paul. She had to give the devil his due. He had always been nice and gentlemanly with her. Tony was smooth, like people in financial circles had to be, but he wasn't sweet and considerate. To be honest, Tony was pretty crude.

Paul would never knock a girl out with drugs and help himself to her secrets! Besides, sleeping with Tony hadn't been planned. She wanted to go to dinner somewhere that had good food and a place to dance. Have a few laughs. She had never cheated on Paul before. She didn't count flirting. What pretty girl didn't show off sometime or other? Of course, going to Bob's Drive-In Sunday night hadn't turned out very well, but she wound up getting the better of Troy and Joe, by getting that paper signed.

They sure were lucky she was leaving town!

Rita wished she knew more about Philadelphia. Tony said it was close to New York. Her plan of working again in New Orleans would be pretty stupid if she hit the big time instead. They'd say she'd married a shrimper with no money. That he dumped her for a younger woman. People always thought and said the worst about strippers. Just because a girl took off her clothes in a really nice way, so that people could admire her beautiful body—and only while the music was playing—didn't mean she was bad, or a whore.

Would Paul keep on treating her like a perfect lady, if he knew about stripping at Frenchy's?

As if expecting company, Rita put out a clean tablecloth and laid the table properly. On an impulse, she clipped several white roses from outside the kitchen door and put them in a vase on the table. When she was satisfied with what she considered elegant southern touches, she sat down to her sausage and eggs.

The letter to Paul was propped against the sugar bowl. She read it over twice, the words sounding different in daylight. Most of it was what Tony wanted her to say. What if Paul *did* fall in love someday and wanted to get married? Why should she mess up the rest of his life by saying he couldn't have a divorce?

She finished eating, her mind wrestling with all her problems. Carefully, she tore the letter into small pieces and sprinkled them inside the garbage can. Bringing pen and paper to the table, she wrote a different letter:

> Dear Paul,
> A big dyke at the beauty salon told me the bank is taking back your shrimp boat.
> The last thing you need right now is a wife to support. I also found out you have Miss Clayborn living with you on the boat and how you had to take her to the hospital. (Which is looking for her, by the way.)
> I'm leaving for good. Don't try to find me because you can't. I might go to California. Then again I might not. I'm taking the car since it's in my name and you don't need it. (You probably won't need a house either, now that you have company on the boat, so why don't you try to give it to the bank in place of the boat?)
> I hope you will be very happy after I'm gone because you are a very nice gentleman, even if you won't give up shrimp fishing. Ha-ha. Lou is also. Rita
> P.S. If you want to get a divorce that's O.K. I don't have another man in my life so it doesn't matter to me if you do or not.
> P.P.S. I hope you find some shrimp before long and pay off the bank. In case they turn down this place here.

She read the letter again and was putting it in the envelope when there was a knock at the door. For a moment she was frightened, then she remembered it was Thursday, the cleaning woman's day to work. She had her own key, but she always knocked first.

Rita was glad she had already put her suitcases in the car. She saw no point in broadcasting the fact she was leaving.

By early afternoon, with Rita's help, the house was spotless. Miss Clayborn wouldn't be able to say that Paul's wife was a sloppy housekeeper.

Clean sheets were on the bed, as always. Rita wanted the blonde to know she was crawling into another woman's bed so she sprayed perfume on the pillowcases!

Rita needed to see Lou and get some money. He might get suspicious if she stopped by on Friday morning, all dressed up. Or he could be off in Beaver City, the fish house closed up.

After a hot bath, she put on white boots, a white blouse, and the miniskirt with small bells on the fringe. Paul had bought it for her, saying it gave people an excuse to look at her pretty legs. She applied makeup until she was pleased with herself in the mirror.

Rita left for the fish house. Driving to River Street, she looked at the clutter of houses in the main part of town and reminded herself again that nothing interesting ever happened in Bonaparte.

Before his second cup of coffee on Thursday morning, as Fisher had predicted, Duke pocketed a ninety-day lease on Beau's Island, which included an option to buy. Elated, he counted out the money in the agent's Beaver City office. He would have shelled out twice as much, without batting an eye.

Earlier, he had followed the agent's car through the open gate, across the narrow marsh road, and into the island's heavy stands of timber. At the dock, he glanced around, showing a little interest, and then the deal was made. He had been agreeably surprised at the price, readily consenting to the clause that prevented him from cutting trees during the option period.

From the real estate office, he drove around until he found a hardware store. There he bought a length of heavy chain and a padlock. From a floor display, he selected signs that apologized for remodeling and promised legal prosecution for those who trespassed. He stopped at the Holiday Lodge for coffee, before returning to the fish house.

Fisher was on the dock, sitting in front of the fuel pump housing. "I'm installing a new switch, Duke. The old one's worn out and you don't need the aggravation."

Duke inspected the work. "I forgot to ask if there's any other place where boats tie up around here."

"Not at Bonaparte. Closest docks are in Beaver City, but no one's fishing out of there. We're all hoping for a spring run this year."

"What's that?"

"Schools of shrimp, when they're migrating along the coast. Usually, we have a good run in the spring of the year."

"Do other boats pass our dock here?"

"Not any more. The government dredged a straight channel out to the bay from Beaver City and put in navigation aids. That's why most captains like to fish over there. Saves time going and coming."

Lou completed the work and tried the switch several times. "That's better. Did an agent show up this morning about the island?"

"Yeah, we talked some."

Inside the packinghouse, a man in coveralls met them. "Everything's okay, Mr. Fisher," he said. "Good as new. We only found one small ammonia leak in the return line."

"Glad it wasn't inside," said Lou.

"She's all ready to pull down, just shove in the starters." The mechanic closed his toolbox and left. Lou explained that the refrigeration people had come in to defrost everything and check over the equipment. Duke nodded, boredom on his face.

"Now's a good time for me to show you in there," said Lou. "While the freezers are warmed up." Lou led him into a long room with a low ceiling. "This is the storage freezer. You should keep it from ten to fifteen below zero." He opened a heavy door inside the room. "In there is the blast freezer."

Duke looked into the small space, at the galvanized racks on metal wheels. *Hell, I know about this crap!* He remembered the Fulton Fish Market.

"All the controls are on this panel, out here on the wall."

A black form flashed in front of them and Duke jumped backwards. Lou laughed. "That's Moonbeam."

"I don't go for black cats," said Duke. "Bad luck is something I don't need."

"Don't worry about Moonbeam. Besides, we haven't seen a mouse around here in ages. She belongs to Catfish."

Who the hell was Catfish?

Lou opened another door and pointed inside. "This is the main cooler, where you store ice. There's another one up front for loading and unloading trucks." He indicated a bottle of milk on a cooler shelf. "There's Moonbeam's milk supply."

Lou closed the cooler and showed him the cat's bowl. "Maybe I should have asked, Duke. You won't mind, I hope, seeing that Moonbeam gets her milk?"

Duke was already planning to get rid of the black cat. "No trouble, Lou. I'll take care of it."

Lou closed the door to the storage freezer and turned out the light. Duke followed to the control panel, where he was instructed in the various switches and fuse boxes. Lou started the machinery for the blast and storage freezers. "We can turn off the blast room tomorrow. You won't be needing to use it until you start freezing." He pointed to the workshop area. "There's a good stock of tools. I could write out an inventory?"

"No need, I can see what's there."

Coffee was on the hot plate in the office. Duke didn't want any, but Lou had a cup. "Judge Black is getting the lease assignment today, no problem there. You have four more years and renewal rights. The yearly cost is very low."

"What about debts?"

"They're all paid, mailed the checks myself this morning. The sales contract relieves you of any liability."

Duke asked about the boats and Lou took a ledger from the file cabinet. "I haven't written off these old accounts. If the boats ever come back, you can collect. Shrimp captains are fairly honest, but they forget to pay up sometimes. What you don't collect can be used as a tax deduction, if you start making a profit."

Duke was pleased with the thought of collections, but confused about the tax thing. "Is the boat that's out there now square with the house?"

Lou hesitated. "I'm not selling Paul's account with the business. You start out even with the *Helen S.*"

"How much is he into us for?"

Duke saw that Fisher was avoiding an answer. "I've marked his sheet paid, and headed up a new page for him. Paul Stark is a fine man, and one of the best shrimpers on this coast."

Lou returned the account book to the file cabinet and unlocked the desk's bottom drawer. "I keep cash in here." He lifted two flat metal boxes on the desk.

"The brown one belongs to the house and holds some pennies. I hope they bring you good luck." He opened the green box. "These forty-six dollars and eighty cents belongs to Catfish Davis."

"You mentioned him before. Who is he?" "

Fisher seemed to be thinking. "Catfish is more like a mascot, I guess. He showed up one morning years ago, when I was building the dock. He's a mute, must've been born without vocal cords, and he can't hear. We tried to find out something about his people, but never could."

Duke didn't like surprises. "He works here?"

"Actually, he's a deck hand for Paul."

"Is he any good on the boat?"

"He's all the crew Paul has, this time of the year. He can't hold a course or manage the winch, but he's the best shrimp header around. Catfish must be over seventy."

Duke nodded knowingly. "Free labor is hard to come by nowadays."

Fisher shook his head. "Oh, he gets paid all right. When the fishing's good he gets a share, like any other deck hand. And when it isn't so good, Paul pays him a small salary."

"What would an old idiot like that do with money?"

Lou's face darkened with the nasty comment. He picked up a stack of bankbooks held together by a rubber band. "We've always put his money in the Savings and Loan at Beaver City. Nothing has ever been drawn out. Some day, he'll be too old to work."

Duke wanted a drink. "Anything I need to do?"

"Paul is being named his guardian because I could be gone for months, maybe longer.

Like permanently, Duke thought. "How do you get his pay into the bank?"

Lou explained the process. "The cash here in the box is for odds and ends. Paul gets whatever the old man needs from time to time. Mainly new tennis shoes every few weeks. Catfish couldn't leave here with dirty tennis shoes."

Duke said nothing, wanting Fisher to get it over with. "Judge Black is bringing the order naming Paul guardian, but Paul doesn't know it."

Fisher smiled slightly. "He sure will be surprised when he finds out about our deal."

Duke toyed with the idea of asking Fisher where he hid the bourbon.

"I can't think of anything else, unless you have some questions."

Duke was relieved. "Can't think of anything," he said. He produced the envelope from his jacket. "I still have that deposit."

"That isn't necessary, we can handle everything tomorrow, when the judge gets here with the papers." Lou was growing pale, his face strained with pain. He stood, holding onto the desk. For a moment, it seemed he was going to faint.

Duke helped him down the steps. "I can drive you home."

"I feel better now, thanks." Lou looked back at the building. "You won't mind locking up when you're ready to leave?"

"I'll take good care of things." Duke watched Fisher drive away. As soon as he was out of sight, Duke locked up and drove to Beaver City, where he had two drinks before lunch.

He brooded about the black cat. He wasn't hung up on spooky stuff, but only a fool would bet against the odds. His clean record proved that.

His anger mounted as he drove back to the fish house. He put milk in the bowl and watched from the office door.

The cat wasn't to be seen.

The bottom drawer had been left unlocked. Inside, Duke found a large envelope from some medical place in New Orleans. He glanced through its contents, whistling from time to time.

He had guessed right: Fisher was on his last legs...and knew it.

He pulled out the green metal box and thumbed through the bankbooks. The one for Catfish Davis showed...he looked closer at the figures. *Over thirty-one thousand!* That shrimp captain and Fisher had to be nuts. He replaced the box, then took the account book from the file cabinet and flipped through the sheets. He punched the unpaid balances into the adding machine, saw that they totaled over seven thousand dollars. The last sheet was the *Helen S.,* with a balance of over thirty-eight hundred. It was marked "Paid in Full" and signed by Fisher. Many entries were listed simply as "Cash Adv."

No wonder Fisher was in bad shape, thought Duke. In the front of the ledger was a new page for the *Helen S.*, entered in Fisher's clear handwriting. It showed a zero balance.

Duke knew Fisher couldn't have collected from Stark overnight, so the shrimp captain wouldn't know that Fisher had sold the business and dismissed the debt.

Duke heard steps coming along the walkway and a faint tinkling noise pass by the locked door. He replaced the envelope, the tinkling sound becoming more pronounced.

"Lou, it's Rita."

She appeared in the doorway, looking at him curiously.

He took in her long dark hair, white blouse, tan miniskirt, and white boots.

"Oh, sorry, I was looking for Lou Fisher."

He smiled and shook his head, admiring her figure.

"Is he here?

"He's gone for the day, wasn't feeling so good."

She turned to go and then hesitated. "Did he say if he'd be here in the morning?"

Duke lied easily. "He's not planning on it, maybe I can help you. I just bought him out."

Her eyes widened in genuine surprise. The fringe of small bells hanging from her skirt jingled whenever she moved. He spread his hands apart. "He sold out to me lock, stock, and old shrimp nets. When I heard those bells, I thought it was Santa Claus."

She looked confused, then laughed, turning her body slightly and causing the bells to tinkle. "I don't understand, you bought this old place?"

He explained about his chain of restaurants. "Whatever it is you wanted, you can take it up with me. You can start by having a seat." He rose and pushed a chair behind her, then he resumed his place behind the desk. He watched her cross her legs and smooth her miniskirt.

"My husband has his boat here, the *Helen S.* I don't suppose you've met him yet?"

Duke's mind shifted into high gear. Stark's wife! He looked at her, conscious of those bare thighs. "Haven't seen any shrimp boats yet."

"Do you suppose Lou's out at his place?"

"He might have already left town," Duke lied, then saw the disappointment on her face.

Her critical eyes scanned the almost bare room and stopped at Duke. "And now this belongs to you?"

Duke was feeling expansive. "For our restaurants and nightclubs, we buy a million dollars worth of seafood every year. I needed a place to freeze our own and this place has possibilities."

Rita's face became alive with interest. "Where are your nightclubs? Do they have stage shows?"

"Sure, all of them. We book big name acts."

"Are they in the south?"

"Naw, they're in Baltimore, Philly, New York, and Boston."

"Philadelphia!" Her hand covered her mouth; she appeared to have swallowed a live fish.

"If you've ever been to Philly, you might know our club."

She shook her head. "Never been up North, mister—I don't think I caught your name."

"Richard, Richard Anderson. My friends call me Duke."

"Mr. Anderson, Duke, are you staying in Bonaparte?"

"I'm sure planning on it, until we get things going. I need to be out in the open, away from the rat race."

"You can do that around here, this town's a real drag. Is your wife going to be here?"

"If I had one, she might, but I've been divorced going on three years." Duke had never been married.

"Well, you sure are lucky to have Paul fishing for you. He's here all year."

Duke turned the screw. "Yeah, Lou told me. Maybe he should try somewhere else." He brought out the account book and spread it open. "His luck ain't so good around here. Right now, the *Helen S.* owes me almost four grand."

"Four thousand dollars!" she declared.

He snapped the book shut. "Mrs. Stark—"

She looked dazed. "I didn't know anything about that."

"You wanted to get some money from Lou, like a cash advance?"

She nodded, swallowing. "I'll just wait until Paul —"

He took the envelope from his pocket, exposing the stack of hundreds, and handed her one bill. "Will this get you by, Rita? If you need more—" He made sure the rest was in sight.

The largest advance on the Stark boat account had been forty dollars.

She hesitated, took the bill, and slipped it into her bag. "Duke, I, I don't know how to thank you."

He waved away the comment. "Tell me, are you French or Spanish?" There was one way she could thank him and the idea was growing. The captain's wife was a knockout.

Rita smiled. "I'm some of both, but Irish on my father's side. My folks had a big plantation up near Lafayette, but they took me away when I was eight. I'm boring you with all this."

"Go on, I want to hear all about you."

"There's not much to tell," she said, then went on to tell her story. When she got to the part about her parents being killed in a plane crash, he decided her story was as phony as a three-dollar bill. "When you first come in, I thought you were one of the girls in my art gallery." He indicated the calendars on the walls. "I knew you weren't from this neck of the woods."

He saw her relaxing. I'm halfway home, he thought, looking at her legs. "So are you planning on staying here?"

"Just between us, I want to find a place on the water, where I can build me a house. I always wanted one of them big houses, with them white columns out front. Like in that movie I saw one time. "

Gone With the Wind," she supplied eagerly. "Tara."

"Yeah, that's the one. I've been trying to remember that name ever since I come here."

Her face lit up as she leaned forward. "There's a place for sale, an island right on the river. It would be perfect for you!"

"Lou mentioned something about it, but I forgot the name."

She was anxious to be helpful. "Beau's Island, and I think there's a good price on it."

He frowned. "You get there by boat?"

"Or by car, there's an old road. I've been there on picnics. If the gate's locked, you climb over the fence and walk out to the island."

Tony had told him not to get his cock up, but he figured that the more information he could get about Paul Stark the better. His cock won.

"It isn't hard to find. I could draw a map."

He shook his head. "I can't go this afternoon, in case that boat comes in with a big load of shrimp."

She laughed. "You'll have a long wait: Paul won't be in before tomorrow night."

"You always know when he's coming back?"

"When Lou's radio is working, I do."

"It's my radio now, only it's in the shop."

"Paul keeps on fishing, in weather like this. He won't think of stopping until tomorrow."

Duke's erection was throbbing behind the desk. "It must get mighty lonesome."

She gave him a funny look. "It's not so bad, and I have a car."

He put his hands flat on the desk and half rose, smiling. "Since I don't have to hang around and shovel shrimp, how about showing me how to crash that gate?"

She hesitated and then said, "Why not?"

CHAPTER 20

Duke sure was handsome. He was also rich!
Rita guessed he was around thirty, maybe thirty-five, but not more than that. Whatever his age, he was young to be so successful. And divorced! The old hags around Bonaparte were sure to hit on him like a pack of wild dogs. Little good it would do that lot! He'd come in handy up in Philadelphia. "Oh, yes," she would say. "Mr. Anderson is a friend of mine. He's living now on his estate in southern Louisiana, a beautiful colonial mansion that's a near copy of the home where I was born."

The green sedan was still in the rear-view mirror, quite a ways back, and Rita thought that was smart of him: Bonaparte was full of gossips.

Showing him the island would kill two birds with one stone. If she spotted home-wrecker Clayborn's car back in the woods, she could make some excuse so he wouldn't follow her.

When Rita turned into the dim trail leading to the gate, there were no other cars in sight. The gate was closed, so she parked off the roadway. That way, Duke would think she wasn't planning to go out to the island. She mustn't seem eager, then he would have to insist.

She waited for him, enjoying the warm sun and the afternoon hum of crickets. He joined her at the gate and she explained that the lock was rusted.

Duke pulled the loose chain through the gate and swung it open.

"You keep going straight ahead," she said, pointing. "You can't get lost."

He grinned and gave her a basset-hound look. "Ma'am, I'm just a stranger in these parts and I'm already lost."

She enjoyed teasing him. "Follow your nose," she said." That road can't go anywhere else."

"How am I gonna know where to build the house?"

"You haven't bought the island yet!"

"C'mon, leave your car here. I'll bring you back in a few minutes."

She pretended to be making up her mind and then she smiled. "All right, but I'll drive ahead of you."

When both cars were through the gate, Rita was slightly annoyed to see him stop, get out of his car, and pull the gate across the lane. Now she'd have to open it on her way out. Chances were, he'd want to spend time looking around the island.

Beau's Island seemed miles out in the marsh, when she reached the edge of the woods. Paul had mentioned that the single lane causeway ran three miles through the marsh and cost a small fortune to build.

She drove slowly over sandy ruts that were carpeted with pine needles. There were no cars parked in sight. When she reached the clearing above the dock, Rita circled until she saw Duke's car, then she drove a short distance from the road. If a boat happened along, the red convertible would be hidden in the trees.

She left the motor running and Duke caught up with her. He got out of the car and walked over.

"The place to put your big house is right over there," she said, as if she were about to leave. Reaching in, he turned off the key. "What's the big rush? I need your advice on a lot of things." He opened the door and waited.

The bells tinkled as Rita stepped onto the ground. Turning, she placed her sunglasses on the seat. Before she could straighten, his arms were around her and his hands were clutching her breasts.

She tried to duck his grasp. "Keep your hands to yourself!" She began to pull herself into the car, one hand grabbing the steering wheel, but he dragged her back and twisted her around, trying to kiss her mouth.

She was more surprised than frightened, hoping it wouldn't be necessary to slap him to make him stop.

A moment later she saw his eyes and they were alive with pure lust. He had her pressed against the rear fender and she turned her face from side to side. "Duke, don't! What makes you think—"

His arm tightened and she couldn't breathe. He hunched against her, grinding her into the fender. Anger was building in her and she tried to claw his face.

He slapped her hard. "You're already paid for—a hundred bucks worth!" His eyes were like Tony's the night of the storm.

Terror ran through her as she realized that he was going to rape her. She knew it would be impossible to stop him; he was an animal with one thing in mind. Rita felt her skirt being jerked onto her hips. She struggled with all her strength. The bells sounded like an excited rattlesnake. He leaned her over the car trunk and her back felt like it was breaking. She beat on his head and he drew back an arm, threatening with his fist.

"Be still, damn it, you want a busted jaw?"

Only then was she certain that he would hurt her. Bad. Badly enough so she couldn't leave and get that job in Philadelphia. She became rigid. She was no match for brute strength. She felt his knee between her legs, heard a tearing sound and then her skirt was down and his erection was pressing into her stomach. He was positioning her on the trunk, his hands gripping her buttocks. Rita jerked her legs free and almost eluded him, but he was too quick. Holding her with one hand, he slapped her hard and she let her body go limp. Her face stung from the blow.

She was no longer fighting when he carried her into the trees, stretching her out on a carpet of brown leaves and pine needles. Through her tears she saw him kneeling and waited until his pants were around his ankles before she tried to roll away. He grabbed the flesh above her knee and squeezed, until she cried out. He began grunting, like a pig rooting in a trough, and then he straddled her, ripping open her blouse and forcing the bra above her breasts.

"Sonofabitch!" he panted, smoothing his hands over her breasts, pinching each nipple. Suddenly, he buried his head in her breast, his wet mouth sucking hard on her nipples.

His weight flattened her painfully against the hard ground. When she felt him shifting, she struggled to get up, but he pushed her into the pine needles and jerked her panties down. He mounted her again, this time forcing her legs apart and thrusting huge inside her.

Damn him! Damn him! Damn him!

When she sensed he was approaching his climax, Rita opened her eyes wide and stared at him, watching the agony in his face. Her eyes looked into his. He was frenzied in his orgasm and then fell on her, his head across her shoulder. Moments later, he pushed up and looked at her with a sickish smile.

She continued to show no display of emotion.

"Don't say you didn't like it," he told her.

"You bastard!"

"Hey, you had a ball."

"You dirty, raping sonofabitch!"

His face flushed. "Shut up, I've known women like you. You're all cock teasers."

She squirmed under him. "Are you through now, Mr. Richard Anderson? Will you remove yourself so I can leave?"

"I like it here."

She felt him slipping out of her. These so-called studs were all the same: on the way out, limp and slimy.

"You're nothing but a pig who has to rape for what he wants! Paul is going to kill you." She saw a flash of fear in his eyes.

"You keep your mouth shut or his fishing days are over." With both hands she pushed his chest, but he wouldn't move. "I'll just let the bank go ahead and grab his boat." He saw something in her face. Surprise? "You don't know that the bank is taking his boat?"

"I know about that rumor. Don't you believe that Paul will ever give up his boat. Anyway, how could you know Paul's business ?"

"Well, I *was* planning to pay off the bank; I got a finance company back east. I need to keep the boats around here fishing, especially the good ones like Stark's. I'm sorry Rita, that this happened like it did. You led me on, showing me your legs. When you came out here I thought—"

"Of all the lousy nerve!" Rita knew that she was trapped, and in more ways than one. "Did you really mean what you said, about paying off the bank?"

"You got my word."

He rolled off and lay beside her. "Next time, I swear, no rough stuff, even if you are the sweetest piece of ass in Louisiana."

She struggled to her knees. "You must not listen," she said. "There won't be a next time, not ever, even if I wasn't going away."

"Where you going?"

She remembered his promise. "Away, but I'll be back soon and I'll know what's going on around here, in case you don't hold up your end of the bargain."

She stayed on her knees, adjusting her bra and buttoning her torn blouse. She watched Duke get to his feet and stroll toward the water, clad only in a sleeveless shirt, jockey shorts, and socks. He looked silly and she threw one of his shoes at his back. He got to the edge of the bluff and then jumped down and disappeared under the dock. Probably wants to pee, she thought. She needed to go, too, and stood up, brushing leaves and pine needles from her backside. He hadn't hurt her. At least, there would be no ugly bruises to show under stage lights. She'd been lucky there.

She smiled to herself, imagining a conversation with her husband. "Oh, by the way, Paul, I've had my own fling on the island, so we're even. Only I got *raped*. But don't get mad, he's paying off the bank so you can keep your boat. Your love boat!" While Duke was on the beach, it was a good time to look for the girl's car. Rita studied her surroundings, figured a car could get between the trees further back. She saw a pile of tangled vines and branches where a large tree had fallen. Behind that pile was a good hiding place.

There was no car. From where she was standing, she couldn't see the dock, so she squatted.

Birds were chirping and whistling for their mates.

She started back to the clearing and saw a shoe inside among the vines. Curious, she stepped closer, and then she stumbled backwards, retching, a scream rising in her throat. She ran toward her car in a blind panic.

The shoe was on a woman's foot! There was a woman's body face down in the mound of vines. Rita glimpsed a white skirt and something tan. *And blonde hair!* Even in the second when she had stared, horrified, she knew the body was that of a young woman.

She stumbled against her car and hung on, gagging. Duke was coming up the embankment just as she got into the convertible. Starting the engine, she raced it and the car leaped forward. When Rita reached the gate, she left the motor running and she got out. The chain was locked. She jerked at it frantically and then heard a car approaching from behind. Duke rolled up to the gate, climbed out, and unlocked the chain. He was still without his pants. He handed her the miniskirt and then opened the gate, waving as she drove through.

Out on the highway, Rita tried to get control of herself. Instead of finding a car on Beau's Island, she discovered the body of a young woman with long blonde hair.

Paul's girlfriend?

Rita thought she was going to faint, but she gripped the steering wheel. Paul's girlfriend was dead?

Had she never made it to Paul's boat from the hospital?

The police! When they found the body, they'd think Paul had murdered his mistress and hidden her body!

Oh, dear God, no!

The police wouldn't think a man would murder his own mistress, they'd think the man's wife did it, *the jealous wife!* And then they'd ask her what she was doing at Beau's Island and she would have to tell them she was with Duke. Her mind raced in circles. Admitting she had been there could be seen as a confession.

She had to leave. Paul would find the letter and it would be too late to come after her.

The letter!

She had accused him of running around; it would show her jealousy. The police would say he killed his girlfriend to keep from losing his wife, or his wife had killed the girl to keep her husband! She had to tear up that letter, flush it down the john, and write another one..

If Paul came home right now, she would throw herself in his arms and cry her eyes out. Paul and Lou would take care of her; they knew how to manage trouble.

Rita stopped for a red light and was soon near the fish house. It was dark inside, with no cars out front. She could not see the *Helen S.* at the dock, so she kept on driving until she reached home. She drove into the carport and ran up the front steps, holding her skirt to keep it on. Trembling fingers dropped the key and she had to feel around for it. She entered and found it dark. Locking the door, she leaned against it and pressed her knuckles to her teeth.

Gradually, her heart stopped pounding.

Rita went into the bedroom. She was glad the cleaning woman had pulled down the shades. She wanted a bath and clean hair, but first she needed to rest. She fell across the bed, not bothering to remove her boots. There was soreness in her back and legs.

Damn Duke! Had he stumbled on the body? If he had, he would've said something at the gate. It was almost dark and Rita worried about spending the night alone.

Her mind was going around in circles again when a sound caused her to freeze. From the corner of her eye she saw the bedroom door closing. She was frozen helpless as a person appeared from behind the door. Screams were trapped in her constricted throat.

Light flooded the room and Belle Potter came toward the bed, her bloated face twisted with hatred. She looked even more ugly than she did the day she and Rita had the run-in at the beauty salon. Her bare arm was drawn back to strike. The whip cut into Rita's arm and Rita fainted.

CHAPTER 21

After leaving Duke at the fish house, Lou drove slowly along River Street.

The pains that began in the office were stabbing inside his chest, causing his body to turn damp with sweat. On the edge of town, he parked and swallowed two pills. The noonday sun warmed the interior of the truck and the hurt gradually backed off, like an animal retreating to its cave. Lou waited patiently, relieved that the attack was a brief one. Feeling better, he pulled away from the curb and drove onto the highway.

An idea was gaining headway in his mind. Death was not a final going away, but a returning, like a sailor comes home from the sea. I have crossed the oceans, he told himself. I have fought the wars and lived among the people, but now is the time of my own homecoming. He found comfort in these thoughts.

He decided to have a Carolina relative suddenly die, the perfect excuse for a journey. A crisis of that magnitude would make Maggie understand why he wasn't waiting when she came home. The truth was, he couldn't risk seeing her again, not even for an hour. Those last minutes might bring up emotions he couldn't hide, and she would sense the truth. No, Lou was steeled to this decision, painful as it was.

As for Paul, he would see him tomorrow. By then his bags would be stowed in the pickup. It would be dark when the *Helen S.* reached the dock and they would talk in the wheelhouse, or while walking on the dock. Paul would understand how selling the fish house made it possible for Lou to travel after the funeral. Undoubtedly, Paul would be excited, full of purpose concerning the octopus, and anxious to go home to Rita.

Lou could glance at his watch, announce that he had a plane to catch; ask Paul to explain everything to Maggie. Paul would do that for him. And then he would be gone, out of their lives forever, and they would feel sadness, knowing he was never coming back to them. He wanted to spare them from having to share whatever secret devils were waiting to confront Lou Fisher.

Planning his every move helped Lou take his mind off a future without Maggie, helped ward off the black emptiness crowding his hours. Her pictures would go with him, wherever he went, and his last days would be comforted by memories of her calm, lovely face.

The pickup would make it to the airport. Then...where? Time for decisions was fast running out.

Going back to the land of his youth would be his first choice, except for the confusion that would cause. The Harris Clinic envelope contained a list of places, several in the Pacific Northwest. He would select one of them and simply go there. On Friday night he would be flying to be with strangers in a place he had never been. Somewhere north of New Orleans he would pass back into winter. He wondered if another spring would make it up there in time to where he would be. A picture of melting snows and mountain flowers filled his mind.

He knew that whatever high mountain or rugged coastline he managed to reach, his heart would remain with the green marshes and the live oaks he was leaving, with Maggie and Paul and Mel, and with those who returned from the sea at sunset. Lou's pain was gone by the time he drove through the trees to his house. There was work to do inside, but he preferred to walk among his trees. The earth felt good under his feet and he walked into his park that bordered the marsh.

The rye grass would soon need cutting. Each year he planted grass in the open spaces, where trees were once felled for his larger house. In that second year of their marriage, he and Amelia had paved the walks, working on hands and knees, and then bordered their efforts with green boxwood. The house had never been built, but the little park was a place of beauty throughout the seasons.

During the last week of her life, Amelia had supervised the placing of the sundial and birdbaths, along with a masonry bench. "For outdoor romance," she had said.

Lou sat on that bench and looked through the tunnels of his memory. Tears welled for everyone he had loved and for all the futile regrets that one suffers when it is too late.

He scolded himself for doing what he was determined not to do and went to the shed that covered the pumps and the tanks of his deep well. After he had explained to Amelia the mysteries of the emergency fire pumping system, she took to calling this Lou's Waterworks.

The long hose was neatly coiled. He picked up the nozzle as he turned on the faucet. A fair stream of water arched into the flowerbed. One press of the emergency button and the nozzle shuddered and hissed, the high-pressure pump jumping to life. A distant tree, presumably engulfed in flames, was extinguished for the thousandth time.

Unable to put it off any longer, Lou entered the house. Through the windows of the kitchen he saw the first color of the sunset. A terrible loneliness swept over him. The stillness of the house, the end of day, these were indescribably sad. He shook it off, refusing to be overwhelmed, and began a search of the house.

Papers.

He was amazed at what he had saved: letters, bank statements, hundreds of documents, each one a tiny milestone of his life. Most of it was added to the box to be burned. A few essential documents went into a metal box in the pantry.

Far back on a closet shelf, Lou found a box with his old war medals and citations. He looked at each one and then put it in his box.

With the paper work completed, he packed two suitcases and stood them beside the kitchen door, ready to go when he returned on Friday afternoon.

Finally, using a cup of fresh coffee to cheer him up, he began writing the letters, the ones he intended to be found with the papers left on the shelf in the pantry.

On Thursday afternoon, Paul watched the red hose shimmering down into the sunlit brilliance of saltwater. Far below the surface he saw the muscular power of the pulsing hose.

The octopus was again alive in the sea.

He envisioned the tentacles of the slow moving monster advancing across the drowned plateau. Needles of air were puncturing through the bottom sediment and panicky shrimp were being herded by broad blades of air flashing above the arms of the octopus. The moving walls of light were blocking the escape of the sea creatures. No longer were they shooting ahead of the lead line to safety. Fleeing the boiling silt and the blinding air turbulence, they were being trapped by the octopus and caught by the net.

His invention had succeeded beyond his wildest dreams and he was still getting his mind around that reality. The deck-side pressure gauge was flicking and the compressor was quietly coughing behind the deckhouse. There were hundreds, thousands, of possible combinations of interval, pressure, and nozzle designs. People would be learning new techniques for years, but it would be Paul Stark who pointed the way!

He tasted victory in the salt air. Only then did a wedge of worry enter his mind, a concern that had been growing each time he sent his monster down to plunder the undersea riches, but had not yet formed itself into words. Now he knew what it was.

The shrimp would not stand a chance!

The octopus was deadly and efficient, the contest would always be one sided. In time, the schools of shrimp would be ravaged to a point where even the octopus would be out of business.

He thought about the great whales, the seal herds; of salmon, halibut, sardines, and other species endangered by the greed of man. He wondered if some day the ocean would put a limit on its bounty and if the sea might be too fragile to withstand the destructive rapacity of the human race. Each year, man was taking more and giving back only the waste of the continents. He remembered the buffalo that had survived the spears of the Indians, but were no match for the slaughtering rifles of the white man.

Would the octopus be such a doomsday instrument, spawned from his mind in search for wealth?

These were serious questions that he would take up with Lou and Mel.

Solutions would have to be found.

All day Wednesday and Thursday he had alternated the drags. The air pulses increased the catch fifteen to twenty times the non-air efforts.

Even the gulls had located his position and had come winging in for their share of the harvest.

The ocean had cooperated, favoring him with calm seas and cloudless skies.

When the fishing day had ended, he prepared a feast of shrimp and fish in honor of his success. He topped off the celebration by opening a bottle of wine that had come with the boat, donated by the builder. "It's a good boat, Paul," the shipyard owner had said. "There will come a time when only a great wine can say how good."

It seemed proper, thought Paul, to acknowledge the wisdom of the shipbuilder and toast the skills of the octopus.

Catfish grimaced when he tasted the wine. Still, when Paul had saluted the boat, the invention, the sea, his deckhand, and their return to Rita and Lou, he turned up his glass and drank. Then Paul ceremoniously dropped the bottle off the stern. By then the trawler had drifted near the marker and the small anchor had again been lowered to the bottom, until the pennant was holding at the same place. Paul believed the "lunch hook" would hold another night in the quiet sea.

The deckhouse doors were locked open.

A faint breeze carried no taint of papermaking and no scent of petroleum. Paul and Catfish sat outside, under the stars shining down on them from the heavens, and watched the moon rise up from the sea.

CHAPTER 22

After Tony's Thursday night call, Duke stretched out in his hotel bed with a detective mystery. He got a big laugh reading about a crook who went around feeling sorry for the people he cheated and robbed. *Bullshit!* He flung the paperback at the wastebasket. Either the crook or the writer was nuts!

Duke knew that a really professional criminal—himself, for instance—had to play it cool, the same way a doctor or an undertaker did. *Neutral.* You didn't give a shit.

Take Rita.

He was sure now that nailing her this early in the game was good business. It put her on his side. Tony would probably say the same thing. If she got wised up to her old man's source of unexpected prosperity, friend Duke would keep her pacified the way dames liked it most. She'd soon be begging for it. Hell, she wanted to get laid when she agreed to show him that old road. That talk about going away was more of the same old act. Keeping Rita Stark in line was a way to pass the time.

He laughed out loud, remembering her face when he promised to pay off the bank. She had fallen for that crap because that's what she wanted to believe. Hell, she probably still believes in the Easter Bunny. Later on, he would tell her he had already known the way to Beau's Island and hadn't needed her help, but she'd been so anxious to get him out there, he wanted to help her out.

He also had five bells that had been lost from her skirt in the excitement. He'd have some fun with that. Whenever she came to the fish house, he'd jingle them. Especially if her husband was there.

The biggest laugh was that he had to pay off the bank, regardless, because they couldn't run the action without the fucking shrimp boat. By then, her old man would be suckered into making the payments from whatever his part of the take happened to be. That is, until he was no longer needed. That was up to Tony.

"We need that boat in our hands by midnight tomorrow," said Tony when Tony and Duke last spoke. "I'll fill you in next time I call."

The big show was about to begin!

The day had been full of good surprises. The cat was gone, he found out about the dummy's bank account, old Fisher was on his last legs, and the unpaid boat accounts were almost four grand. He'd be collecting from Stark big time! Getting money from Stark would be a pleasure. Another look into the account book revealed that the old *Helen S.* sheet was no longer there; zero balance had been transferred to the new sheet written out by Lou Fisher.

Fisher had asked *him* to tell Stark his bill was all paid up. Oh ya! Fisher was going to grab his money and haul ass. Anyone on his last legs wouldn't be hanging around this dump a minute longer than he had to. When word was out that Fisher had croaked, a statement would be handed to Captain Stark.

Bonaparte wasn't going to be so hard to take after all.

CHAPTER 23

Rita felt bright light on her eyelids. She knew she had been in a deep well, that she was back in the sunshine, and that she was lying in a soft place. Her eyes blinked at the overhead light.

Belle Potter was sitting astride a chair, her arms folded on the backrest. She had a mean look and a whip dangling from her hand. Rita knew it was a nightmare and she needed to move closer to Paul. Belle Potter couldn't be real, sitting there with that whip in her spotted fist, and saying nothing.

Belle's lips were moving. "I come fer that paper Joe and Troy give ya."

Unreality lingered a moment longer and then dissolved. Fear trickled along Rita's spine as she sat up. The paper, Joe and Troy? *The confession!* She remembered putting it in her suitcase, which was locked in the trunk. "W-what paper?"

"I ain't got all night!"

"They broke in and raped me," Rita said, and then her voice grew stronger." How did you get in my house?"

"Ye's a-lying, Joe Riley ain't touched ya. His name is on that paper and ye's ain't got no right."

"My lawyer has it locked in his safe."

"Ye's lawyer? Who?"

"Judge Earle Black."

"Ye's lying." Belle held up the rumpled miniskirt and a pair of panties. "Ye's bin on yere back agin, there's trash all over ye's behind."

Rita looked down, horrified at her nakedness, then back at Belle. The woman's eyes were narrowed to slits.

"Ye's gimme what I come for 'n I won't whip ya."

Rita cowered, trying to pull the spread over her. "You get out of my house before my husband comes in! He's due right this minute."

"Then how come ye's prawn boat ain't in yet?" Belle rose from the chair, grimacing and towering.

Rita scrambled to the far side of the bed and the whip cracked inches from her ear. She heard Belle's half-strangled voice.

"I'll fix that whoring face of y'ern for good!" The big woman was backing off, dropping the lash behind her. Rita crawled away at the last moment and again escaped the bite of the whip. "Ye's ain't got no gun this time, I done looked."

The gun! On the closet shelf, hidden in the folds of an extra blanket Belle was crouching and weaving at the foot of the bed when Rita hurled the alarm clock. The old woman threw up her arm, ducking, as Rita sprang from the bed and darted into the closet, slamming the door.

Rita hung onto the doorknob with one hand, the other plunging frantically inside the blanket. She withdrew the pistol just as Belle jerked the door open. The woman stumbled, the whip no longer in her hand.

Rita fired over Belle's left shoulder. The sound was deafening and Belle struggled backwards, mouth slack and eyes sick with fear. Rita moved out of the closet, holding the gun with both hands. "I'm going to kill you, you ugly old bitch!" Rita's chest was heaving. "I'm going to fill your big fat ass with bullets!"

Belle cowered, raising an arm to shield her face, falling to her knees, her jaw moving soundlessly. She raised her palm and then sagged forward, her face on the floor; liver spotted hands covering faded yellow hair. "For God's sake, don't shoot me, Miz Stark! I ain't got myself ready t-die. I never meant ye's any harm!" Her voice was muffled, each word stressed with terror.

Rita heard herself screaming as she picked up the whip and brought it down hard on Belle's wide back. "Who are you going to whip now, Belle Potter?" In spite of her own terror, she felt savage delight when she saw the red stain on Belle's uniform, blood coming from a cut on her upper arm. Rita stared at the wound in disbelief, and then looked at the red smear on her own arm. With an angry gesture, she threw the whip down and dropped onto the bed, pulling the spread over her lap.

"Get up, Belle. Go sit in that chair."

Belle turned and saw that Rita was no longer pointing the gun.

"I said get your big fat ugly ass back on that chair!"

Belle backed toward the chair and pulled herself onto it, never taking her eyes off Rita. "I dint mean no harm, Miz Stark. As God is my witness."

"Shut up, Belle, I'll do the talking. What did Joe say?"

"He's a-drinkin' and he don't sleep none. He's gonna lose his meat cuttin' job. Ye's know it was all Troy's doings."

"Joe lied to me about his car being broken down," snapped Rita. "He was in on everything, right from the start."

"How kin ya say that? It *was* broke down, else he wunt come to call the tow truck."

"He's lying. He told me himself he drove out to Sandy Point to spy on my husband."

"Joe ain't said nothing to my sister Emma about no Sandy Point."

"Belle, you were spreading the same lies in the beauty salon. I heard you say my husband was living with a woman out on his boat. You said he brought her to the hospital."

Belle was nodding her head. "He's the one what brung us Mary Beth. She was bad off."

"Who?"

"Mary Beth Claiborne."

"What was the matter with her?"

"Dope. She was a-ravin' outta her mind afore morning."

"Where is she from?"

"From right here in Bonaparte. She's Hank Claiborne's kid, at the bank."

Rita felt strange and shook her head. "I don't guess I know her."

Belle was anxious to be helpful. "Hank's had her off in some fancy school, which is how she got on dope."

"Why was she on my husband's shrimp boat?"

"Yore man found her out there after she's a-tryin' to drown herself. He brung her in."

"Listen to me! Where did he find her?"

"Dint I say? He seen her a-lying on the bank when he come by Beau's Island in his prawn boat."

Rita sagged against the bedpost, her voice thin and far-off sounding. "How's she doing?"

"She done run off, Miz Stark. Tuesday, after I went off duty. They's a-lookin' everywheres."

"What was she wearing?"

"They's done ast me that. I hung 'um up in the closet after I dried them in the laundry that night. It was a tan sweater an' a white skirt."

Rita already knew, but her heart was pounding anyway. The body on the island still had on the white skirt and the tan pullover sweater. She forced her voice to sound casual. "Well, surely they've found her by now. She could die without medical attention."

"They say she run off with Letty Cameron's boy. She was seen a-drivin' his car. They's a-lookin' for both of 'um."

Rita's brain was spinning and she wanted Belle out of the house. A trickle of blood circled Belle's arm. Rita went into the bathroom and returned with a dampened washcloth, which she threw in the woman's lap. The woman mopped away the blood.

Rita stood up, no longer caring about her bare legs. The gun was pointing at the floor. "If something bad happens to my husband, or to me, Joe and Troy will be executed and you'll be spending the rest of your life behind bars!"

"Ye's never hafta worry, Miz Stark. I swear to ya on a stack of Bibles."

Rita noticed the line of hairs on Belle's upper lip. "I told Joe and Troy, now I'm telling you: Any Riley, Baker, or Potter that ever sticks their nose in my house again, gets their head shot off."

She was breathing hard when she herded Belle along the hallway and down the front steps. The white uniform was soon lost from sight.

Rita locked herself in the house and went into each room, switching on lights and checking window locks. The kitchen door was unlocked. The cleaning woman had often failed to lock it. Why bother? Nothing bad ever happened in Bonaparte!

She put the pistol on a chair within easy reach in the locked bathroom and proceeded to shampoo and set her hair. Then she got into the tub. The hot water was soothing; it gradually relaxed her tight muscles and helped calm her ragged nerves. The wound on her arm was smarting. It was a small cut and wouldn't leave a scar. Rita sank further into the water and relief flowed over her. Paul was innocent! The pathetic creature had not been with him out on the ocean. All he had done was save her life.

The letter would have to be changed, with no mention of Mary Beth Claiborne.

And Paul was not going to lose his boat. He could thank her for that. It was foolish, but she wished he had some way of knowing how she helped. When the water was no longer hot, Rita stepped from the tub and dried herself in front of the bathroom heater. She unlocked the bathroom, put the gun on the bed, and opened a drawer to search for a teddy. The whip was still on the floor. She picked up her skirt and saw that the zipper could be repaired. Several bells were missing and she wondered if she could find more in Philadelphia.

Her chest tightened with alarm. The bells had to be on Beau's Island. She saw her face turn white in the mirror. Her knees were weak and she sat on the bed, holding the skirt and counting the torn threads. Five bells were missing.

Everyone had seen the skirt with the little bells. She'd worn it everywhere, especially when Paul was home. The police would find them and know that there had been a struggle. They'd come for her! And they'd want to know what she was doing on the deserted island with a dead body. Who was she fighting with, and why? She would be arrested, while Paul was still fishing. Who would she turn to? Lou and Maggie were gone; Mel and Lois were out of town. Duke would be of no help. She preferred having the police and Paul think her guilty, rather than admitting that she had let Duke rape her. She was best keeping quiet. This way, Duke would see to it that Paul was off the hook at the bank.

Rita leaned against the bedpost for a second time and fought for control. She needed to leave at once, get a head start; disappear from Paul's life with a new name, a new routine. She jumped up and looked in the mirror. She was still young, she could do it.

From that point, everything happened in a rush. Rita made up the bed, removed blood from the spread; she replaced the chair and picked up the bloody washcloth. Ticking off each detail in her head, she packed cosmetics and other essentials in a travel case, located the hundred dollars she had hidden, and made a final check on the clothing she would leave behind.

In the kitchen pantry, Rita took the fishnet orange sack and, carrying it outside, put in some rocks. Returning to the bedroom, she stuffed in the panties, the torn mini, the whip, and the washcloths.

Leaving the key on the kitchen table, where Paul would find it, she turned out the lights and stood at the front door. With the gun in her hand, she stared out into the darkness. Telling herself that she was no longer afraid, she closed the door and made sure it was locked.

Rita drove past the fish house and wondered where Paul was

anchored. Was he lonesome, with only Catfish to keep him company? She looked in the direction of the ocean, beyond the dark marsh, and saw the moon coming up.

Ten miles past Beaver City, where the highway crossed a wide stream, Rita stopped the car and dropped the weighted bag into the water. It made a small splash as it broke the yellow track of the moon.

It was past midnight when she reached New Orleans and telephoned the Royal Orleans and was told that Mr. Milano was not registered. She got the night manager, who verified the operator's claim.

"But he must be there."

"I'm sorry, but he checked out Wednesday afternoon."

"But he told me he's coming back."

When she was told that no reservation was being held, she hung up. Giving up the suite would be the sensible thing for a smart businessman to do. Besides, she was returning early.

Rita drove around and then remembered a good hotel with cheap rates. At the Hotel Crescent City, she signed the register as Jean Brown, of Lafayette. The bellboy insisted on carrying her baggage, which consisted of a travel case and rain cape. Minutes later she was driving around the neighborhood, looking for an inside garage. It wouldn't do for the police to find her car in the hotel's parking lot. Finding one, she pulled in and made certain the glove compartment was locked.

Certainly Tony would check in by Friday night. It would be foolish to drive all the way to Philadelphia without seeing him one more time. The bed was hard and smelled of disinfectant, but she tried to sleep.

CHAPTER 24

Duke began his Friday with a big breakfast at Mike's.

"You had any luck buying seafood, Mr. Anderson?"

Duke held up a ring of keys. "Fisher sold out to me. I plan to use the place for freezing and shipping."

Mike stared in open-mouth astonishment. "I never thought I'd see the day."

Duke nodded and paid his check. "I'm closing up to enlarge the freezer. Good time to do it since there's only one boat fishing from my dock right now."

"Cap'n Stark," acknowledged Mike.

"Damn," said Duke. "I forgot to ask Fisher where Captain Stark lives."

Mike supplied the information and Duke drove past the house. The red car was not in the carport and no one answered his knock.

He didn't think she would come to the packinghouse, not if his car was parked out front. Rita was the type who made men come to her. When he did, he planned to rattle those bells. Duke unlocked the packinghouse and pushed open the doors. A sailboat was suspended from overhead rafters and he made a mental note to ask if it went with the deal. He had seen the same type of boat around Miami.

The red and green lights of the electrical panel attracted his attention. Fisher had said something about shutting down the blast freezer. Duke hit the switch and somewhere outside a large motor stopped running. When he turned on the light, opened the freezer door, and saw something black on the floor. The cold bit his ear lobes as he went closer; the missing cat was stretched out. Duke tiptoed, expecting to surprise the sleeping animal. There was no response; the cat was dead. Its ice-filled eyes were open and its legs straight out, as if it had died yawning.

Duke touched the fur and found the body rock hard. Using a pair of ice tongs, he pulled the animal from the floor, leaving fur stuck to the concrete. Dropping the cat off the dock, he watched it float away, its body slowly turning, glassy eyes staring.

Duke returned inside, closed the freezer door, and washed his hands. Despite everything breaking his way, a strange feeling was beginning to gnaw at his gut. Fisher had shut the black cat in the freezer. Duke threw back his head and roared with laughter. This would be one hell of a joke on old Fisher.

He looked at his watch and saw that he still had two hours to kill before driving to Beaver City. After that, Bonaparte Seafoods would be his.

Lou waited until one o'clock to leave the house, ignoring the carton containing the papers to be burned. That could wait until he returned.

He had spent the morning resting, reading the clinic's report, and going easy on the pain medicine. He had also decided on a treatment center on the Oregon coast. He was glad Maggie was still out of town.

Several people waved as Lou drove through town; he whispered a silent goodbye to each one.

He arrived the same time as the judge and his secretary. "Sue Ellen insists on driving me to the airport," said Judge Black. "Tell her I'm perfectly capable of taking the bus."

"He'd go right on through to Mobile," laughed Sue Ellen.

"You're going to have a fine trip," said Lou. "Best time of the year to be in the Yucatan."

The judge looked around. "Is your man here? The papers are ready."

Lou pointed at the station wagon and they proceeded to the dock. Introductions were made.

The judge squinted suspiciously at Duke. It was nothing he could put his finger on, except years of experience on the bench. Maybe he thought, he should just chalk it up to old age. "Would you excuse us a minute, Mr. Anderson? I've got some personal matters with Lou, then we can get on to your business."

Duke nodded. "I'm in no hurry."

Inside, Lou read and signed his will, signed the papers for the guardianship of Catfish Davis, and heard about the judge's conversation with the Washington patent attorney. Their business completed, he put the will in his zippered pouch and left the papers dealing with Catfish on the desk. Duke was called in.

The judge insisted on reading the entire contract. When he seemed satisfied, Lou signed and Sue Ellen guided them through the formalities of notarization. This process completed, Duke handed an envelope to the judge. The old man counted the money twice and passed the envelope to Lou, who folded it and buttoned it inside his shirt pocket.

Duke's eyebrows rose as he watched Lou acting so casual. Putting the money in his pocket without counting it. Offering coffee, tea, or bourbon. Pretty cool, actually.

Sue Ellen and the judge stood up and they all walked outside. Lou shook hands with the judge and Sue Ellen, then watched them drive away.

"I have to catch a plane myself," Lou said.

"Tonight? I didn't know you were leaving that soon."

"My plans have changed," said Lou. "I have to attend a funeral."

"Need a ride to the airport?"

"Thanks, but I'll take the truck. I'll be leaving right after Paul gets in." Lou looked at the darkening sky. "Weather's about to kick up and a squall's due to hit after dark. Knowing Paul, he'll fish as long as he can, so he should be here tonight."

Duke nodded. "I can stick around," he said. "No need both of us being tied up."

"Thanks, but I need to talk to him about our arrangement. I'll wait at the house. When I see his running lights, I'll come on over."

Duke began to laugh. "Did you know you froze your cat?"

Lou looked at him without comprehension. "I did what?"

"That black cat? You must've shut him in the freezer yesterday. I found him stiff as a board." Duke chuckled.

"Frozen?" There was disbelief on Lou's face.

"Dead as a mackerel; quick-frozen pussy."

Disgust flashed over Lou's face. He turned to Duke. "Is the poor thing still in the freezer?"

Duke laughed. "Hell no. When I worked in the fish market as a kid, we froze a bunch of alley cats one weekend. The spics claimed they heard spirits after that and wouldn't go anywhere near those damn freezers. Almost got me fired."

Lou was feeling years older. He pictured how frantic Catfish was going to be without Moonbeam waiting to greet him. "Did you bury Moonbeam?"

"Naw, I threw her in the river."

Lou winced as anger and pain attacked like a storm advancing down a valley. He stiffened and leaned against the truck.

Duke eyed him. "You got that bellyache again?"

Unable to speak, Lou would not allow Duke to help him into the truck. With an effort, he started the ignition and drove off.

Duke watched the truck disappear and crossed to the workshop, where he found a hammer and nails. In minutes, the signs announcing "Closed for Remodeling" were tacked onto the building.

Back in the office, Duke studied the court order regarding Catfish's guardianship. If he filled in his name in the space intended for Paul, he'd have complete control, including the right to deposit or withdraw funds held in trust. He needed time to work out an angle.

Duke sat in the swivel chair, leaned back and looked around. He liked the sexy pictures on the walls; they reminded him of paintings behind a bar.

He was pleased with himself: The base of operations was set up and he would provide cover for the important action.

From now on, he was one of the big-time boys. Millions were raked in each year from narcotics, and this took brains. He wondered how much his cut would be.

Miami was no longer important, but Bonaparte had deals all over the place. Just look at how many he had uncovered in three days. First, Fisher had five grand in his pocket and the two other people who knew were gone. Second, this Catfish idiot had over thirty-one grand in the bank and Bonaparte Seafoods managed it. Third, he was about to get four grand from the shrimper, Stark. And finally, there was all that dough he'd collect from the skipped-out boat captains, half of which would pay collection muscle. Still, it'd be like picking money up from the sidewalk!

That made a total take of more than forty grand!

One thing for sure, he couldn't allow Lou Fisher to tell Stark about the Catfish papers, or about the paid-up bill at the fish house. That five grand burning in Fisher's pocket would never make it out of town.

Duke looked at his watch. He still had plenty of time. He was the only one who knew Fisher planned to see the shrimp guy that night.

Lou Fisher came out on the porch when Duke drove up.

Duke smelled smoke coming from inside the house. "You got something burning?"

Lou waved toward the front of the house. "Spring cleaning: I'm burning old papers."

Duke noticed the suitcases and the medical report on the kitchen table. The pocket of Lou's khaki shirt was still stuffed. "You all ready to go?"

Distaste was written on Lou's face, that he had to even talk with Duke. "As ready as I'll ever be. I'll leave for the airport after I've had a few minutes with Paul." He reached toward a shelf where he kept his bourbon.

When Lou turned to take down a bottle, Duke moved fast. He grabbed Lou around the neck, locking his arm around his throat. He was surprised at Lou's strength as he pulled him backwards. Lou clawed at Duke's arm, but the younger man tightened his hold. And then, suddenly, Lou dropped and Duke was pulled forward, off balance. He felt himself flying over Lou and into the kitchen wall. When he turned, he found Lou standing, a chair raised over his head and his eyes blazing. Duke tried to move along the wall, but the chair struck his arm and shoulder. Lou raised it once more and Duke dived toward him. Lou moved faster, jumping behind the table. This time, he swung the chair and missed.

Duke crouched, arms held up in front of his face, and he inched toward Lou. The chair wavered and he saw his opportunity. Before he could move, Lou's face shifted into a horrible contortion, and then the man slipped slowly to the floor.

Duke watched, fascinated, as Lou died.

Within seconds, he took the envelope and stuffed it into his own pocket. There was no urgency: It was late in the day and would soon be dark. Duke wandered into the front room and found a smoldering fire, fueled by a cardboard box half filled with papers. In the kitchen he found a large dishpan, which he filled with water. Remembering the gloves, he pulled them from his pocket and pulled them on. With a smaller pan floating in the dishpan, he returned to the front room and looked around. He touched his lighter to the parlor curtains and flames curled against the ceiling. After the lightweight curtains and heavier drapes burned, there were blisters of paint on the woodwork. He transferred a burning rag to the couch and a red rose of fire began to eat into the cushion. Coughing from smoke, he placed the box of papers on the hearth and set it afire, then he backed into the hallway to watch.

The house faced the marsh, so there was little danger of the smoke being detected. With a handkerchief over his mouth, Duke used the pan of water to douse the fire in the couch and on the hearth. The place was a mess. Duke used a cloth to wipe his fingerprints from the dishpan and then pressed Lou's fingers against the shiny metal. He found a small glass and closed Fisher's hand around it. Then he took the bottle of bourbon and poured a few ounces into the glass, which he placed beside the report. Anyone reading would see the warning: No alcohol.

Duke took a quick swallow from the bottle and spilled a good amount into the dead man's mouth. He continued to pour until the bourbon was running down Lou's chin.

"Cheers," said Duke, taking another swig.

Recapping the bottle, he closed Lou's fingers around it and then set it on the table.

A quick inspection confirmed that there were no marks on Lou's neck or throat. The eyes were bulging, but Duke guessed this was normal for a man who got all steamed up about a fire and had conked out from a heart attack.

They sure as hell wouldn't need an autopsy!

Duke put both hands under Lou's armpits and dragged him down the hallway, past a bedroom door, and then left him, face down.

Old Lou Fisher sure as hell wouldn't be rocking on his porch tonight, watching for the *Helen S.* Duke made a final check and turned out the lights. Before locking the kitchen door behind him, he spotted a reel of water hose mounted on the corner post of the shed.

He turned on the faucet, rotated the brass nozzle until the water was shut off, and then dragged the hose up the back porch, through the kitchen, and into the hallway. Standing at the living room doorway, he activated the nozzle and drenched the parlor and its contents.

Duke stepped over Lou and slipped the hose under the body. As he turned to go something brushed his leg above his ankle and he stumbled back in quick panic. His blood ran cold.

The black cat was back, right there in the hallway, arching its back and staring at him. The eyes were no longer ice-filled and he was circling, meaning Duke would have to cross his path to get out. In a frenzy, Duke grabbed the animal and hurled it with all his might.

Duke strolled into Mike's and looked at his watch. The whole deal had taken less than an hour and he felt calm now, over his scare. He sat at a table and picked up a newspaper.

Mike arrived with the menu. "Got real fine gumbo, Mr. Anderson. Warms a man up for a rainy night."

"Sure, Mike, and you got fried prawns?"

"Fresh this afternoon."

"Gimme the gumbo, a big platter of prawns, and a double order of fries."

"You want coffee with that?"

"Yeah, I could use some coffee." He tapped the face of his watch. "What time you got?"

"Seven-fifteen, by my time," said Mike. Duke ate and pretended to read the paper. Fisher's money was locked in the glove compartment. His plan was to tell Stark that Fisher had split. No sweat there. It might be days before the body was found. If anyone found out about the money being gone, it would be one more unsolved mystery. Duke arrived at the darkened Texaco station just as the phone in the booth was ringing. Tony sounded impatient.

"Is Stark's boat in yet?"

"It's expected around ten. We got a bad storm starting down here."

"Yeah, and we got a boat in the gulf that has to come in. She's running out of gas and we have to make that transfer before daylight."

Hot damn, thought Duke. "All you gotta do is clue me in, Tony."

"We got some people that should be there by now. They're in a dark green van with dual wheels. I told them to park close to your motel. When they get there, get the van out to that new place of yours. Where the old dock is."

"Hey, Tony, what about the shrimp boat?"

"Duke, we ain't got time to make a deal with Stark tonight. We got to get that other boat cleaned out. You can talk to that shrimp captain tomorrow. For now, play it like we got it set up. The guys in the truck know the score."

"What if Stark wants no part of it?"

"Can you run the fucking shrimp boat?"

"Hell no."

"So you hafta keep the captain healthy, understand?" The phone went dead.

Duke stood there, trying to remember everything Tony had said.

A dark van was parked across from the motel. Duke stopped and spoke to the driver. "You here for shrimp?"

"Yeah, we're looking for Duke."

"I'm Duke, you wait here. I'll be back in a coupla minutes."

Duke got a rain slicker from his room and asked the clerk for directions to a Beaver City restaurant. Mike and the boy at the motel might come in handy if Duke needed an alibi. It wouldn't be the first time Duke had arranged in advance to cover his tracks.

The green van followed him to the gated road on Beau's Island. The trees were whipping in the breeze, but no rain was falling. Duke left the gate unlocked.

They drove without lights across the marsh-lined stretch of roadway until they reached cover. Using his parking lights, Duke led the van through the twisting route to the clearing at the dock. He killed the lights and peered across the marsh toward the gulf. Nothing. The only sound was the steady humming of wind. Duke walked back to the van.

The driver, a heavy-set man of medium height, opened the rear doors and two men slid out. One of them was tall and slender, the other short and slight. Duke figured he'd make a jockey's weight.

"What about the boat?" asked the driver.

"She'll pass here before she gets to the fish house."

The driver squinted into the darkness and lit a cigarette. "This ain't gonna be no picnic."

"You better get your van into those trees over there," said Duke.

"Shit! I can't even see it, from where I'm standing."

"If you had a fucking searchlight, you could," snapped Duke, disliking the heavy-set man.

Duke signaled with his flashlight and the truck was backed out of the clearing. He parked the wagon in the trees and turned it in the direction of the mainland. The van driver got into the back seat.

"What's the score?" asked Duke.

"You sure we ain't missed that shrimp boat?"

"I said he ain't come in."

"You sure he has to go past us here?"

"Unless he can fly over all that grass," answered Duke, gesturing toward the expanse of field.

"Once he passes here, how long to the place he's goin'?"

"About fifteen minutes. Why can't we get the boat to stop here?"

"That ain't the way the shot was called."

"It would save time," Duke argued.

"You're supposed to be in the clear," explained the van driver. "So no one knows you're tied in with us. " The driver outlined the instructions he'd been given. Duke was amazed by what he heard. It had taken real brains to work this out. "So you rob me," he said, going over what he'd heard. "And then you grab the shrimp boat."

"That's it, friend. The guy on that boat has to think we're gonna knock you off."

Duke was intrigued. "But suppose he don't want to play ball?"

"Me and Slim'll take care of that. When we get back, he's your boy."

Duke turned and looked at the man in the back seat, his face lit up by another flash of lightning. "How're you gonna find that other boat, out there in the dark?"

"That ain't our worry; Tony told us where to go. Said the other boat would find us."

Duke was glad he was staying on solid ground. He looked at his watch, briefly flicking his lighter: Eight-fifty. Suddenly, two lights, one red and one green, glimmered out in the marsh.

"Maybe that's him now," said the burly driver.

"We wait and make sure," said Duke. "Get the others in the wagon before they get hit by lightning." Duke went to the edge of the bluff and stood behind a live oak.

Like glowing eyes, the boat's lights grew larger. Duke soon heard the sound of the engine. He stayed behind the tree until the boat was past the dock. A moment later he ran, hunched down, to the wagon.

"That your boy?"

"That's him," said Duke, starting the motor. "It sure as hell is!"

CHAPTER 25

Paul awakened before dawn on Friday. The boat, tethered to the bottom, dipped fore and aft in a light swell. For a few minutes he allowed his senses to get adjusted to the beginning of a new day. The creaking of the vessel and the low hum of the generator blended with the rustling sounds of nets hanging in the rigging. A sea bird protested and was answered.

He slid from the warm bunk, stretched, and stripped before going on deck. The marker was off his starboard rail and a shimmering silver trail led to a half moon low in the indigo sky. The breeze explored his bare limbs. He dropped the upended deck pail over the side and it set off clouds of tiny lights as it turned under the surface, spilled its pillow of air, and gulped itself full of seawater. He pulled it up and tilted it over his head, water cascading over his body, washing the warmth of sleep from his muscles, stinging his eyes.

His last day at sea had begun.

An hour later, with a fire-red sunrise off the bow quarter and Paul and Catfish eating breakfast, the octopus worked the first drag. The trawler shouldered the heavy cables, like a draft horse bent to its plow, pulling smoothly on a westerly course. The weather broadcast told of an approaching front and Paul estimated they needed to be secured and under way no later than two o'clock. That would still put him at the dock well after dark, but he wanted to fish until the first winds of the front caught up with him.

The octopus produced the largest catch ever, the cod end of the net bulging with hundreds of pounds of huge prawn. With the rig put back into the sea, Paul turned off the air and let the red monster loaf along the bottom. During this drag, he and Catfish headed and iced the shrimp. Paul kept count of the baskets from the first drag, then whistled and held up eight fingers. Catfish smiled. Even with the octopus working half time, there were more than eight thousand pounds of jumbo shrimp in the hold. It would have been impossible to head the catch if his invention had been used each drag. As if to confirm these thoughts, the second drag produced only a half basket. Nodding understandingly, Catfish pointed to the octopus as it slithered over the stern, tapping his cheek puffed up with air and pointing to the valve. Paul laughed as he turned the valve. Curtains of bubbles widened into a large V as the trawl boards spread the arms of the octopus and guided them once more to the ocean depths.

Storm clouds were amassing toward the Yucatan when the final catch was on the deck. Paul passed the marker for the last time and checked his bearings again from several shore stations, verifying the position on his chart. He swung the bow on course for home and switched on the autopilot. "We'll be cutting it pretty close," he told Catfish, as they continued to head shrimp on the rear deck. Flocks of gulls sailed behind the boat, screeching and scolding as they dived for the vessel's discards. Paul studied their noisy competition.

Some of the birds he knew by sight, those who had remained with the trawler for days. When it was anchored, they also rested. When the net came aboard, they winged in from the sky or shot in low over the water, ready for the leavings. After each deck wash-down, they became quiet, content to float in sight of the trawler, waiting for man and boat to supply the next feast.

Paul studied the overcast sky; saw the wind building from the southeast quarter. The weather station was advising all small craft to seek immediate shelter.

It was well after nine when the trawler entered the river, the wind sending undulating waves through the marsh grass and whipping the lines in the superstructure. The incoming tide was flooding the marsh. Paul didn't need his searchlight as he threaded the bends and long reaches of the river.

The overhead light was out, at the Bonaparte Seafoods dock, and Paul coasted past the pilings, swung wide, and then came in against the tide. With the engine in reverse, he gently edged the bow against the dock, dropped a line over a cleat, shifted into neutral, and allowed the current to bring the stern in. A moment later, the boat was fast to the dock and the engine was stopped.

His plans for the evening had been worked out during the long run in. First, he would call Rita and ask her to come to the dock. After she arrived, he planned to show her the coiled red monster and tell her about his invention. Money she understood! Pretty clothes, a fine house, music and dancing. The octopus would make it all possible.

Paul sprang lightly from the gunwale to the dock and fumbled with his key ring. As he turned from the dock to enter the catwalk, there were quick steps behind him. Before he could react, a hard object was shoved into the small of his back.

"Keep moving, friend!" said a husky voice. "And put your hands over your head!"

"What the hell?" Paul swung around as his assailant backed away.

"I've got a gun here and I'll use it," growled the stranger. "Best you do like I tell you."

Paul saw the pistol. He tensed to swing and then checked himself. "Who the hell are you?" he demanded. "And what are you doing on this dock?" From the glow of headlights on the highway, Paul saw that his assailant was holding the gun in both hands.

"In the office, friend, and don't try no funny stuff!" Paul pushed through the door, followed by the gunman. The door closed, light suddenly flooded the room, momentarily blinding Paul. Seated in Lou's old chair was a man Paul had never seen. The man was well dressed; his arms were forced behind him and his ankles were tied together. Sitting a few feet away was a smaller man wearing black pants and a black trench coat. He was pointing a gun at the constrained man. On the edge of the desk sat yet another man, tall and gaunt, his gun pointing at Paul.

The burly one ran his hands over Paul and pushed him against the wall.

"Are you Stark?" asked the man in Lou's chair.

Paul was not frightened, but was furious. *Who were these crazy people?* He studied each one in turn and then shifted his attention back to the one who had asked the question, the one bound with rope.

"I'm Paul Stark. Who the hell are you?"

"Richard Anderson, Duke. And don't cause me any more trouble. These guys already have my money."

Paul noticed that their captive was wearing an expensive watch. "What do they want from me?"

"Damned if I know," said Duke. "They musta thought I was Mr. Fisher."

An alarming feeling gripped Paul. He spoke to the room, turning to look at all four men. "Where's Lou?"

"He left to catch a plane outta New Orleans," said Duke. "I bought him out, as of today. This is my place now; I was working here on the books."

"You what?" Paul leaned forward. "You're lying, this place wasn't for sale."

Duke nodded at the desk. "Maybe it wasn't before, but I paid cash for this broken-down fish house. Some guy called Judge Black fixed up the papers. You can see for yourself."

"That's all the talking for now," said the leader. "You come with us," he told Paul. "Your new buddy stays here, where Shorty can look after him. If we get back okay, maybe Shorty turns him loose. Else he goes in the water, chair'n all."

"Captain, for God's sake," begged Duke. "Do whatever they want, don' push our luck. Remember, they already got all my cash, more than eight grand, to get this business going." Duke's eyes got large with fear. His hands were trembling.

Paul lost all patience. This sure as hell was not the homecoming he had planned. "Just what do you want from me?" demanded Paul.

The heavyset one spoke up. " A little charter job and we're gone." He motioned at Duke with the gun. "Shorty, we ain't back by daylight, throw this fish off the dock." Turning back to Paul, he said, "We ain't got all night, Captain, so who else came in with you?"

"Nobody," said Paul. The last thing he wanted to do was put Catfish in danger.

"How can you run a big shrimp boat without help?"

"Hasn't been any shrimp," said Paul. "Now what's this nonsense about a charter? Is this some kind of stupid joke?"

The gangster ignored the question. "Slim, lead the way and I'll look after the captain."

Again Paul felt the gun jab his back. The three of them stepped into the roar of the wind, Slim leading the way back to the trawler. Paul was worried about Catfish, until he glimpsed a head peering above the end of the dock and then disappearing. Anger was burning his guts, but years in the military had taught him caution. The thought of having his boat violated by these seedy characters made him furious. More than anything else, they had interfered with his plans to be with his beautiful Rita.

"Better start 'er up, friend," said the leader, when they were in the wheelhouse.

In seconds the throbbing diesel was spitting out cooling water near the waterline.

"Get out there, Slim, and unhitch this thing!"

Slim leaned into the wind and went on deck. The trawler was soon drifting with the current.

Paul considered going upstream, where the marsh river got smaller and ended in the grass, which would cause the boat to go aground. The gun shoved against his throat convinced him to spin the wheel and back into the channel. When he was well clear of the dock, he threw the clutch into forward and they moved downstream. If he caused them to run aground in the mud—

"Friend, you get this thing stuck in them weeds and I shoot you in the leg."

"You need to tell me where we're going," said Paul, switching on the anchor and running lights. He felt hands around his ankles and a rope tying his feet together.

"Take us to North Point Marker and I'll say where from there."

Paul wondered if the gunman knew that the beacon was only a few hundred yards past North Point. "That'll take three or four hours," he lied.

"Where's the flashlight?" demanded the leader.

His captor found it and moved its beam around the wheelhouse, finding the radio transmitter's microphone. He pulled the cable from its jack, slid open the door, and threw the mike into the river. He turned to the fathometer and ripped the transducer wire from the instrument.

"Do some more crazy things like that and the engine stops," growled Paul. With the beam exploring the wheelhouse, Paul strained to stay focused on the river's channel.

Paul gripped the wheel and thought about his predicament. His captors knew little about boats, which was in his favor. Once they were into the open bay, they'd be crazy to disable him. They had to keep him healthy to get back, unless they planned to board another boat. If that were the case, it was likely that they planned to shoot him. If he had to guess, he'd say this trip was about drugs.

The ship's clock sounded ten bells as they passed the Beau's Island dock.

CHAPTER 26

Friday morning, Rita was tired from a sleepless night. The sounds of the old hotel had frightened her. Even now, a drunk down the hall was banging on a door, shouting at the barricaded woman inside. Rita pulled the covers over her head and closed her eyes. The drunk was let into the room and the hall fell silent again.

Each time the elevator door opened on her floor, she tensed until she knew no one was walking down the hall towards her door. She worried less when people were ringing for an elevator to leave on. Those passengers would be johns or pimps having completed business with the girls.

By noon Rita was awake and hungry. The Creole salad provided by room service was just what she wanted. The pot of hot coffee on her tray was almost empty. She smiled and thought, days were for sleeping and nights were meant for fun. Just before eight in the evening, Rita left the room carrying her purse and makeup case. She paid her bill, impatiently waiting while the elderly clerk made change. She neared the front entrance and saw a familiar figure getting out of a taxi. It was Tony!

From instinct, she darted into a phone booth in the hallway. A shadow hesitated near the booth and her heart almost stopped. Tony was in the next booth. She crouched against the pay phone and heard him making a call to Bonaparte! The number he gave the operator wasn't hers.

"Duke," he said. "Has Stark's boat gotten in yet?"

Rita was dumbfounded. How would Tony know Duke? She pressed herself against the wall and listened. As if in a bad dream, she caught snatches of the conversation: A boat running out of gas...had to make the transfer before daylight...got some guys coming to help...dark green van...no time to make deal with your shrimper... ten o'clock.

Her mind was spinning and she began putting the pieces together. Tony and Duke were plotting to grab Paul's boat. So Tony was not an important businessman, just a lousy gangster in cahoots with Duke. If they wanted a shrimp boat, it was just for one thing: drugs!

She saw Tony leave the booth and go into the lobby.

Paul was coming in around ten, she had to warn him. She had less than two hours to drive home. A quick glance toward the lobby and Rita darted outside. A taxi pulled up to the curb.

She jumped in and instructed the driver to take her to the bus station. From there, she could phone Lou, let him know about Duke and these plans. Lou could radio Paul. Yes, this was faster than driving to Bonaparte. Rita grimaced. No matter what, she still had to get to Lou, or the police.

Tony was leaving the hotel just as the taxi drove away.

Rita got to the bus station and called the shrimp dock. No answer. She tried Maggie, but the phone rang and rang. Frantically, she called Mel Wilson in Beaver City, but with no success. She looked at her watch, saw that it was eight-twenty. She could still get to Bonaparte before Paul came in, but there wasn't a minute to spare.

A taxi took her to the garage. She drove through the French Quarter and then twisted and darted through the streets and traffic until she was on the highway. The wind roared against the car, trying to push it off the road. Lightning flared, blue jagged streaks puncturing the ground. She had to get to Lou's before Paul got in.

Duke's thugs would be lying in wait for Paul, ready to hijack his boat and make him haul their damn drugs. She knew Paul; he wouldn't give up without a fight. Rita had no idea what she was going to do. All she wanted was to keep Paul safe.

She opened the glove compartment and put the gun in her purse. It was still loaded, but with one less bullet, thanks to Belle. That left five.

Three miles from Beaver City, Rita hit a sharp curve in the highway. The car began a long slide before shooting off the hard surface, crossing the grass shoulder, and flying into the low, wet, soft land. The world backed off as Rita lost consciousness, her car slowly sinking into the watery marsh.

CHAPTER 27

Before the *Helen S.* reached the bay, the weather front smashed into the coast. Rain-blurred lightning gave Paul glimpses of the twisting river. The wind roared across the marshes, pushing the tide near the top of the grass. A rough chop began slapping the hull as the trawler moved out the river entrance into the bay.

Rain turned to wind-driven deluge, coming down in great slanting sheets and shooting red and green bullets through the glow of the running lights. Paul was grateful for the storm. His captors had said nothing since they had passed Beau's Island.

Out on the bay, rain blotted out the world. The frequent lightning caused only a dull glow beyond the windows and Paul knew that the trawler was invisible from a hundred yards. The boat cleared the sandbars at the rivers entrance and Paul gradually held pressure to starboard until the compass inched to higher numbers. When it registered a southwesterly course, he eased the wheel. This new course should take them ten miles to the west of North Point Light and still clear Shell Keys.

Paul knew that, in the open gulf, there would be thirty- to forty-foot waves. Only in the cove in the lee of the island could vessels lie alongside each other in such rough weather. The other skipper was probably waiting there. There was no chance of being boarded in the gulf. With those waves, hulls would be smashed like eggshells.

No, his best chance was with the sea and his boat.

The reason for this hijack was undoubtedly drugs, but why the *Helen S.*...or any other boat? It seemed clear that they'd use him and then kill him. Paul wondered about Lou. Selling out and leaving didn't make sense. But he had seen the documents. And this Richard Anderson, tied up in the office. What connection did he have with the hijacking? At eleven-fifteen, they passed beyond the shelter of the barrier islands and reached the open sea. The trawler again began to act like a stallion, rearing up and then plunging down and forward, climbing the next wave and falling from the crest into the trough. Rain drummed against the boat and the world outside the wheelhouse was black between lightning flares.

The big man yelled over the roar of the storm, "Friend, where's that damn light?"

Paul shouted, "Up ahead somewhere! Can't make much headway against this wind. We should put back in port before we capsize and sink!"

"How long before we're there?"

"Maybe an hour, two," yelled Paul. "I can't stand up much longer; there's no feeling in my feet." A hard jerk on the line almost tripped him. "You do that again and you can take over this wheel!"

His anger matched the fury of the storm. They had spoiled his triumphant homecoming and they may have hurt Lou. They had control of him and his boat, and they were forcing him to commit a crime. But the *Helen S.* still held some aces. The storm was one of them. Paul heard the fog horns on an oil platform and judged it to be dead ahead. He turned on the searchlight and the light swept from the top of the platform to the bottom, just as lightning flashed. Paul spun the wheel and passed the rig downwind.

"What the hell!" The gunman's voice was electric with fright.

"Oil platforms!" he called out. "There're all over the place! In this storm, the chances are we'll never make it."

Slim lurched into the wheelhouse and clawed at the starboard door. Finally releasing the latch, he staggered to the rail, retching and convulsing over the side. Rain sprayed through the opening and the big man slid the door shut.

Slim pounded frantically until Paul released the latch. The man entered, wet and groaning, trying to keep his balance as he fell back into the deckhouse.

Paul knew that they were below the horizon, relative to North Point. Figuring that the *Helen S.* could take more punishment than the hijackers, he allowed the trawler to fall off a few points. It no longer bucked straight into the mountainous seas, but began to roll more violently. The wipers were sluggish, as if moving under water and the bow quartered into the sea and wind, wave tops curling over the gunwales and cascading tons of water onto the deck.

A hand dug into his shoulder. "Friend, you get us outta this and I ain't going to tell you but once!" There was raw hysteria in the big man's voice.

Paul took one step back. "Here, you run the damn ship!" In a cold fury, he switched on the searchlight, its beam punching into the rain. "Listen, you bastard, if we hit an oil platform, we sink in one minute!" He pointed to the overhead control ring of the light. "You had better start operating this!"

The gunman clutched at the ring, hanging on with both hands, Paul bracing for his next move. He glimpsed the sloping greenish wall of water one moment before a giant wave towered over the bow and began lifting the vessel.

"Look out!" Paul screamed, swinging the boat broadside to the wave. A mountain of saltwater smashed into the deck and then the trawler was swept up at a dizzying rate, rolling violently, almost capsizing. Another giant wave crashed into them and Paul waited until they were rising before he spun the wheel. The ridge of the wave swept solidly under the hull, pitching the trawler like a cork before throwing its burden into the next trough. The vessel rolled and the gunman swung from the light ring, like a monkey on a trapeze.

An ear-splitting sound pierced the storm's roar as Paul swept the air nozzle into the gunman's face. They fell to the deck together and the big man screamed, both hands pressed over his eyes. Paul recovered the gun and twisted his body around.

In the doorway, Slim was trying to brace himself. The boat wrenched free of a wave and snap-rolled at the same moment Slim fired. Paul saw the blue spurt of flame as he brought his own weapon up and pulled the trigger. Slim fell forward, his head striking the untended wheel, and slumped on top of Paul, who was now lying across the big man.

Paul removed his thumb from the air nozzle button; the screech of escaping air stopped. Slim was jerking convulsively. The man on the bottom was flailing his arms, searching blindly for his gun. Paul laid its barrel against his cheek and the man froze. Slim felt rubbery as Paul heaved him against the far wall.

"When I move," said Paul, "you're going to untie my feet." Finally freed from his bondage, he pulled himself up by the wheel, switched on the overhead light, and turned the helm, putting his stern into the waves. To lessen the danger of broaching, he shoved the throttle forward. He suddenly realized that Slim's gun was sliding around the deck. The big man dived for it as Paul fired. Once more, the gunman froze. Paul took the second gun and slipped it into his pocket.

Still holding the first gun on the man, Paul steadied the boat on course and switched on the autopilot. Moving now with the waves, much of the violent motion stopped. He secured the searchlight ring and bent over the cowering gangster.

There was blood on the man's jacket. "Friend, I been shot!"

Slim was against the bulkhead, lying on his side, with his blood forming red lines across the deck. Paul looked at the wheel, where Slim's bullet had split a spoke.

"Good," said Paul. "That means the sharks will find you quicker!"

The gunman seemed to be having a convulsion. " I'm hurt bad and I can't swim a lick! Get us outta this!"

Paul looked closely and nearly laughed. "That's not even your blood." He tied the man's wrists with the line used to bind his feet, and then he turned Slim's face up to the light. Paul felt for a pulse before opening the starboard door and dragging the corpse outside. Waves were breaking against the stern, but the rain had stopped. The wind was beginning to back off. Paul knew the storm had moved past his position: The sea was already calming. Leaving the dead man on the side deck, he returned to the wheelhouse. The other gunman was still on the floor. Paul studied the compass, reset the autopilot, and then adjusted the throttle until the boat was climbing the backs of the swells pushing under its hull.

He took a coil of line from a drawer and tied one end to the lashings around his prisoner's wrists. He threaded the other end through the searchlight ring and pulled until the man on the floor began to whimper, then he loosened the line before making it secure. Seated on the edge of the couch, his feet on the blood-smeared floor, he leaned over the trussed-up gunman and, using the compressed air nozzle, blasted air across the hijacker's head. The ear-splitting sound stopped and he put the nozzle against the man's ear.

"I want some answers or I'll blow your brains out, *friend!* I'm going to count to three."

The gangster squirmed. When he spoke, his voice was muffled. "Slim's the boss, Cap'n. He'll tell you what you want to find out. I don't know from nothin'."

"Slim's dead; I turned him over to the sharks."

"Gawd Almighty!"

Paul held the nozzle just inches from the man's squirming buttocks and pressed the nozzle button for a split second. The man screamed and Paul leaned closer. "Now, shark bait, start talking, or I'm blowing up your gut and throwing you in the water. What's your name?"

"Joe." The gunman was quick to answer. "Joe Lucas."

"Who're you working for, Joe Lucas?"

"I don't know his name. Some guy in New Orleans."

"I'll help you remember," said Paul, releasing a short blast between Joe's thighs.

"Name's Tony. Tony what, I never asked. Never laid eyes on him in my life. I swear, that's the God's truth!"

"You're lying!"

"I'm giving it to you straight. This Tony phones when he wants something done. Like tonight."

"You close your eyes when you get paid?"

"He mails us the money, all cash. I swear, that's how it is!"

"Joe, let's talk about tonight, about why you tried to steal my boat and where we were supposed to go."

"All I know is Tony phoned and said for us to grab this shrimp boat and make you take us to that North Point light place. He never said another fuckin' thing. And that's the truth, so help me God!"

Paul placed the nozzle in the gunman's ear. "If my thumb slips—"

Joe Lucas was quivering. "I'm telling you all I can. I ast Tony how come we gotta grab a stinkin' fish boat in the middle of the night and all he said was we gotta help out this other boat in trouble out here."

"Tell me about that other boat."

"I don't know nothin', I never seen it. All Tony said was it's a big white job with a lookout guy on top."

"You mean a tuna tower?"

"I don't know nothin' about boats; I was raised on a farm."

"What's so important about this big white boat?"

"Tony didn't say."

"What's your guess?"

"Maybe grass, but Tony never tells us stuff we don't hafta know about."

"Was there another man at the fish house tonight, before I came in? A man named Fisher?"

"Just that Duke dude, the one Slim and Shorty tied up. You seen him, Cap'n."

"How much money did you rob from him?"

"I can't say, but I sure ain't got it. Search me and you can see I ain't lying. Slim took it. He was supposed to split with Shorty and me. Good God, Cap'n, when you put Slim with them sharks, the dough was still on him!"

"Well, Joe, before it gets daylight, you'll be out there looking for him. Dark as it is, you won't be seeing the sharks, but they'll find you by your smell!"

"Now look, Cap'n, I've done a lot of rotten things and I ain't saying different, but you can't put me in the water. I don't swim a lick. Gimme a break! I could turn state's evidence; you might need me when we git back."

"How did you and the others get to the shrimp dock? Where did you come from?"

"In a van from New Orleans. Shorty stole it."

"After you unloaded the other boat, what were the other plans?"

"We'd come back on the other boat, something about interstate waters, and they'd put us off and we'd ride back on the bus."

"You mean the Intracoastal Waterway?"

"Yeah, that musta been what Tony said."

The interrogation continued, but Paul got nothing out of him.

Paul turned his attention to the direction finder and checked his position on the chart. He changed course a few degrees and reset the autopilot. The wind had died with the coming of daylight and the surface of the gulf was glassy. Only widely spaced swells remained of the storm's fury. Small schools of flying fish shot from the smooth waters and skittered ahead of the trawler. Everything seemed normal, until he turned back to his prisoner.

"Joe, I'm kicking your lying ass off my boat. Maybe your friends will come along before the sharks do, or maybe I'll use this." He reached for the air nozzle.

The face of Joe Lucas turned green; he swallowed and licked his lips, as if expecting the worst.

"I'll give you one more chance," said Paul, his voice menacing. "Tell me the truth: who was going to run this trawler after we met up with your buddies?"

"Tony said that you would, and that they were hopin' to make a deal with you. Like they would be renting your fishing boat and paying you good money. More'n you could ever make just fishin'."

"If that was the plan, why was it changed? Why did they decide on hijacking instead of chartering?"

"Tony said they had this emergency and had to do it this way, on account of you was out there, out of touch. That's the only reason I come on this job in the first place, 'cause I figured you'd be working for us. I mean, for Tony and his boys. After you made this first trip and got paid a pot full of cash, we'd all be one big happy family, ya know? Otherwise, I never would'a done it. You c'n see that, right?"

"Who was supposed to make the deal with me?"

"Tony said he planned to show you how you could make more dough helpin' him than you could with ten fuckin' shrimp boats."

"Suppose I'm not interested in working with scum like Tony? Suppose I wouldn't run your kid-killing drugs? What then?"

"Tony said that nothin' bad happens to his shrimp man or Slim and me get the ice pick. He said we maybe shoot you in the leg, but not bad, so's you can't run the boat."

The trawler's course was set for the Shell Key entrance to the bay. A warm front had moved in from the land and wisps of fog were rising from the water. Paul decided to put into the salt docks at Avery Island, rather than risk returning to Bonaparte. Those waiting to unload the drugs were surely looking for him at Beau's Island. Meanwhile, the other boat was probably fog-bound in the cove at North Point. He slipped a bunk cushion under Joe's head.

"When we get in, Cap'n, turn me loose and you can have them five bills I got on me. I got myself a record. They'll throw away the key, on account of I'm on parole."

Paul turned his attention to the radio. Without the microphone, it was useless for transmitting. He spliced a severed wire and the receiver came alive.

Coastal and lower Mississippi shipping was being advised of the dense fog conditions. Another news bulletin revealed a collision between an oil tanker and a small freighter. The freighter had sunk, but its crew had been picked up. Oil was spilling from the damaged tanker. The Coast Guard frequency crackled with messages.

The *Helen S.* entered a fog bank and it seemed as if she were standing still and the mists moving past. This continued until they entered a space with blue sky and a sparkle of sunlight on the swells. Ahead was another towering wall of gray fog. Before reaching the wall, Paul got a cup of water and held it to Joe's lips. Slim's blood was sticky underfoot. Paul went outside and looked at Slim, whose rigid face was whitened with salt spray. Back in the wheelhouse, he took the helm off the autopilot and strained to see ahead. In some places, the fog was thinning near the surface. They were entering and leaving huge amphitheaters, with invisible domed ceilings, places without substance. Paul felt as if he were lost in a vast and improbable palace, moving from room to room across an undulating liquid floor from which vapors were rising. The engine sounded muffled.

A white sport fishing boat was a mile away, coming through a fog curtain. It appeared veiled and indefinite, as if suspended above the water, and then it dissolved. In that one moment, Paul had a clear view of the flying bridge.

Radar!

The white yacht was on an interception course. Paul knew his trawler could not escape in the fog, with its presence a bright spot on the radar screen. The sports fisherman would have twice his speed. Paul considered trying to ram the other boat, but this idea was quickly discarded. Spinning the wheel to starboard, he set a new course straight for North Point, and engaged the autopilot. Raising the cover of his bunk, he removed the shark rifle and dropped a box of ammunition in his pocket. He took a machete from the locker and bent over his prisoner. "We got company, Joe."

"More'n likely they got machine guns, Cap'n." Paul worked swiftly on the afterdeck. From a locker, he took a coil of wire cable and tools. Within minutes he freed the flotation and lead lines of the shrimp nets from the trawl boards and changed the bridles on each board, before connecting them with twenty feet of cable.

At the afterdeck controls, he reduced speed as he winched the boards up and over the stern. They skimmed the surface until he allowed the big winch drum to rotate. The boards began to sink. At three hundred fathoms of cable, he slowed and stopped the winch. The trawler passed slowly in the fog-free space. He increased speed gradually, until he saw the boards surfacing like cavorting porpoises, with the connecting cable frothing through the swells, then he slowed the trawler until the boards were swimming just below the surface.

At that moment, the yacht came speeding out of the fog; bow high, in the middle of the trawler's wake. Walls of spray shot out from her bronze hull. At the last possible instant, Paul shoved the throttle into maximum rpm's and the *Helen S.* dug her stern into the water to tighten the cables. The trawl boards, like giant barn doors, rose from the water just ahead and on either side of the speeding yacht, whipping the connecting cable under the lifted bow.

Paul heard the rasping sounds of punished metal and the sudden high scream of diesel power freed from her load. Then the engines were quieted and the yacht was turning. Paul hoped the yacht had at least one wheel or shaft damaged. On one engine, it could not keep up with the trawler. He waited for his gear to pull loose from the sports fisherman.

The yacht was swinging to its starboard, rocking in its following sea, when the trawler stalled, reared and shuddered. The cable whipped above the surface, and the heavy boom strained with the unaccustomed load. White water swept back from the churning wheel. The yacht was being pulled stern first. Paul realized that the cable had become entangled in the underside of the gangster's craft. Quickly releasing the brake on the cable drum, he allowed the big spool to turn until only the bronze attachment fitting was gripping the end of the cable. Once more, the trawler felt the load and seemed to stall. Paul saw a small wave rolling against the gangster's stern.

He watched three men in the open cockpit as another climbed to the flying bridge. A patch of fog drifted between them and Paul ran to the wheelhouse. The breakers at North Point were dead ahead. He reset the autopilot to pass through the channel. The Coast Guard frequency was still loaded with traffic about the tanker accident. He switched to the international emergency channel and turned up the afterdeck speaker.

"Cap'n, what's going on out there?" Tied securely, Joe was sitting up on the couch.

"We got us a fish."

As Paul returned with a hacksaw to the afterdeck, a bullet smashed off the deckhouse. Others whined past, followed by popping sounds. Crouching low at the air compressor, Paul lifted the rifle and squeezed off three shots. The men on the yacht took cover. Paul went to work on the cable with the hacksaw. Again, streamers of fog floated between the boats. When visibility returned, Paul saw two men on the swim platform with a boat hook. Again he fired the rifle and both men tried to climb the platform ladder. "Calling the *Helen S.* This is the *Honey L.,* calling the *Helen S.* Come in, Paul."

Mel was nearby on the *Honey L.!* Paul felt a surge of excitement: Another shrimper might even the odds. He pounded his fist on the cable. There was no way he could answer. He rushed to the wheelhouse locker for flares and heard the whine of an outboard motor. Glass shattered in the wheelhouse windows and he dropped to the deck and crawled back to the rifle, pushing its barrel through a scupper opening. An outboard boat flashed in view, coming at an angle, one man standing in the bow with a submachine gun, another crouched at the control pulpit. The gunman was swinging his weapon as Paul fired. White material exploded from the bow of the small boat. It veered away, out of Paul's line of vision, and came back from another angle. The submachine gun was spurting flame as an electric sensation telegraphed along Paul's left arm and his shoulder jerked, as if someone had smashed it with an iron pipe. His answering shot went wild as the outboard passed astern.

Paul managed to pull off his jacket. A deep red furrow was on his forearm and blood was welling from the gash. His left side was growing numb. Once more he crouched as the speedboat came in sight and bullets banged into the trawler. He waited, aiming carefully, holding the rifle with his right hand. When he fired, the man with the machine gun spun around and dropped to his knees. The boat then veered from its course and headed back toward the yacht.

Dragging the rifle, Paul crawled into the deckhouse. He took the first aid kit from the wall and carried it into the wheelhouse. Glass was scattered everywhere.

"My God, Cap'n, your bleedin' to death! If you untie me I c'n give ya a hand with that first aid stuff."

At least the bullets hadn't found his prisoner. "I can manage."

He fumbled for antiseptic and bandage materials, while straining to see the *Honey L.* The *Helen S.* was passing North Point, still towing the gangster vessel stern first.

"Calling the *Helen S.*... Come back, Paul."

He no longer heard the outboard. Blood poured from his left hand as he held one end of an elastic bandage with his teeth and he painfully wrapped the strip under his armpit and around his arm. He pulled it tight, until blood no longer spurted with each heartbeat.

He was growing weak as he sounded his air horn. Through the rear door of the deckhouse, Paul saw the small boat alongside the yacht. Water was still pushing up through the latticed treads of the swim platform. His eyes focused on the range markers past the Point. Already safely past the breakers, he pressed the right rudder button of the autopilot and held it until he could see the cable pulling into the breakers. Again he set the autopilot for a straight course. This done, he returned to the rear deck and leaned over the winch drum with the hacksaw. As he sawed on the cable, he watched the other vessel go aground in the breakers. The metal was hard and his memory became lazy, black dust floating inside his eyes.

He dropped the hacksaw and fell to his knees.

He was dreaming in some corner of his mind. The outboard was coming back. He heard voices, but he no longer felt a part of reality.

"Our boy's tied up in here!"

The voices were far away. "Is that the shrimper?" Then Joe saying, "He's dead. Nobody c'n lose that much blood and live." Then a scream, somehow familiar. "No! God, no! I can't swim! No!"

Paul tried to take it all in: the roaring sound of the outboard, the noise of the trawler's churning wheel; and in a distance, someone saying, "Wake up, Paul, wake up!"

CHAPTER 28

Shorty returned to the office and announced that the boat was gone.

"Don't turn on that light!" demanded Duke. "Close the door and get me outta this damn chair!"

Shorty fumbled with the loose knots and freed Duke, who stood and stretched, then turned off the light and went out on the catwalk. No cars were passing on River Street. "Close that door and let's go," he said. "And leave it unlocked."

"What if somebody walks in and helps their selves?"

"Somebody already did, bird brain. I've just been robbed, remember? Ever heard of burglars locking the door when they leave?"

The wind was moaning around the fish house as they left in the station wagon. Neither of the men spoke during the drive to the island. Once inside the fence, Duke locked the gate. He drove without lights on the marsh portion of the road, guided by silver-purple lightning that flared through dark clouds. Wind gusts rocked the car. He parked in the trees, away from the green van.

"Rain's coming," he told Shorty. "Wait in the van and keep your eyes peeled."

Duke heard the trawler heading out and stepped behind a live oak, out of sight as the craft passed the dock. He wondered how the shrimp captain could make it through the crooked river without headlights. When he returned to the car, Shorty was in the front seat.

"I said for you to stay in that van!"

"When they gettin' back?"

What's it to you, thought Duke, wondering how long they'd have to wait. Joe said they'd return before daylight. He leaned back and stretched, cracking his knuckles. "Three, four hours maybe. Now, get your ass into that van while I get some shut-eye. And don't bother me if the squirrels come after your nuts." Duke chuckled. "And if I catch you sleeping I'll wake you my way!"

Duke lit a cigarette and turned on the radio. Storm warnings told of the approaching front. Small craft not safely in port were advised to seek immediate shelter. Duke listened to the rising wind, glad Tony hadn't sent him along on the shrimp boat.

Most of the important jobs were finished. He bought the shrimp house, leased the island, been robbed. Now the boat was on its way as planned, no slip-ups. All he had to do was stay out of sight until the cargo was in the van and on its way. That would wrap up this deal. Then he would tell some cock-and-bull story about a robbery and getting loose from the dude who had orders to drown him. Even telling his story to the police, he had nothing to worry about: he didn't have a record like the meatheads Tony had sent.

Somewhere there was a banging noise and Duke was annoyed. He opened his eyes and saw Shorty outside the window. It was light, yet he had no awareness of having slept.

"Duke, wake up!"

Duke rolled down the window. "That boat ain't here yet and you said three or four hours."

Duke got out stiffly and walked to the dock. He could see only a short distance into the marsh: Cotton-like fog blotted out the world. He stretched, tried to see down river.

"How long we gonna wait for the fuckin' fish boat?"

Duke whirled. He didn't hear Shorty walking up behind him, and hated people sneaking in close like that. "Listen, asshole, you see that white stuff out there? That's what they call fog and boats get slowed down in it. We gotta stay outta sight, so haul ass back to the van and I'll keep a lookout."

Shorty mumbled and then left in the direction of the van. Duke jumped down onto the narrow sand beach and urinated. He washed his face, tasting salt. He wanted coffee.

The river gurgled where it was split by the dock's pilings. Duke was beginning to get worried. If the shrimper couldn't make it through the fog, they could have problems, big problems.

In the station wagon, he flipped on the radio.

"...found dead in his rural home near Bonaparte."

He turned the volume down and listened to the report that Lou Fisher had apparently died of a heart attack while putting out a small fire at his house. He felt pleased. No mention of violence, so it might be weeks before anyone knew about the cash.

He would send flowers from the new owner of the fish house. The new owner, and he had the papers to prove it. Had he known of Fisher's illness? No, but he was having some kind of attacks, like he was ready to have a stroke. Face all screwed up and turning stone white. Sure was a shame; a damn fine man.

Old Fisher had been burning things he didn't want people to find out about, after his cancer laid him in the sweet peas. Most people, Duke knew, had a lot to hide.

With Lou Fisher no longer around to make trouble, Duke had only the shrimp captain to deal with. If they knocked him off, it would be an accident. "Shrimp boat explodes in Gulf, Coast Guard recovers body of Paul Stark." If Stark got greedy or hard to manage, Duke would have to work him over. He'd enjoy that. But there was another angle: If the law did close in, Stark would be the one they'd grab. After all, the shrimper was the one on the take, breaking the law, not the owner of the fish house. And Stark had no way of knowing that Duke was tied in with Tony.

Duke looked at his watch and frowned.

There was more news on the radio. "The two vessels collided in a dense early morning fog. The Coast Guard reports the freighter sank in fifty feet of water. The crew escaped in lifeboats. The oil tanker is losing its cargo of crude oil. Maritime investigators are heading for the scene."

Duke walked around the bluff, the waiting getting on his nerves. He went under the dock and looked at the timbers. No sweat backing the van out on the dock. When he came from under the dock, Shorty was on the bank.

"Down there on them posts? Oysters, maybe? My stummick thinks my throats been cut."

Duke looked at the barnacles. "Yeah, small oysters, don't eat 'um myself." He felt amused when Shorty scrambled down and began chipping off barnacles with a piece of driftwood. Dumb sonofabitch!

The roar of a plane was overhead and Duke ducked. It flashed through the fog, low over the marsh, and he saw a diagonal red strip on its fuselage. He began sweating in the cool morning air.

"You better have some of these oysters." Shorty held out a gritty hand full of barnacles. "Don't taste bad."

Duke shook his head, noticing the cigarette butts on the ground. He picked up some of the filter tips and put them on top of the barnacles. "Your ass's where your head oughta' be."

"Sorry, boss. I didn't think."

Duke wondered if the little squirt was on his last day. If it were a big shipment, all three bums would be hit, it was good business. The organization used lots of temporary help. Ex-cons had a hard time, usually didn't have a snowball's chance in hell of making it on the outside. Connections at penitentiaries kept the organization posted on prisoners being turned loose, even from the women's places. Shorty and his pals were the only three from New Orleans; in Miami, he had lists of at least a hundred. The ex-cons were expendable. That's why they were used for the cruddy jobs, like stealing cars or hijacking a shrimp boat. They weren't smart, which is why they got caught. To protect it, the organization disposed of them and nobody gave a damn. If Duke were in charge, Shorty would never make it back to New Orleans. He watched the little guy crack barnacles with his bad teeth and turned away in disgust.

It was then he heard the sound, faint at first, then growing louder, like a ski boat passing by. He pushed Shorty ahead of him, behind the van.

Through the mist came an open boat, with a rooster tail of water spraying behind the outboard. It neared the dock and slowed, turned, then bumped onto the sand. Two men were aboard. The one in the bow stood and stepped into the water over his ankles, a leather jacket covering his broad shoulders. Cradled in his arm was a submachine gun. His left sleeve was bloody and more blood glistened on his pants. Duke had never seen him before.

The man running the boat was dark-skinned. As he stepped into the water, Duke saw that he was short and built like a gorilla. And strong: He dragged the bow higher on the beach.

"Duke!"

Duke had not expected a small boat. He stepped from behind the van and trotted to the bluff. The boat was piled high with canvas sacks.

"Where's the shrimp boat?"

The armed man ignored the question. "Get that van out here quick, we ain't got all day!"

Shorty came to the riverbank and joined the others.

"Back it over here," Duke barked.

The barrel-chested man began passing the sacks up to Duke, who stacked them on the ground. Shorty backed the van close to the bags, jumped out, and opened the double doors.

"Put all that up front," commanded the injured man. Shorty scrambled into the van and Duke slid the sacks along the metal floor. He counted twenty of them.

The gorilla started to remove the outboard motor, jerking loose the fuel and steering lines. Shorty and Duke helped put the heavy motor in the van and then three of them pulled the boat up the bank and shoved it into the van. Shorty closed the doors.

"Drive back in the trees there," said the man with the gun.

Duke was on the beach with a pine branch, sweeping at the footprints and the marks made by the boat. He threw the broom into the water.

The man with the bloody pants hefted the submachine gun. "I gotta hide this and then we get our asses outta here."

"Put it back in the woods," said Duke. "Nobody ever comes out here."

"You stay here, Duke, and keep your eyes open. There's a chopper snooping around. Ted, you drive the van." He jerked his head at Shorty. "You come see where I put this thing so you can pick it up later." They ran into the woods. A few moments later there was a burst of gunfire and the stranger returned with the gun. "Damned if he didn't go right up to a big old hole in the ground, like a well they dug. He was an even dumber temporary than we thought. Duke, open that door for me."

The gunman handed Duke a walkie-talkie. "Get us out of here. When you get to New Iberia, turn right on thirty-one to St. Martinsville. You run into any trouble, you call us on that thing and take off. Make the cops take off after you. If we get separated, we'll phone you later."

Duke nodded and got into the station wagon, glad to be leaving the island. The man with the gun hadn't said what happened to the shrimp captain and the others, or how he got shot. Duke had seen a bullet hole in the speedboat.

He had been right about Shorty!

The getaway was clean.

Several times, passing through small towns, he drove right past police cars. In New Iberia, he had no problem finding the highway. It turned out to be a paved country road, with no traffic in sight. The van had not caught up with him, so he slowed down. In a few minutes he saw the van catch up and wondered why the delay.

The guy they called Ted was probably the bodyguard for the other man. Duke wondered when he'd get the word to drive back to Bonaparte. He turned on the radio.

"... bringing you the latest on the burning vessel at Point LaCroix Island. According to the Coast Guard, the large yacht is still on fire. Rescue units are on the way to the scene to search for survivors. A shrimp boat tentatively identified as the *Helen S.* is towing a yacht. Here's another bulletin just in: The Coast Guard has taken an injured man from the shrimp trawler. There are reports that another body has been removed from the trawler and both are victims of gunshots. For all the latest news, keep tuned to this station."

Duke felt cold fingers of fear around his neck. By now, cops would be crawling over the whole area. The chopper might have seen the speedboat coming up the river. If they did, Beau's Island would be the first place they would look. They would find Shorty!

Murder One!

He gripped the wheel, trying to think. He could step on it, outrun the van, make it to the airport, and hire a small plane. He had plenty of cash on him. He told himself that he was losing his grip, that the organization would take care of him. He wasn't an ex-con and he didn't have a record, so that helped. They needed him for their new management team. Like Tony said. And the guy with the submachine gun knew Duke had a future, otherwise—.

The van's headlights were flashing in the rear-view mirror. Duke read this as an order to get off this road fast.

A sign on the side of the road advertised a farm for sale. Duke slowed, saw that the house sat back from the road and looked deserted. Behind it was a large barn. Duke turned into the weed-covered road and drove to the rear yard. Windows were broken; a door sagged from one hinge. He stopped at the barn and got out, pulling the wide doors open. The van moved in behind him and Ted hopped out and pulled the doors closed. The place smelled of old manure and straw spilled from a loft.

The man with the gun walked along the empty stalls. A plane passed low overhead.

"Duke, get out in them woods. I saw another road, find out where it goes. We have to hold up until it gets dark."

The road began at the edge of the clearing and became little more than a dim trail thick with underbrush. The trail led into a swamp. Duke stepped into the water and a snake swam from behind a stump. He jumped back, cursing the slimy thing. Birds were making a racket. He returned to the barn and found Ted up in the loft, his face pressed against a crack. "From up here, I can see a road," Ted said.

Duke was sent out again, this time to check for a path through the woods that bordered the driveway. He found one and followed it to the public road. From a tangle of undergrowth, he could see in both directions. There were no cars on the highway, which he reported to the gunman.

"Get in your wagon, Duke, and turn on the radio."

Duke climbed into the car and thought about the money in the glove compartment as he turned on the radio. A disk jockey was talking fast and the man with the bloody arm leaned in the window. "I wanta hear some fuckin' news."

Duke turned the dial. "A search is underway for Richard Anderson, also known as Duke. He is believed to be driving a late model green station wagon, Louisiana tag A dash N-four-five-three-one. Stay tuned for more developments."

Duke felt paralyzed as the nightmare closed in. The cops were already looking for him!

"They got other stations, Duke?"

"Captain Stark is expected to survive. However, dead bodies of a young woman and a man have been found on Beau's Island. Rita Stark, wife of Captain Stark, is still unconscious. She was injured last evening, when her car skidded off Highway 90 and hit a tree."

The news went on to say that the ruptured tanker was creating a massive oil spill at the mouth of the Mississippi. The fire on the stranded yacht had been put out and another body found near the yacht had been identified as that of an ex-convict, recently paroled. The yacht had been used to bring in illegal drugs. An all-points search was underway for the smugglers. The captain and mate of the yacht had been brutally murdered.

"Turn it off," said the man.

Duke was sweating. The radio didn't say *why* they were looking for the station wagon, but all hell had busted loose. He opened the passenger door. "Maybe you oughta get off your feet," grunted the big guy.

The man got in the car, leaving the submachine gun on the barn floor. A package of cigarettes appeared in his hand and he shook one up, catching it with his lips. Duke pushed in the lighter as he studied the man. He seemed to be in his early forties, his heavy, coarse features topped by coal black hair. He wore a short beard, which made his skin appear blue. In spite of the cigarette and the barn smells, Duke was conscious of the sour odor of sweat. The man looked like a rough construction worker without his hardhat and Duke wondered how high up he was in the organization.

"Where's that money you took off that guy? You know, after you went out there last night and choked him," the man asked.

Duke was stunned. This must be a bad dream and the nightmare was getting worse. He licked his lips. "What the hell are you talking about?"

"That phone call back there, when we turned off the main highway? We got a friend inside Treasury and somebody talked to some old judge down in Mexico. The cops had the all-points out for you ten minutes before I phoned in."

Duke started to speak, but his jaw muscles were frozen. His hands clenched the little bells in his pocket. Suddenly his door was opened and a gun butt glanced off his head. He fell onto the dirt floor. "The dough's in the car!" he gasped. "Every damn cent. It was Tony's idea to knock off Fisher." Then he was sobbing. "Gimme a break, you can take the cash! Noooo!"

Ted knelt beside him, an ice pick in his hand. Duke tried to escape, but a huge arm clamped him around the neck and he struggled, unable to get his breath. And then he screamed, deep in his gut, feeling the ice pick touch his ear, feeling his brain explode.

CHAPTER 29

After driving Maggie home from the mortuary, Mel returned to the hospital. At the reception desk, he was told that Captain Stark was out of surgery but still in recovery. It would be hours before anyone could talk to him. Mel headed toward the car and was stopped by a stranger.

"Captain Wilson?" he asked, holding out an identification wallet.

"Yes?"

"I'm Ed Brooks, from the Treasury Department, and I need a statement from you."

They sat alone in a corner.

"If you'll please start from the beginning," prompted the tall, muscular man.

Paul's fellow shrimper told of finding Catfish under the dock. When asked, he offered that he had found the man after eleven, perhaps eleven-fifteen.

"Did you know about the car accident? Had Mrs. Stark been admitted to the hospital?"

"I didn't, not until I got back this morning."

"Why did you go to Bonaparte?"

"To make certain Paul was safely in. A blow like that can be very dangerous."

Brooks asked why he'd gone out into the rain, when the dock was clearly visible. "I thought his trawler might be coming upriver. Also, the dock light was out, which I thought was strange. Lou's mighty particular about his lighthouse, kept it going night and day."

Brooks was writing in a notebook. "What happened then?"

"I checked the light, saw that the bulb had been broken."

"Is that when you saw Catfish Davis?"

"Something moved at the end of the dock and it turned out to be him."

"Who is this Catfish?"

Mel gave the treasury man a brief history of Catfish. When he was asked if he had suspected anything out of the ordinary, he answered, "Damned right! I knew Paul wouldn't leave him. The old guy was scared to death."

"But he knew you?"

"He came up the ladder, wanted me to help find his cat. Then he pointed toward the coast and kept shaking his head. By then, the wind was up to thirty knots or more."

"Is that when you went to Fisher's house?"

"Yeah, I thought Lou might know something. I took Catfish with me."

"And you found—" The agent waited for Mel to fill in the blanks.

"The place was dark, so I thought Lou might be at Maggie's, here in Beaver City. That's when I saw the hose going into the kitchen. It was dark, but my headlights were on." When the agent remained silent, he continued.

"I turned on the kitchen lights and smelled smoke. I heard water running. Then I found Lou in the hallway. He was lying face down and the hose was running."

"How did you know he was dead?"

Mel looked at the man for a moment. "I was in Special Forces."

"Did either of you touch anything?"

"Catfish was still in the car. All I did was turn off the water."

"And what about the rest of the house?"

"I checked all the rooms. There had been a fire in the front room, but I didn't see any sparks. I guess Lou put it out before he…"

"Did you know he was dying of cancer?"

Mel's eye widened, and for a moment he couldn't speak. "You must be wrong, he seemed in good shape."

"He found out last week that he had only a short time to live."

Mel tried to remember small details. "We all just assumed he had a heart attack." After a moment, he added, "There were two suitcases near the kitchen door."

"He was going on a trip. Any idea where?"

"I can't believe he'd leave without telling Maggie or Paul, or me."

"Did Mr. Fisher drink? That is, excessively?"

Mel looked at the man quizzically. "Lou hardly ever took a drink.

Sometimes, when we'd come in from a trip, he'd take a nip, but nothing more."

"The doctors warned him about alcohol, but there was a bottle on the table and evidence that he'd been drinking."

"Maybe he was in pain?"

"We may never know." The man checked his notepad. "Did you notice anything else?"

Mel scratched his head and gave a big sigh. "I didn't think about it at the time, but Lou had a special fire pump and a reserve water supply. The switch hadn't been turned on and I wondered about that."

"Perhaps he forgot about it, in the excitement."

"Not Lou, he was a B-52 pilot in the war. He would never forget his own fire emergency system."

Brooks wrote for a moment and then asked, "After you left his place, you got on your own shrimp boat and went looking for Stark?"

"Lou didn't have a phone, so I called the highway patrol from Potter's Service Station. After the patrol showed up, we took off."

"The boat's back at Fisher's dock, but it's off limits until we finish our investigation."

"I need to get aboard," said Mel. "The windows are shot out and more rain means more damage. All I need to do is throw some tarps over the wheelhouse."

Brooks wrote something and tore out the sheet. "Give this to the guard," he said, handing it to Mel. "I'm asking you not to disturb anything, understand? And according to the Coast Guard, she's not taking on water."

"What about Catfish? He lives on that boat."

"Find him another place to stay for now."

Mel rose to leave, stretching against the stiffness in his back. "Is that all?"

Brooks stood up as well and slipped the notebook into his coat pocket. "We hope to question Stark soon. Until we do, we can only guess at the details. Captain, can you meet me back here around midnight? You could be a big help."

"Anything," said Mel as he headed for the door. He was worried about Rita and wanted to make sure that Maggie was going to sit with her.

"One more thing. Did Lou Fisher have any pets?"

"He had a dog, but it was killed last year. Why do you ask?"

"A dead cat was under Fisher's bed. Its neck was broken."

Mel clenched his fists. Nothing was making sense: Paul hijacked and shot; Rita in a bad wreck; Lou dead. And now this, a cat with a broken neck! He suddenly remembered the black cat at the dock. "It belongs to Catfish," he told the agent. "But I don't see why Lou would take it home."

The agent smiled. "In our work, we find that people do the most illogical things when they're under severe emotional stress. Fisher just found out on Monday he was dying. It seems he'd been drinking, perhaps so much that he accidentally set the room on fire. And then there's this cat. You can be sure it didn't crawl under there with its neck broken."

Mel studied Brooks face. "Good God, man, I see you have it all worked out."

"I'm sorry. I know that all of this has been a great shock, but we have a job to do."

Flashbulbs were popping as Mel drove up to the wooden barricade at the fish house. Cars were parked on both sides of the street and a small crowd was milling around. A patrol car came from the west, siren wailing, and whipped off the road. Willing hands moved the barricades; the patrol car stopped at the catwalk steps.

Mel walked through the yard, hearing scraps of talk.

"got the damn Air Force looking for them gangsters"

"Coast Guard's bringing in more dead people"

"I hear they got a morgue set up in Beaver City..."

"Ain't that Captain Wilson?"

"Hold it, Wilson," demanded a photographer, planting himself in front of the man and walking backwards.

The flash was blinding and Mel covered his eyes with his arm. He was grateful when a patrolman stepped forward and moved the rope.

There was a floral wreath on the office door and a portable floodlight shone on the *Helen S.* A man approached. "She might be fixin' to rain afore sun up, Cap'n." He pointed to the trawler. "Every blessed window up front is shot out."

"Are you in charge here?"

"Right now I am; my relief comes on at midnight."

Mel stared at the boat. "I need to see if the bilge pumps are working, and the stuffing box might need attention."

"Make yourself at home" said the stranger. "Anywhere, that is, 'cept up there in front. They're waiting for daylight so they can look in there some more." He gave off a shiver. "I have never seen so much blood."

Mel heard the bilge pump humming. When he loosened the catches around the afterdeck hatch cover, a spurt of water hit him full in the face. He jumped back feeling a little foolish.

With the cover off, the unmistakable aroma of fresh shrimp filled his senses. He climbed down the ladder and turned on the light. At first he thought the bins were full of ice. Looking closer, he brushed away the ice, plunged his hand into a bin and discovered large shrimp. Lots of it.

"Well, I'll be damned," he said softly. All the bins were filled with iced-down shrimp. On deck, he battened down the hatch.

"There's some shrimp on the boat," he told the guard seated on the housing of the fuel pump. "They'll spoil if they're not unloaded soon."

"Well, Captain, I don't hardly know 'bout that."

"You want those shrimp to go bad? You want the responsibility? They need to be re-iced...now."

"Lemme ask the officer about that." The guard wandered away.

Mel brought a tarpaulin from the pickup and threw the folds over the wheelhouse, tying the corners with strong line. By the time the guard returned with the patrolman, the tarp was firmly in place.

"How you plan on getting in there?" asked the patrolman, pointing to the closed door of the packinghouse.

"I have a key."

"Tell you what, you bring something in writing. This ain't no parish investigation, y'know? The United States government is running this show, maybe on account of drug running and piracy on the high seas and all. Us boy's ain't doing nothin' better'n walking guard duty."

"I'll get the authorization," said Mel. "Have you seen a small, dark-skinned man around the dock?"

"No, I ain't seen no nigger."

"He's not black," replied Mel, his temper about ready to explode. "Just sunburned from living on that boat. He never learned to talk, so he's not much for being around strangers. Can't say that I blame him."

"I ain't seen 'um, Cap'n, but we'll keep our eyes open."

Just then, Catfish climbed from under the dock, with relief flooding his face, and ran up to Mel.

"Is that your boy?"

"My man?" asked Mel. "Ya, I'll take my man with me."

Catfish clung to Mel's arm as they walked down the steps and past the curious crowd.

CHAPTER 30

Two men were with Brooks at the hospital when Mel got back at midnight. The lobby was deserted and Mel was glad for the chance to sit down.

"You've had a rough twenty-four hours," said Brooks. "Sorry to impose on you again, but we need more information and Stark's still unconscious."

"I'll help all I can," said Mel. "But I have to unload Paul's shrimp before they spoil."

Brooks looked up from his notebook, frowning. "Shrimp? You want to unload shrimp?"

Mel was on edge. "That's what these boats do: they catch shrimp and then unload the shrimp at the dock."

"Can't that wait until we finish our investigation?"

The shrimp were well iced and would be safe for several days, but Mel wanted to get the load off the boat and away from curious eyes. If word got around, hundreds of trawlers would be there in a matter of days. He looked at the agent. "I suppose the government will take responsibility for a load of spoiled shrimp?"

Brooks looked thoughtful before speaking. "I'll give you a note for the guard. Will you need help?"

"Catfish and I can manage."

Brooks scribbled, tore out the sheet and gave it to Mel. "If you have trouble, phone me at the motel. Now, getting back to where we left off: You came back for your boat about midnight, after you left Fisher's. What happened then?"

Mel sat down and took a minute or two to sort through his thoughts. "Well, the wind and rain had gotten stronger and I stopped at the dock. If Paul were in the marsh, he would have been using his light, but I didn't see any sign of him."

"But you figured that he'd come in, left Catfish behind, then gone out again? In the teeth of that storm?"

"No other way Catfish could have been there."

"Maybe Stark sent him in on another boat."

"That doesn't add up; Paul would have no reason to do that."

"Was your vessel at the dock?"

"No. Not at Bonaparte. It was on the ways here in Beaver City."

"Did you call the Coast Guard?"

"For some reason, Lou's office was unlocked. So yes, I did call the Coast Guard. They tried several times to reach Paul, but with no luck."

"When the Coast Guard got no answer, did you request other assistance?"

"I decided to go myself." Mel shifted in the hard chair, anxious to be finished with the conversation. "The Coast Guard won't send out a cutter just to look for an overdue boat. I made the request, but got turned down. They were working the Delta."

Brooks pulled his chair closer to Mel. "Yeah, I heard about that tanker collision."

Mel nodded, "I hear we're getting another load of crude oil over our fishing grounds."

Brooks ran his finger over a list of questions and then asked, "Did you leave right away?"

"First, I called Maggie and broke the news about Lou, then I went to the boatyard and got the manager out of bed. He rounded up a crew and put me in the water. By the time we took on fuel and water, it was about four this morning."

"Did you have any ideas then, about Captain Stark?"

"I thought he had run into some garbage out there, maybe flooded his batteries. Even with a busted shaft, the radio wouldn't go dead. There's a lot of junk out there, most of it uncharted. Our boats lose dozens of nets each year."

"It sounds like the *Helen S.* was undermanned."

"A shrimper needs at least two experienced crew members, what we call strikers. Paul only had Catfish."

"Why doesn't he use a full crew?"

"Strikers work on shares and shrimping's been bad around these waters for some time."

Brooks gave Mel a hard eye-to-eye look. "How do you manage?"

"I leave my boat tied up," said Mel. "The truth is, I haven't been out in a long time. Paul's keeping me posted."

"Sounds like your friend's an optimist."

The shrimper considered this. Maybe Paul was an optimist; maybe a man had to keep going on faith. Or guts. Paul had both. Mel wondered about the fantastic catch in the hold and how it got there.

Brooks looked up from his notes. "Do you think there might be a connection between Fisher's death and the missing trawler?"

Mel slowly ran his fingers through his hair. "No, I can't think of any."

"At least we know why the cat was at Fisher's house. Fisher bought it Friday morning in case something happened to the animal at the fish house. Yesterday afternoon he came by for the cat, saying the other one met with an accident. The people said he left with the new kitten in his truck."

"But you said its neck was broken..."

"We're working on that," responded the agent. "Who went on your boat with you?"

"Catfish and my young brother, Sonny. Sonny's an experienced crewman."

Brooks was all business. "When did you reach the bay?"

"Just after daylight. The fog was so thick in the channel we couldn't make any speed."

"Did you try to radio Stark?"

Mel was getting tired of being peppered with questions. "All channels, but the Coast Guard frequency was jammed with traffic because of the tanker accident."

"You had no answer from the *Helen S.?*"

"Nothing. Some boats on the waterway came back, but none of them had seen or talked to Paul."

"So you felt he had to be south of Bonaparte?"

"He would have been logged, going through the intracoastal bridges, so I knew that he had to be in the river or the bay. Or out in the gulf. But in that storm?" He shook his head.

"After you entered the bay?"

"The fog was breaking up and the Coast Guard reported a vessel on fire at North Point. I was about ten miles away. A boat was being sent from the base here in Beaver City. For a time, I was afraid that the burning boat was Paul's. When I finally made out Paul's boat, she was less than a mile from the point. I could see she was kicking up water but not going anywhere. The one on fire was in the breakers, with flames shooting up and the tuna tower hanging over the side."

Brooks eyes took on a flicker of excitement. "Did you see any other activity?"

Mel thought about this for a moment. "No, the patches of fog got in the way."

"And you saw no signs of a small boat or survivors?"

"No one. A Coast Guard plane came over, and then a chopper flew in low, over the fire. After that, it moved on to Paul's boat. I steered toward the fire, but when we got close to the *Helen S.* I sounded my horn. Paul wasn't at the wheel, or on deck. Then I saw that the other boat was aground, and it looked like Paul's boat was pulling it stern-first across the bar. I couldn't figure out why he wasn't tied to the bow and pulling in the other direction. That way, she'd come off with the tide."

"And it never occurred to you your friend was hurt?"

"I saw his boat digging in and didn't think of the autopilot. But he was going about it ass backwards, and that's not like Paul. When he didn't answer the air horn, I assumed he was below."

"So you proceeded to the burning vessel."

"Couldn't get closer than a hundred yards, not enough water. And my deck pump wouldn't reach. Besides, the Coast Guard was sending a fire pumper."

"And you saw no signs of life in the water or on the beach?"

Mel stood up and paced the floor. "I looked around with the binoculars, but there was no one, then I turned back toward the *Helen.* When we got closer, I saw Paul on the afterdeck. Even at that distance, there was lots of blood. That's when I told Sonny to start putting out the Mayday. Sonny put me alongside and I jumped aboard. Paul was breathing hard, in a bad way. There was a bandage around his shoulder and arm, but it was a clumsy job, like he tried to doctor himself."

"Did you go in the wheelhouse?"

"No, the Coast Guard was coming. I closed the throttle to slow forward, so she'd hold steady on the pilot and not foul the cable."

The agent nodded and looked a bit sheepish. "I don't know much about boats, sir. Don't you need to operate the controls from the wheelhouse?"

"No, you can use the auxiliary controls on the afterdeck. My boat has the same arrangement."

"How did you find Stark? I mean, was he on the floor?"

"On his side, doubled up with a hacksaw next to his hand. I didn't know what to do, so I waited until the Coast Guard took him aboard."

Brooks wrote something down and then asked, "Did you notice anything else that seemed different or unusual?"

Mel thought of the strange equipment and that pile of heavy red hose. "The net was cut loose from the doors and there was a machete on the deck."

"Did you say *doors?*"

"Trawl boards, but they look like thick doors. They hold the net on the bottom and spread the sides."

"Were they on the boat?"

"They were gone and all the cable was off the winch. Paul's boat was still tied to the one on fire. To be honest, nothing made sense. And then they found a body on the trawler, on the starboard deck. We left him for the coroner and I put the anchor down and shut off the diesel."

"And all this time the big boat was still burning?"

"Her fuel tanks erupted," said Mel. "I could hear explosions and they sounded like ammunition going off. I figured she was taking on water. Sonny put me as close as he could, but her stern was hard on the bar. No one could have been alive on that boat."

Mel and Brooks sat quietly for a moment, contemplating the tragedy. "When you first reached the bay," said Brooks. "Did you see or hear any other boats in the fog?"

"Only the patrol boat, which was behind me. The chopper came back and I could see that it was from a TV station and they were taking pictures."

"Anything else you can remember?"

"About the burning craft? Yeah, there was one trawl door washing around her stern starboard side, and the other door was slapping up against the yacht on the port side. It looked like Paul's cable was hung up in the underside gear. The strange thing," he added, "was that this can't happen because the doors there are weighted with steel. They have to stay on the bottom for the net to work, so they're built to sink. There's just no way that glass boat could get hung up like that unless—"

The agent leaned closer, eyes alert.

"—unless the bridles had to be changed. If they were changed, the boards would plane on the surface." Mel sat back down and leaned back and rubbed his eyes. "When Paul can talk, maybe we'll find out."

"Captain Wilson," said Brooks, "just before you came, we heard from the divers. It seems that those boards, or doors, were joined by a length of cable that had twisted around the wheels of the yacht. Both her shafts were broken."

"To hell you say!" Mel shook his head, and then held it with both hands; the night closing in. "How was the connector cable attached to the boards?"

"They said there were cable clamps on each bridle. We think Paul Stark meant to catch himself a pleasure yacht."

"You mean it wasn't a rescue?"

"Maybe just the opposite. Our best guess is that your friend was hijacked when he came in last night. We think that when they tried to force him to attempt a rendezvous with the yacht, he turned the tables on them."

Mel was dumbfounded. "Hijacked! The hell you say! That's why he couldn't use his radio!"

"That other boat was carrying narcotics; we found quantities of marijuana on board and the sacks were burned and waterlogged. We think the main cargo, the expensive stuff, was removed before the vessel was torched. We also found two bodies that were burned beyond recognition. Both had been shot. We suspect these were crew members who were murdered and left to burn with the marijuana." He paused a moment, giving Mel a chance to absorb this news. "Another man's body was found in the marsh grass near the shrimp boat. He drowned, but he had a large contusion on his head. We think he was also one of the hijackers. As for the others, we're guessing that they left in the outboard."

"Do you have any idea how Paul got hurt?"

"There was a rifle in the wheelhouse that's been recently fired, and the bullet marks on the deckhouse indicate a rapid-firing weapon, such as a submachine gun. Our guess is that the ones who escaped in the small boat also shot up the *Helen S.* Your friend might have been firing the rifle through a drain opening and caught a bullet. The coast guard's plane probably foiled their plan to escape on the trawler. We think they went ashore at Beau's Island."

"How many are in custody?"

"No one yet, and the operation has all the earmarks of organized crime. Right now, it's our guess that your friend threw a monkey wrench into their plans."

"What about the sports fisherman?"

"She's the *Patty Two*, owned by a Texan who's visiting in the Middle East. The captain and mate lived aboard. The marina manager in Galveston says the captain was a heavy gambler. I'm thinking that overdue gambling debts forced him to make the boat available for running narcotics."

"But if the crew was working with them, why were they murdered?"

"For one thing, there would be less weight in the getaway boat. And dead people don't make good witnesses." Brooks hesitated. "We understand Captain Stark was in financial trouble?"

The question hung between them. "What the hell are you getting at?"

"We have to check out all angles. The bank was foreclosing on the *Helen S.* Stark was informed on Monday."

Mel was stunned. "You're not implying—"

"An increasing number of boats and planes are being used to smuggle drugs into the country; very few of them are stolen. There can be a fortune in a single cargo."

"You're damned well barking up the wrong tree!" Mel forgot his weariness. "It might be hard for someone in a job like yours to understand, but Paul Stark broke his back paying for that boat. Something has happened to shrimping around here, as well as fishing and crabbing. Did you know that the oyster beds are being wrecked by pollution? Maybe it's the oil people you should be checking." A pained look spread across Mel's face.

"Last year, Paul went up to Baton Rouge to get more enforcement of the pollution laws, Mel said I should have gone. Hell, I have a masters in marine biology, but I didn't think a couple of shrimp fishermen would get to first base. The thing is, Paul not only went, but he made a fine case!"

"All very interesting, but I don't see the connection."

"I'm giving you the big picture, okay? You wanted background, so listen and I'll set your mind straight. Paul's appearance before the legislature was played up big by the state press. You know, simple fisherman takes on big oil. It was the old David and Goliath angle. Some of the merchants around here got the crazy idea that Paul was trying to pull the plug on the whole petrochemical industry, not to mention paper mills and other sources of pollution. And money. Pressure was probably put on the bank."

"Before I reach conclusions," said Brooks, "I assemble my facts."

"What I'm trying to say is, a fine vessel is more than a possession to Paul, it's his life." Mel ran a hand across his damp brow. Mel looked exhausted. "Now it seems he is the victim of another colossal failure."

"Another failure?"

Mel was boiling mad, but his voice was low. "The failure of pompous jackasses who are hired by taxpayers to protect them from the kind of human scum that took over Paul's boat. Dirty leeches who turn kids into drug addicts. If I were you, Mr. Brooks, I'd reach the conclusion that Paul Stark was badly hurt doing your job. Who are these men sitting in the corner of the room, doing nothing but drinking coffee?"

"One is my assistant. The other is with our public information office and he'll be meeting with the press."

"I can already see the headlines: 'Federal Agents Smash Big Drug Ring, Arrests Expected'. Maybe Paul should have a press agent."

The circles under Brooks eyes seemed to have grown darker. "Captain, we try to stop the play in one place and it breaks loose in five others. Organized crime is becoming more organized. They hire people with good brains, the same way as big business does. They've got the money and millions are being raked in every week." Brooks looked old and tired as he released a huge sigh.

"Mr. Brooks, I'll give you one more fact," said Mel. "But it's very confidential. There's a load of shrimp in the *Helen S.* that will bring Paul over forty thousand dollars. I don't know how or where he did it, but that's the most valuable catch I ever heard of. Paul was down to his last net, but he just wouldn't give up. When word of this gets around, fleets of boats will come here. Shrimp catches worth millions each month may be landed again along this coast. That is *if* Paul recovers and tells us where to fish."

"I'm real pleased to hear that."

Mel's hands flew upwards in exasperation. "But Paul cannot be comprehended by some pea-brained, scared little banker. His government can't enforce its own pollution laws and a spineless and inefficient bureaucracy can't protect him from gangs of cutthroats who are getting fatter all the time. He's being raped by the whole damn system!"

"I understand how you feel, but I have to ask him about his financial situation."

"I've got a pretty good idea who blew the whistle on Paul and made the bank call in his loan."

"I'm sorry, Captain, but that's a local issue. Right now, I'm trying to get to the bottom of a crime."

"And I have a fishing boat to unload."

"Technically, that cargo is the property of Paul Stark and is in the protective custody of the government. I have no authority to permit you to remove the shrimp. However, I'll go out there and personally help you do whatever needs doing, and to hell with the regulations!" Brooks put out his hand and Mel shook it.

"Thanks, but Catfish is all the help I need."

"One more question: Are you familiar with Beau's Island?"

"I went there often, until the oil company put it off limits. That's where I'd guess the small boat landed."

"We found bow marks in the sand and two dry areas where vehicles had been parked during the rain. One was a truck or van with dual wheels. We've got roadblocks up and two helicopters, but they had a good head start. Do you know a Richard Anderson? He likes to be called Duke."

"Doesn't ring a bell."

"A man using that name checked into the Bonaparte Motel on Tuesday afternoon and talked with Lou Fisher before dark, which was the day after Mr. Fisher learned about his condition. The next day, Wednesday, this Duke arranged to purchase Bonaparte Seafoods."

Mel was stunned. "Lou sold the docks?"

"On Thursday, this Anderson fellow got a ninety-day lease on Beau's Island and put a new lock on the gate. Yesterday, he paid Fisher five thousand in cash. Judge Black handled the transaction, but the money never got to the bank and it wasn't found on the body."

Mel was remembering Lou's hallway and Lou lying face down.

"Fisher made a will this week, leaving his estate to Paul Stark. He also made Stark the legal guardian of Catfish. We talked to Judge Black in Mexico and to his former secretary, Sue Ellen. She prepared and witnessed all the papers. The judge is on his way back here now."

"Where's this Duke?"

"Mr. Fisher didn't die of a heart attack; we think Duke murdered him. We also believe Duke started the fire in the house and left the hose running. It was a clumsy job."

"And you think this Duke was connected with the hijacking?"

"Apparently, he set up the deal, planning to either force or buy Stark's cooperation. We have an all-points out for him."

"Are you saying Duke paid Lou and then followed him back to his place to murder and rob him? To kill a man who was dying?"

Brooks nodded. "It all fits."

"What about the black cat?"

"Duke probably disposed of the animal at the packinghouse and later encountered the identical cat at Fisher's place. Many criminals are very superstitious."

Mel recalled words overheard at the funeral home. "Was a woman's body brought in?"

"She was found near the Beau's Island dock. The medical examiner said she had been dead for several days, apparently of a drug overdose."

"Does anyone know who she was?"

"Her father, Henry Claiborne of Bonaparte, identified her as his daughter."

"Mary Beth Claiborne! But it couldn't be her, Mary Beth wasn't on drugs! She was just a kid!"

"Her father confirmed her addiction and said she had talked of suicide. Captain Stark found her unconscious Sunday night and brought her to the hospital. She left before being discharged and was last seen driving with Johnny Cameron."

Mel turned to leave. "I'll be at the fish dock."

When he joined Catfish in the car, his mind was whirling. The sweet smell of honeysuckle made the night air heavy.

CHAPTER 31

She wanted the bells to stop ringing so close to her head. Her arm was aching. Someone was touching her shoulder and she tried to open her eyes. The room seemed full of marsh mist.

"Rita. It's Maggie."

"I don't feel well, Maggie." She closed her eyes. She liked Maggie.

"She's still a little disoriented, Mrs. Gamble," said the nurse.

Rita was trying to clear her head; she heard distant voices. Someone was calling Maggie Mrs. Gamble. What was Lou's girlfriend doing there? "Maggie?"

"You're going to be fine, just rest."

"Paul! Where's Paul?" Rita tried to sit up.

"He'll be here when you wake up, after a nice nap."

"I need to see Paul now. When—"

It was the middle of the night when Mel finally made it home. He fell asleep the minute he hit the bed. His eyes flew open in what seemed like a few minutes to him, to see patterns of sunlight dancing on his covers. "Lois! I've overslept. What happened to the alarm?"

Lois came in from the kitchen, biscuit flour still on her hands. "I turned it off and put a pillow on it to keep it quiet. I never realized before how loudly it ticked. Dear, you've been up two nights in a row. This morning, when you came in with Catfish, you were half dead."

"What time is it?" he asked, looking around for his watch.

"Just after twelve, so take a hot shower and I'll make you a good breakfast."

He struggled to get out of bed. "I have to go to the hospital."

"You can see Paul later, you have plenty of time. Besides," she added. "I called and both of them are out of danger."

He felt a wave of relief. Out of danger. He was suddenly hungry. "Is Catfish stirring yet?"

"He's gone, Mel. He left just after you went to sleep."

"He'll be back at the dock." Mel knew the little man would be trying to find Paul, Lou, and his warm playmate, Moonbeam. Catfish would have traveled for seven miles of walking and hiding from passing cars.

The Sunday editions of the papers were on the table. The headlines read:

SHRIMP BOAT FOILS DRUG SMUGGLERS

There was a full-color picture of Paul lying on the bloody deck of his trawler. Other pictures showed the burning yacht awash in the breakers at North Point. There was even a picture of Paul testifying in Baton Rouge.

Mel turned the pages in disbelief. There was a special feature, with a drawing that showed how the shrimper managed to catch the gangster's craft and disable it. Statements made by so-called experts said it was highly improbable, one chance in a thousand, but it might be managed. Especially by someone like Paul Stark. There was a cartoon showing a tiny tugboat dragging an ocean liner, stern first, onto jagged rocks. The villains were shown running in panic round the liner's decks.

Mel wondered why the artist left out the sea serpents.

"It's been on all the TV stations, Mel."

"I was there a few minutes after they took all those pictures."

"I know, and I'm so grateful that you're not hurt." She leaned over and kissed his forehead. "Did you hear about Mary Beth Claiborne?"

Mel shook his head in disbelief. " She was just a kid, the last time I saw her."

Lois poured a cup of steaming coffee for Mel. "I suppose the gangsters will keep right on bringing in those awful drugs, regardless of someone like Paul getting in their way."

Brooks had said the same thing earlier.

"When can Rita have visitors?"

"Later today, Maggie's there now. They say she'll be okay."

"Does she know about Paul?"

"No, but she sure wants to see him. When I saw her this morning, she kept saying his name over and over. I could tell by her face how worried she is."

Rita was awake when Mel came in. She wore a gauze turban on her head and her left arm was in a cast. The flawless face was unmarred, except for black shadows under both eyes. Rita looked at him, and then at the door. "Paul?"

Mel took her hand. "He'll be fine in a few days."

Her eyes widened. "Was he, was he badly hurt?"

"Paul was in a fight out in the gulf," said Mel. "He was shot in the arm, but he's out of danger now."

She tried to get out of bed. "Where is he? I have to see him!"

Maggie had come back in the room with a fresh cup of coffee. She eased Rita gently against the pillow. Mel's worried face broke into a kind smile. "He's here in this hospital, but no one's talked to him since surgery. He doesn't know about your wreck."

"Oh, Mel, please! Are you keeping anything from me?"

Mel placed his hand over hers. "Paul's got a broken shoulder and his arm was hurt. He was very weak when they brought him in, but they said I can see him a minute or so this afternoon. I'll tell him about your accident and that you're doing fine."

"What day is this?"

"Sunday. Your accident was Friday night."

"The nurse said I have a broken arm."

Maggie gently stroked Rita's cheek. "Plus a nasty bump on the head."

Rita's eyes filled with tears. "I went to New Orleans to see about a job. On my way home, it got real windy. All I remember is going off the road. When can I see Paul?"

Maggie answered softly. "When the doctors say you can, Rita. They know best. Anyway, he's on this same floor. He's close."

"Why can't I be with him now? I'm feeling better, I can look after him."

A nurse came in and put her fingers to her lips. Maggie and Mel immediately headed toward the door, Rita waving her good arm as they left.

An hour later, Mel came back to the hospital. He climbed the rear stairway to the second floor, rather than take the crowded elevator. A nurse's aide was coming down the hallway with the Sunday papers and they reached the door of Paul's room at the same time. Mel blocked the door.

"The papers are filled with things about Captain Stark," she whispered.

"There's a lot he doesn't know, Miss."

Her mouth formed an O. "He doesn't know about his wife?"

Mel smiled at the sweet little aide. "He hasn't been told yet. Tell you what, why don't you save the papers for the Captain? He'd appreciate that."

She nodded and hurried down the hallway.

Mel knocked softly at Paul's door. A nurse opened the door and looked him over. "You're Mel Wilson?" When he nodded, she opened the door wider. The captain's expecting you."

Paul was propped up with pillows, his arm bandaged and a dressing covered his left shoulder. He gave Mel a weak smile. "Hello, Mel. Where's Rita?"

"She'll be here later. How's the one-man Navy?"

"Ready to get out of this hospital." Paul shifted his weight as if testing his ability to get out of bed. "Where did you say Rita is?"

Mel sat down on the edge of the bed. His face looked very serious. "Paul, I don't want to alarm you. Rita is okay, but she was in a car accident."

Paul tried to sit up, but fell back against the pillows. "How bad is she hurt?" He looked hard at his friend. "Give it to me straight."

"She has a broken arm, a simple fracture. For a time they were afraid of a concussion, but that danger's past. She's here on this floor."

"Help me up, Mel, I can make it. I want to go to her." Paul held his right hand.

"The doctors are saying that you're both staying put a little longer. She's sleeping now, and I know you want her to rest. So just lie back and take it easy."

"Damn it, I shouldn't have left her. She's wanted me to sell the boat, get in some other line of work."

"You know you can't give up shrimping, Paul. Why not talk her into going with you on the boat? A pretty mate sure would make time pass!"

Paul managed a smile, thinking how nice that would be, but knowing better. "How long have I been here?"

"Since yesterday morning, compliments of the Coast Guard."

"The last thing I remember is sawing on that damn cable!"

Mel wanted to calm his friend as best he could, but also wanted to keep him up to speed. "When you get stronger, there'll be plenty of time for the details. The police and a Mr. Brooks are waiting to ask you lots of questions."

"I heard you calling on the radio," said Paul. "But those bastards threw my mike overboard and I couldn't answer." The machine wired to Paul started to go faster as Paul got more excited..

"I know, Paul. Oh, and Catfish and I unloaded your shrimp before daylight."

Paul smiled. "What did you think of the catch?"

"Eighty-seven boxes and a piece. You sure found the shrimp convention."

"That's why I wanted to see you and Lou when I got in Friday night. Lou knows everything, except whether my invention worked or not. Did you see anything different on the boat?"

Mel recalled seeing Paul unconscious and a dead man on the side deck. He remembered blood, a chopped-up net, and some very unusual things. "Yeah, Paul, you could say that. You mean like the air compressor and that big cage of red hose? I thought you were rigging up to build an oil platform." Mel gave a little laugh.

"Lou and I put that compressor on Monday afternoon. He had more confidence in the octopus than I had."

"The octopus?"

"My invention, Mel. That's what we call it. It's the octopus that caught those shrimp. I was hoping we could all have a party Friday night and celebrate."

"We can talk about everything tomorrow. As of right now, you've been involved in several major crimes, murder, narcotics, smuggling—and you somehow managed to wreck another vessel. The hospital is crawling with people waiting to get in here and get the scoop! After all, your boat was hijacked and you were shot, which makes you the lead story. We can talk about your invention later."

"I realize all that, Mel, and that's why I insisted on seeing you before anyone else. I hoped Lou would be with you, and Rita, too. But Mel, we caught those shrimp in three days, using that new equipment only on every other drag."

Mel was dumbfounded. "You caught shrimp with compressed air? That sure as hell is one for the books."

"Let me finish. I didn't mention it to you until I could try it out. If it didn't work, then only Lou and I would know about it. No use telling everyone you're a fool!"

"Paul, your catch should bring over forty thousand." He told him how he and Catfish had made sure it was all iced down in the cooler.

Paul thanked him. "They're way out there, Mel, real deep. I found a flat place with no coral. Like a plateau, maybe twenty feet higher than the average. There might be two hundred square miles of new fishing ground. And you make only one-hour drags, or the nets are too full to haul them in."

"You certainly proved the shrimp aren't inshore, at least not on the regular grounds. Did you know there's another bad spill in the mouth of the Mississippi?" Mel told him about the ruptured tanker. "She was in violation of three regulations," he said, ticking them off his fingers. "Defective radar; she didn't anchor in the fog; and there was no pilot aboard. They'll probably just ask the skipper not to do it again!"

"You go where I tell you, Mel, and you won't have to worry about the oil beating you there. You could put the octopus on the *Honey,* but it will be quicker to patch up my boat. While I'm laid up, you fish the *Helen* and order all the parts for your own octopus." More color was coming into Paul's face. "Find my notebook in the chart drawer; it has all the information. I've marked the seamount on the chart. Meanwhile, I'll bust outta here."

"Okay, I'll do whatever you say. But first, well, I've got some other bad news, and it's best you hear it from me."

"Rita? You're holding something back?"

"No, Paul, Rita really will be fine. You'll see that for yourself soon. It's Lou, he's gone. Friday night. Did you know he had cancer?"

Paul turned and looked out the window. He was silent for several minutes. "I didn't know. I just can't believe—why didn't he tell us?"

As he told of going to Lou's house, Mel made no mention of Brooks version of Lou's death.

"You and Catfish found him when you were looking for me?"

"That's right, but it was too late. I'm sure it was very sudden. Probably no one knew."

Paul was back on his pillow, the eagerness gone from his face. "I brought Mary Beth Claiborne into the hospital Sunday night. Do you know how she's doing?"

"You might as well know it all: She disappeared from here Tuesday morning and apparently took her own life. They found her body yesterday."

Paul's voice was a whisper. "Found her body...where?"

"Back from the dock on Beau's Island."

"My God, what's happening? Has the whole world gone crazy?"

Mel didn't answer; he didn't know what to say.

Paul became grim as he watched Mel's face. "And you're sure Rita's all right?"

"I've told you everything," said Mel. "In case you're interested, she must love you very much because she can't wait to see you."

"I shouldn't have left her alone."

"Paul, all of us have certain things we must do. You and me, we have to fish. Others have to fly planes, work in their office, whatever. Our wives, they have to put up with our absences. Lou would sure as hell want us to get the *Helen* and the *Honey* out there with your octopus, so we better think about getting on with living. There's not anything we can do now for Lou or Mary Beth."

"If I had only come in Thursday night."

"That wouldn't have helped Mary Beth. Maybe some things just have to be."

The nurse returned and Mel took Paul's hand. "I'll be back tonight. Do you feel up to meeting with this guy, Brooks, from the Treasury Department? I've already told him what I know."

"Yeah, hell, send him in."

In the hospital lobby, a man stepped in front of Mel. "I understand you saved Stark's life."

Mel got the man's face into focus: close-set eyes, the face of a rodent. He had a pencil poised over a notebook of blank paper. Mel disliked him instantly. "Then you heard wrong."

"I'm just quoting the Coast Guard; it's another angle I'm checking out."

Mel shrugged his shoulders and started to move past the reporter.

"Stark was about to lose his boat —."

Mel whirled. "That's a damn lie!"

"It's one we can print. We have a copy of the letter Stark got from the bank. It says he either pays up, or his shrimp boat goes on the auction block."

Mel's face went chalk white. A cold, hard, frightening anger spread over him. "Did you get it from the bank?" He swore to himself that Claiborne would pay for telling this crap. Ethics hell. Claiborne didn't know the meaning.

"We got our sources, captain."

Mel bit down hard, the muscles in his jaw bulged. "You print that and you'll be publishing lies."

"Now hold it, captain. We're not saying there was any deal between your friend and the underworld, but if he was pushed against the wall?"

Mel realized he was being baited, knew that silence was the best policy. He started past the rat-faced man, but the reporter again blocked his path. "Would you say Stark was being foreclosed because he stepped on some toes last year?"

Mel thought of Baton Rouge, the oil slicks and brown sludge. He saw mountains of diseased oysters and smelled the fouled gray sediment. "Tell me, you cockroach, have you ever seen a marsh weasel?"

"Can't say I have, captain. I heard Stark kept fishing without getting any shrimp, after all the other boats had tied up or left."

Mel tried sarcasm. "So he makes a deal with the mob and then wrecks their boat. How does your warped mind handle that?"

"Could be there was a falling out with his new buddies and they fought over the cut."

Mel leaned toward him, fists balled. "You dirty bastard."

The reporter kept on writing. "Yeah, yeah, cockroach, weasel, bastard: I've been called worse. I'm not saying *yet* that Stark had himself a deal."

Mel grabbed the mans jacket and screwed the cloth in his fist. He pulled the man close. "Now listen well, and I'll give you a story you can print. You want to shut up and listen?"

"You're supposed to answer *my* questions," said the reporter. His voice was taunting, but alarm was evident on his face.

Mel shook him slightly. "Your brand of muckraking reminds me of sewers. So that's what we'll talk about, sewers."

"My editor only wants to know about Stark."

"The biggest sewer in North America starts out in Minnesota as clean water, then it becomes the gut of the country, getting bigger and dirtier as it moves south. Thousands of sewers dump into it from cities, factories, any place with garbage and poison to pass along. By the time it pours out here, it's loaded with every kind of filth man can create."

"Hell, we all know about that, but no one's real interested in pollution right now."

"Well, I'll just be damned," jeered Mel. "You are pollution, that's your job, isn't it? Finding a stink to publish. So here's how to find smells that will make even you gag: Go to the state capitols and you'll find laws against killing a river, then go smell the waterways." Mel released the man.

"I got the background on Stark; I hear he was busy changing all that."

"Paul Stark asked the legislature to take action before the coastal waters are as dead as some lakes and rivers."

The reporter scowled. "Yeah, I have clips of his testimony, we know what he said."

"Did you also know that the papers didn't report it right?" Mel knew this was weak.

With a sneer, the reporter answered, "Sure, captain. The press never gives anyone a fair shake. You don't deny he was fronting for the fish and game lobby. So is he being charged with conspiracy? We understand he's under suspicion in this drug thing."

Mel clenched his fist until his knuckles went white, but didn't hit the man. Instead, he turned and walked away.

"Sure appreciate the information, captain," called out the reporter.

Mel drove toward Bonaparte. When he reached the open road, a putrid smell hit him. It was coming from the pulpwood digesters to the north. Without them, he would have smelled the faint, sweet presence of marsh, the lonesome breath of watery plains and green grass.

CHAPTER 32

Sunday night Rita was lying awake in the darkened hospital room. She was relieved when Maggie and Mel came in. They told her Paul was feeling much better and that he wasn't in much pain, but she could see for herself very soon.

Her head was no longer throbbing and the ache in her broken arm had dulled. Tomorrow she would finally talk with Paul!

Rita had cried over Lou. Not for his sake, though—he was the lucky one, no longer feeling pain or having to worry. No, she cried for Paul, who would miss his best friend so very much. And for Maggie, who would be left behind. Alone.

At the same time, she was going to miss Lou. When she went to him for money, he was always very nice and never made her feel embarrassed. He was always friendly and treated her like a lady. She tried to remember how she acted around Lou, other than flashing her phony smile and walking sexy. The truth was, during her months in Bonaparte, she had thought of him as just one more person in Hicksville. Her taste had always been for sharp, good-looking men like Tony and Duke. Whatever the case, it was too late.

The detectives would soon have their chance at her. They would have those little bells from her skirt and fingers would be pointed at her. All of them—Paul, Lou, Mel, Maggie— would have been better off if she had never come here, if they had never laid eyes on her. She was the one who, by rights, ought to be lying in that funeral home.

Rita shuddered, remembering the telephone booth and Tony's plot against her husband.

The thought caused her to freeze in sudden fear. Tony and Duke were still out there, somewhere in the night, with unfinished business. They would kill again, never giving it a second thought, and she could identify both of them. Fear tingled in her spine. Rita fingered the bell cord and thought about calling the night nurse.

How stupid she had been for falling for Tony's phony line.

Investments and nightclubs! How easy it had been, making silly Rita believe he was rich and would use his influence to help her. She had danced for him in the suite at the Royal Orleans, freaked out. "I'm so ashamed of that, Paul," she whispered to herself.

No wonder Duke had raped her.

Shame spread over her like tar and she swallowed hard, facing another bitter fact: She was the one to blame. She was the one who had spilled the beans to Tony about Bonaparte, who had given what he needed to turn his animals loose to hijack and kill. She was the one who turned her charms on Duke, who turned out to be not only a gangster, but also a rapist. Maybe he had raped Mary Beth, too, and then killed her and hid her body in the honeysuckle.

If only Paul could be saved from the knowledge that he married a stripper. And not only a stripper, but also one wanted by the police. If...if...if.

If only she had died in the accident.

Rita closed her eyes. It came as a shock that she no longer cared about herself. Not her smile, her perfect teeth, not even her beauty queen figure. Only Paul mattered now. It was Paul she was thinking about, caring about.

In the antiseptic hush of the hospital, Paul turned in his bed and thought about Rita. He wanted to go to her, say how sorry he was, that he understood why she had gone to find a job.

Lois had told him about Belle Potter broadcasting the news about the bank's letter, from the bank, and how Rita had rushed out, hurt and angry.

Paul released a heavy sigh. Instead of fighting with Hank Claiborne, he should have made certain that Mary Beth had received proper treatment.

He had neglected his wife and was too self-centered to know that his best friend was dying. He had also left a vulnerable girl to the whims of her stupid father. He had been having a ball out in his own private world, the ocean! He had been too puffed up with his own sense of importance to call Maggie and get a message to Lou. Like a spoiled kid, he wanted to surprise them! His dear friend Lou, and young Mary Beth, and Rita; they all needed him and he wasn't there.

With Lou gone, the excitement about the invention was gone as well. Would Mel be willing to take over and manage whatever future it might have? Mel had a good business head, evident when shrimping had become unprofitable and he used his property to provide a good living. He had also paid cash for the *Honey*, so there were no bank loans to get in arrears.

Paul fought to keep his mind away from the ordeal he had just suffered, from thoughts about how close he had come to having a bullet shot through his head.

CHAPTER 33

The first shock waves of national attention rocked Bonaparte on Saturday. Shortly scenes from North Point were televised. Stunned locals watched in disbelief, huddled in small groups. Cars milled around River Street until the authorities untangled them and sent them away.

By Sunday evening, the ordeal of Captain Paul Stark was burned into the awareness of the nation. Phone calls and telegrams poured into the hospital. The vice president called to wish a speedy recovery.

The ruptured tanker was no longer on the front page, even though its crude oil was spreading for miles along the coast. Investigations were under way to fix responsibility. In Beaver City and Bonaparte, the drama was growing like a firestorm and being fed by the media. There was no man or woman not personally acquainted with the good captain; no one who would hesitate describing the trawler, Beau's Island, Point LaCroix, or any other item needing clarification.

In follow-up coverage, the media played up the angle of the simple fisherman pitted against the powerful gangster overlords. Good and evil in mortal combat, good winning despite impossible odds.

Paul Stark was an overnight hero, the epicenter of a cyclone that swirls around any individual suddenly thrust into the harsh limelight by the working media.

CHAPTER 34

The threat of rain hung in the humid dawn as Mel drove from Beaver City.

Catfish was back on the *Helen S.* The *Honey L.* was back on the ways at the boatyard. The fish house was securely locked, although empty without Lou. The property now belonged to Paul, a fact that Paul had not been told. Judge Black felt it best to wait a few days before revealing the contents of the will.

Men had worked on the trawler, scrubbing away bloodstains and replacing glass. A new microphone and transmitter were back in operation and nets were expected soon from Beaver City.

On Sunday night, while townspeople were at church, the instructions that were found in Lou Fisher's old half-burned folder were carried out. At a few minutes after midnight, a darkened hearse backed up to the basement door at the university. When the driver returned to the funeral home, he carried with him a signed receipt attesting:

> Received on this eighth day of April 2003, one corpse, said to be the remains of Louis Fisher, age fifty-three, delivered to this institution in accordance with the written and signed authority of the deceased. Said remains to be used only for the advancement of medical science.'

Mel called the hospital. When he heard Paul's voice, he smiled.

"Hey, Paul, how's our hero? Pulse, fever, pretty nurses?" Mel was relieved when Paul laughed and asked about Catfish. "Trotting around in his new tennis shoes," said Mel. "Still looking for Moonbeam."

Mel mentioned nothing about the black hair in the storage freezer. "Let's get him a puppy this time."

"Good, and one with seagoing legs!"

Mel reported on the trawler repairs. "Judge Black sent all your papers and drawings to a patent lawyer in Washington," he said. "He got them from Lou last week."

Paul was silent for a moment. "I dreamed about Lou," he said. "Told him we needed help controlling the octopus. Then I woke up and remembered something Lou had said."

"I don't have the answers," Mel said.

"Not to worry, here's what we can do for now. Lou came up with a gadget that controls the air pulses. It works with another gismo that's installed at the end of the cable, next to the octopus. These are precision machined parts, really the brains of the monster."

"It won't operate without them?"

"Right. We can talk about that later."

After hanging up, Mel looked at the girlie calendars on the office wall. How many times had he and Paul kidded Lou about his *art*, as he called it. "This is Patricia, and over here is Diane. This comely wench is Angela."

In the early afternoon, the truck from the freezing plant hauled the shrimp out of the cooler. The check written to Paul was just over forty thousand dollars.

Only minutes later, a workboat from Beaver City pulled alongside the dock. "We got the doors here," announced the pilot. "Had to cut them cables with the torch."

Mel wondered how they managed to use a cutting torch in the breakers, but said nothing. He swung the hoist boom over the workboat and lifted the doors onto the deck. "What about the bridles, Jim?"

"Making them up now, Captain. They'll be finished before me and Jess come over tomorrow to hang the net."

At the hospital, Danny was surprising Rita with a visit.

"Danny! Danny Lapere! Who's running the Fish and Game office?"

"Hey Rita, you're more gorgeous than ever!"

Danny always made her feel good. "You're about the last person I expected to see just now."

"The department sent me down to see if the celebrity needed anything. Like a mess of fried fish."

"Celebrity? Do you mean Paul?'

"Who else? The whole country's caught Paul Stark fever. Young girls are wearing Paul Stark T-shirts."

"Have you seen him, Danny? How does he look?"

Danny seemed confused, starting to point towards Paul's door. "You mean you haven't seen him? He's right down the hall!"

"I get to visit this morning."

"If I had a sexy dame this close, I'd pick up the damn bed and move in here."

"Then you've seen him?"

"Not yet. I wanted a few words with his fascinating wife first."

"Very sweet of you, Danny."

Danny gestured toward her arm. "How did it happen?"

"My car thought it was a plane and went airborne. Almost made it across the marsh."

"I see they gave you a pretty fancy headdress. You look like an exotic princess."

Rita touched the gauzy beehive. "It was a rough landing. I hope you're not here to get Paul to testify again."

"Paul's the best witness we have. I suppose you heard about the oil tanker."

"I heard, but they haven't let me see the papers. I'm supposed to rest my eyes. That means no husband, no radio, no TV."

"Danny, do you—do your people—really want to help Paul?"

Danny leaned closer and took her hand. "What is it you want for him, Rita? You'll never know if you don't ask."

"Paul won't like my saying this, but it's the damn bank. They're going to take his boat and sell it to the highest bidder. That would be just awful!"

Danny laughed. "You really go for that big clown."

"He's my husband, in case you forgot."

"So you want us to go to bat for him, maybe pay off the bank?"

"Danny, he's hurt, and he's so square. Someone has to be on his side for a change. He never even told me about the bank, didn't want me to worry. I've been no help to him at all."

"I'll see what we can do, but I'm not promising. I've been trying to get in to see the elusive bank president, Claiborne, but he's not available."

"Did you know that his daughter's missing? She was here, in this hospital." Danny looked away. For a long moment, he said nothing. "Rita, she isn't missing. They found her body on Beau's Island."

Rita felt paralyzed and every bruise on her body suddenly hurt. "Do they know what happened? What caused her death?"

"According to the papers, she died from an overdose."

"Are you sure it wasn't the gangsters who killed her?"

"No question about what happened. She left the hospital to meet her boyfriend, Johnny Cameron. While they were driving around, she managed to eat a handful of his pills. She overdosed and he panicked and hid her on the island."

Rita closed her eyes. Now the bells wouldn't mean anything and the police would not be coming with questions. She spoke, but her voice was directed to no one in particular. "I want to go home with Paul," she said, then opened her eyes and looked directly at her visitor. "Danny, what can you do about the bank? I want to know right now."

Danny touched her hand and smiled. "Tell you what, the government has money to help fishermen. I'll go see the people in New Orleans, but I can't promise anything."

"Oh, Danny, I just know you can do it!"

"We'll see."

She frowned. "There's something else that's bothering me. Not for myself but, you see, Paul never knew that I..."

"...was an exotic dancer?" Danny laughed. "And a damn good one at that."

"I never want him to know, but I have a real problem. " She told him what she heard in New Orleans about Frenchy's, how the fat man was in prison for blackmail.

Danny was beginning to smile. "Someone's handed you a line of bull, kid. I saw the fat man last week and he tried to hustle me again."

"Oh, Danny, are you sure?"

"I'll take you there, you can see for yourself."

Relief washed over her like a warm bath. "No thanks," she said. "I never want to see that place again."

"Then take my word for it. The fat man's still running the joint.."

"Danny, what did you come to see Paul about?"

He laughed. "A hundred million people know the story about Paul, how one brave man stood up against organized crime."

"So you want to get him back to Baton Rouge and get into more hot water?"

"Rita, the fishing industry always gets the short end of the stick around Washington. If Paul spoke up, lots of people would listen." When Rita didn't respond, he went on. "I'm talking about all sorts of things. Like tanker captains who wash out their bilges wherever they please, and stream pollution, and inedible fish. Paul could really shake things up."

Yes, she thought, people would listen to him now. "He'll probably say no, Danny. He got his fingers burned last time. Why didn't you people make the papers print the truth?"

"We tried, but all we got were promises and double talk. The story got cold before we could do anything."

"I'll make a deal with you," said Rita, trying to sit up straighter in the bed. "You get Paul off the hook with that crummy bank, and I promise to help you with your deal."

He stood up, smiling. "Deal," he said. "You'll be hearing from Danny Boy soon." He moved toward the door and then turned back. "Laissez les bon temps rouler," he announced and walked out.

"Yeah, let the good times roll," laughed Rita, waving as he disappeared into the hall.

A nurse came in. "Mrs. Stark, the people who towed your car dropped off your suitcase and purse." An orderly carried in her belongings, placed the suitcase near the bed, and handed Rita her purse. She had makeup in it, but it shouldn't have felt this heavy.

Then she remembered the gun.

It was time to see Paul. The nurse combed her hair and helped her apply makeup. She would not go in a wheel chair and insisted on walking. She leaned on the nurse until she entered her husband's room, smiling. He returned her smile and she felt tears falling on her cheek. She went directly to his bed. Her hand found his and she lowered her eyes from his gaze.

"Paul, oh Paul..." The words weren't there. Only tears.

He tenderly touched the cast on her arm. "Rita, where've they been hiding you? Are you really all right?" His eyes moved lovingly over her. She had never looked more beautiful to him.

"I want to be here," she said. "With you." The truth was so simple. She searched his face. "Do you hurt much?"

"Not now, not since they told me you were coming."

She ran a hand along his arm and squeezed his hand.

They both laughed and time passed quickly. When she saw that he was falling asleep, she kissed her fingers and placed them on his lips.

When Paul awoke, a nurse was there holding a thermometer. "What's going on? You just *took* my temperature."

"You fell asleep, captain. The telephone chimed and she answered. Paul motioned for the receiver, but the nurse moved away. "I'm so sorry," she told the caller. "The Captain is indisposed. Why not call back in, say, a month or two?" And then she hung up.

"What was that all about?" Paul noticed the nurse's dark eyes and her sweet face. He thought how pretty Rita would look in a white uniform.

The nurse fluffed his pillow. "Some terrible woman with a magazine—the kind that nice people don't read—wants our captain for its centerfold!" Her eyes grew wide. "Oh, I bet she thought I was Mrs. Stark!" Blushing, she left the room and nearly bumped into the doctor.

"I wouldn't pinch *that* hard, Paul," said the man, picking up the thermometer.

Paul smiled. "I didn't lay a hand on her, doc, I promise." His faced turned serious. "When can I see Rita again?"

The doctor was feeling Paul's pulse. "It's not every week we get to play nursemaid to a superstar. If we're lucky, the women will calm down after you leave."

"Did you hear my question?" he prodded. "When can Rita come back and visit me again?

"Only thirty minutes today, sorry."

"Thirty minutes, like hell!"

"All in good time, Paul, all in good time. We still have business to do with that shoulder."

The next day, Rita walked in and, leaning over, kissed him on the lips. "I'm taking up nursing," she said. "It's the only way I can compete."

Paul reaches up for another kiss, and Rita gave Paul the lingering kiss he has craved for a very long time. "Very interesting, because I just happen to be in the market for a live-in, round-the-clock, beautiful nurse."

"After that, captain, I plan an ocean voyage." She pushed hair off his forehead. "Several trips in fact."

"The Louisiana coast is nice this time of year."

"I hear the stars are something else!"

He squeezed her hand. "Like the stars in those beloved eyes! Do you really mean it, Rita?"

"Yes, I do. We're going to make up for lost time. Besides," she added, eyes twinkling. "I don't think you and Catfish have been eating properly."

Paul nodded. "We could use a cabin boy. Maybe I could teach him how to cook."

"And get a first mate. Me!"

Again the time passed quickly. When Rita walked out, Paul was smiling, tears of joy shining in his eyes. He loved her so!

Mel called and said that the weather outlook was good and the *Helen* would be ready to leave early Friday morning. His brother was going along as a crewman. "Sonny's a good boy, Paul. Not only on deck, but also in the engine room. And he can keep his mouth shut."

The octopus would need bright young men like Sonny. The new technicians, Paul thought. "What time do you think you'll get away?"

"About three in the morning; it's a long run. Sonny has to go to New Orleans to pick up a shipment at the bus station. When he gets back here, we'll be ready to shove off."

"Have we covered everything, Mel? I've been sleeping so much—"

"If we haven't, it'll be on the list this time tomorrow. Lois found a puppy for Catfish and we named him Beau Brummell, 'cause he's such a classy little dude."

"Great, and thank Lois for bringing Catfish to the hospital. As we speak, he's in Rita's room, but his eyes are asking to escape the hospital and return to the sea. He's not alone with that thought."

CHAPTER 35

Law enforcement agencies issued a joint statement announcing that the body of a man tentatively identified as Richard "Duke" Anderson was discovered in a deserted barn, along with a rented station wagon and a stolen van. Anderson was linked to the murder of Louis Fisher, near Bonaparte, the dead man's prints matching those found on a bottle in Fisher's house. A small boat, the tender from the *Patty Two,* along with an outboard motor, was found in the van, and bullet marks were found on the boat. The dead man was believed to be involved with a person or persons who had escaped from the burning yacht, after shooting Captain Paul Stark. Other arrests were expected in connection with these murders and for other possible violations.

On Wednesday, one of the nurses delivered a telegram to Rita. "Great news my end Stop Must see you and Paul Stop be there ten Thursday." The sender was Danny.

Rita read the message several times. *Paul will keep his boat!* Thank God!

Rita awakened during the night to find Belle Potter standing there, her head in the doorway. "Hello, Belle," she said, not frightened by the woman's presence.

"Ye's need anything, Miz Stark?"

"Come in and turn on the light. Help me open this suitcase."

Rita found the envelope with the confession. She showed it to Belle and then slowly tore it into pieces. "Tell Joe and Troy they're off the hook."

Tears formed in the big woman's eyes.

"Belle, we've had enough trouble and killing around here."

Belle stood there, wringing her liver-spotted hands. She retreated, sobbing in great gulps.

"You can go home Saturday morning, Rita."

"Doctor, what about Paul?"

"Sunday or Monday, but you have to keep him away from that shrimp boat until his shoulder heals."

"I'll do that, I promise. And when he starts fishing again, I'm going with him."

The doctor shook his head. "Lucky stiff! I wouldn't bother to fish."

"Doctor!"

"You better watch out. Half the nurses are madly in love with the captain."

"What's wrong with the other half?"

"Nothing, they're in love with me." The doctor left, laughing.

Paul wouldn't need any other nursing, Rita thought. She'd take care of him twenty-four hours a day.

Rita was sitting on Paul's bed when Danny arrived. "Two visits in one week," said Paul. "I thought you guys had work to do."

Danny greeted them both and dragged a chair to the bedside. "God, she's prettier than ever!" He turned to Paul. "Why wasn't it me instead of you? I found her."

"Your generous heart. You not only got me a wife, but a deckhand working for board."

Danny pretended to be amazed. "Rita... heading shrimp! The fever is causing your mind to play tricks!"

"She may make a few changes. You know, curtains for the wheelhouse and monogrammed towels for the head."

"Hell, Paul, you wouldn't have to stick around here fishing, you could keep on going."

"Have you two oddballs finished planning my life?" asked Rita.

Paul looked at Danny. "Did she come up with you?"

Danny studied Rita. "Never laid eyes on her before this very minute."

They laughed and Danny opened his briefcase. "I'm all choked up, being this close to someone so famous. Did you know they have a new name for River Street? They renamed it Stark Mad Boulevard."

"Hear that, Rita, Danny's kissed the blarney stone. And all this time I thought he was half Creole and half hush puppy."

Danny took out a legal size document. "I need your signature on these papers, Paul."

"Some kind of bureaucratic trick? I won't sign." Paul's high spirit showed in the big smile on his face.

Danny glanced at Rita. "Due solely to the efforts on your behalf, by your sexy and crafty first mate, the government is going to guarantee a certain mortgage on a certain shrimp trawler, documented as the *Helen S.*" Paul took the papers, read them quickly, and turned to his wife. "So this is what you were doing in New Orleans!"

She was astonished. "No, no, Paul, I didn't. I just asked Danny to do something if he could, but I thought you'd be angry if you knew…" She held a tissue to her eyes.

"Paul, it was *all* her idea. You don't even pay interest until you get back on your feet."

She watched Paul as he turned his gaze toward the window. She laughed nervously. "Danny, he has these spells of not talking; it's a habit he picked up from Catfish." She didn't know what else to say.

Paul looked back at them. "Where do I sign?"

"With that half of the business over, we can talk about the other half." Danny looked at Rita.

"Oh yes, Paul." It came out in a rush. "They need you. That tanker is still leaking oil and no one knows better than you what that will do to the fishing waters. You have to finish what you started in Baton Rouge."

Paul watched her face, as she kept her bargain with Danny.

"Lapere, are you thinking what I am?"

"Yup. Who could resist that appeal? That high voltage charm? Those fluttering eyelashes?"

A nurse who had just come in stuck a thermometer in Paul's mouth just as he was agreeing to do what he could. That is, he laughingly mumbled, as soon as he was well and able to travel.

Danny gathered the papers. "Meanwhile, I'll book Rita for a few speaking engagements. Nearby, of course. She'll get paid with chicken salad and lukewarm tea."

Rita couldn't believe they would want her to make speeches. "I'll make some notes for you," said Paul, smiling at his wife.

That afternoon, Maggie, Mel, and Lois came in. "Greeks bearing gifts," said Mel, brandishing an ice bucket. Mel opened the champagne and filled glasses. "Here's to the good captain and the captain's lady."

Paul held up his glass. "To our very special friends." As they drank to their toasts, each felt pain for the one who wasn't there, Lou. Grief was private, not to be intruded upon. The friends kept their thoughts and drank in silence.

When everyone was gone, Rita took Paul's hand. "I really didn't have anything to do with getting those papers, Paul. I can't let you think that."

"Then hold me responsible. Lois told me about old Belle Potter at the beauty salon."

"What did she say?"

"That when Belle was sounding off about the foreclosure; that you told her off and rushed out."

"How did Lois know?"

"Bonaparte's a small town, Rita. A friend of hers was having her hair done and heard it all."

"Darling, we're going to have to find time to talk. Even before you go home. I have things to tell you, important things you don't know."

"And I have things on my mind, Rita. I might even give up fishing, if that's what you want."

"No, you can't do that, but I would like to go with you on your boat. That is, if…"

"If what?"

"Oh, Paul! You won't love me anymore when you hear what I have to say."

"You want to tell me you were a stripper, and that you worked a few nights at a dive operated by a guy who once worked on a shrimp boat? That is, until he got too fat."

Rita thought she was going to faint. "You *knew* and you never mentioned, never said *anything!*"

"Of course I knew." He was laughing.

"I've been so ashamed. I wanted to tell you. I didn't know what was going on at Frenchy's, that he was promoting prostitution on the side. I would have no part of it. I swear. I was always more of a dancer then a stripper. I mean, it was the dancing and the music I loved."

"Rita, I also knew that you were somewhat past your twenty-fourth birthday and that you were quite a little schemer. Danny never had any idea how hard I'd fall for his Stag Night Sensation."

Her hand flew to her mouth. "You knew about that?"

"Knew about it! Hell, I was there, only you didn't see me across all those bald heads." He paused. "And I must say, I sure liked what I saw, which was almost everything."

"Paul Stark, how could you? All this time you let me think that you thought that I was a lady?" Suddenly she was crying and her face was pressed against his hand.

He raised her face and looked into her eyes. "I knew you had a rough life after your mother died. I also knew about your no-good stepfather, but I believed in a foolish, beautiful way you were hiding a good person underneath that lovely shell. I was willing to settle for either one. You weren't getting any gilt-edged bargain package yourself. I didn't tell you about my problems back home. The car was a bribe, because I thought I might lose you. Hell Rita, I'm just a shrimp fisherman."

"You must have used your boat payment money to buy the car! And all this time I thought the only thing you cared about was your shrimp boat. I was jealous of that damn boat and didn't even realize it! I'm so ashamed. I feel so stupid."

"Don't ever feel ashamed again, not ever! And you are a long way from being stupid. Look at me, Rita. There were a hundred times when I knew I was a failure, that the invention wouldn't work, that I would lose you. I learned things about myself. It was my love for you, and Lou's faith, that kept me going. Everything might have gone the other way. I'm the same person, no better and no worse. There's a fine line between a bastard and a hero. A gamble paid off, so suddenly I'm a hero! If I had failed…"

"I've not been any help, when you needed it most," she said. "I've been selfish, just awful, but I'll make it up to you."

He pulled her closer with his good arm. "Do you have any idea how you look when you're asleep? I've watched your face by the hour and loved every moment. When you move, when you're angry, when you smile, whatever you do, I can't get enough of just seeing you and being glad you're not off in a distance. The very thought of you makes my heart race. When I look at you, I melt."

Her eyes searched his. "Paul, other men—well, to begin with, they never said any of those things to me. I was someone they wanted to…I guess I hated them for trying so hard. Most of my life was that way. You were different."

"No, I'm the one who fell in love with you. I had the same things on my mind, along with something else. Like having kids, if you wanted them, too."

"You would want to have kids with me, even knowing all the things I've done?"

His fingers were on her lips. "We'll never mention the past again. Nothing you could ever do or say will make me stop loving my Rita!"

"I'll be a good wife, Paul. Now, I think I know how."

"Suppose we buy Beau's Island and get a house started?" He proudly showed her the check Mel had gotten for his shrimp, and told her how well the invention had worked. How the invention would give them the means to build the beautiful plantation she had always wanted.

Rita's eyes became misty as she envisioned her beautiful plantation surrounded with blooming magnolias and climbing roses. They would be white roses. The sultry salt-water breeze would wave to her as it danced among her flowers. She and Paul would have children. First, a little girl. She would call her Jean. Maybe her second name would be Elaine. Jean Elaine. Had a nice jingle to it. Paul would want a son to carry on the business. He would be tall and strong like Paul. And smart. She would call him Jaxon. There was nothing someone named Jaxon couldn't do. Rita was startled out of her daydream by someone calling her name.

"Rita. Rita. Have I lost you already? Where are you, anyway?"

CHAPTER 36

Thursday afternoon, Mel called Ed Brooks. "I'm going out on the *Helen*," he said. "I expect to be gone several days. Have you seen the papers?"

"I have, and they're making a legend of your friend. In my opinion, it's an honor well deserved."

"Paul's being made into a law-and-order hero. Everyone's laughing at the drug peddling mob."

"We need more people like him, people willing to fight back. Private citizens who will stand up and be counted."

"Bullshit!" exploded Mel. "I've been keeping up with the circus in the press and they're acting like he's a one-man anticrime wave. Paul's not a crime fighter, he's a shrimper."

"Maybe I shouldn't say this, but the public won't allow Paul to stick to his knitting, whether he likes it or not. We hear he's going to do some television shows. That should do some good."

"Good for what? A couple more drug busts?"

"He's agreed to talk about pollution enforcement. It has nothing to do with narcotics trafficking."

"I'm afraid the interviewers won't let him spend much time on a topic as dull as oil spills. They'll ask him questions about the crime, which won't help our cause at all."

Mel squared his shoulders and forced himself to relax. "I know you mean well," he said, "but you don't get the point. Paul took one hell of a chance out there, and not because he hated the mob, but because they tried to grab his boat and force him into something he'd have no part of. There's a big difference between the man I know and the Superman created by the media. "

"Mel, everyone, including our department and law enforcement people all over the country, needs a few Paul Starks to help put some backbone in others. If he inspires just a few of them to fight back, to go to some helpless victim's aid and show a little personal courage, then we'll all be better off. The people of the media know this, they know that Paul is good copy, but also a man of courage."

"Perhaps it's as you say, but Paul is injured and helpless right now and the public is laughing at the mob. Did you see Leno last night? I don't think the mob will take these insults lying down."

"You're wrong there. Organized crime operates like a business nowadays; crimes of passion are the old way. Bribery and non-violence is the game now and the big bosses want as little visibility as possible. I don't think Paul is in any danger."

"I'm still worried about his safety while he's laid up. I'm hoping you can send some of your men over, in case they put out a contract on Paul or his wife."

"I wish I could do that," said the agent. "We just don't have the manpower, so I suggest you ask the local police to assign a man to the hospital."

"I've already talked to the chief in Beaver City and he's having the patrol check the hospital two or three times a night. That's not enough; I want someone outside Paul's door day and night."

Brooks promised to do what he could and rang off.

Cap'n Stark's room was already jammed with flowers and more were in the service room. They were expensive cut flowers arranged in fancy vases. In the office were wastebaskets of telegrams and letters waiting to be opened. Belle, in her dirty old apron and mop pail, tried to imagine how it would feel to get flowers, or even mail. "Why'd anybody in his right senses write to me?" she mumbled.

At two-ten in the morning, it felt good to sit and rest her feet while she unpacked her lunch. The coffee in the machine was lukewarm. Nelly Sutton, looking sour, put down her clean-up tray and joined Belle.

Belle nodded. She had her own troubles and was not interested in Nelly's whining complaints.

A Beaver City policeman came through and went down the stairs.

By two-thirty, Belle was back on the second floor. She first sensed, and then saw, a man slightly crouched and moving quickly, headed for the captain's room. As the figure was about to enter it, Belle saw the flash of metal. Instinctively, she threw her bucket of soapy water as hard as she could at the stranger.

Someone else was in the hallway.

There was a shot.

Belle rushed towards Paul's room, holding her mop like a baseball bat.

Minutes later, the world outside the hospital was lit by a bright flash to the west, followed by a distant rumble of sounds not unlike thunder.

CHAPTER 37

S omeone else would have to run the power sander. Sonny still waited at the bus station in New Orleans. When the package arrived, he signed for it and drove away. It was a warm night, with only a pale haze of clouds high in the moon's glimmer.

It would be a good morning to leave for the gulf. By sunup, he guessed he, Mel, and *Helen S.* would be past the North Point beacon.

The car was running well. She was old, but the engine had never been hurt. He had the motor fine-tuned so that it responded smoothly to the gas pedal. Hell, if he had a new body to put on the chassis, he would have almost a new car. With no payments!

It was one o'clock in the morning when Sonny left the silent streets of New Orleans and reached the bayou country. The high tide glistened in layers in the marsh, and in the silver dark waters of the roadside canal. He drove with the windows down, filling his lungs with the sweet warm smell of sea marshes, slowing down only for villages and crossroads.

He was glad to be going out again on a trawler. The boatyard had been good to him—good pay and steady work—but the yard was no place to spend the rest of his life. Someday, he knew, he would have his own boat, like Paul and his brother. The shrimp would come back. And how many times had he told people about the sardines off California, how they had disappeared and then, as if by magic, returned? That's how it would be with the shrimp. They'll be back!

He knew big steel trawlers like the *Helen* and the *Honey* would eventually have to leave unless shrimping got better. The hope of better fishing was important to his future plans. He hoped that the rumor heard at the yard was true, that the *Helen S.* had brought in a big load of prawns the same night it was hijacked. The word had come from New Orleans. Mel hadn't said and he hadn't asked. You didn't ask such questions unless you had a boat of your own. Maybe the shrimp were already back! An expert like Captain Stark wouldn't keep going out, week after week, if it were otherwise. Everyone knew Captain Stark was about the best shrimper on the Gulf Coast. You wouldn't get any argument about that.

It was a real honor to be the one picked to go out on the *Helen* while Captain Stark was laid up, and to be crewing on the most famous shrimp boat in the whole cockeyed country! He thought about the dope smugglers and was glad he would be on board with Mel, just in case they wanted to try something again.

Shrimp people from all over were talking about how Stark rigged the doors. He had been listening to the captains around the yard, as they killed time waiting for their boats to be repaired.

"Way I make it, he had to shorten the bottom leg of the bridle. Like so," and diagrams were drawn in the sand.

"Suppose you did rig them doors like you say. Then how about getting them to come up at the split second, so that cross cable hung in them struts and wheels? That sure took some sweet-ass timing!"

"He sure as hell had only one shot at it. Man, I'd of given a week's catch just to see the face of that fancy sports captain when he was running down the *Helen* and his shafts just up and wrung off."

Many people had stopped in the yard since the hijacking, a good number of them shrimpers traveling between Florida and Texas. Some of them had left get-well cards at the hospital.

Sonny liked to be around shrimp people. They talked of boats and engines, about storms and adventures, and they dreamed of far-off places. As long as he could remember, he had planned one day to have his own boat.

On this trip, he would be running the trawler most of the time; Mel would take her down the river in the darkness. There were things a captain had to do himself. When they were safely in the bay and on course, he would be asked to take the wheel. They would drink coffee in the dark wheelhouse and talk about many things.

Offshore, they would take turns; on the drags, they'd be on the autopilot. He would begin training the puppy brought along for Catfish. It was important to get a dog started early. Beau Brummell sure was one cute puppy. Smart, too.

In Beaver City, Sonny turned down the side street and unlocked the yard gate. He left the shipment in the shop and relocked the gate. When he drove past the clock on the bank building, it was two-thirty.

He guessed he'd reach the dock twenty minutes before he was expected, and in plenty of time to help shove off.

Sonny was looking at the steady red lights, as well as the flashing one on the radio tower, when there appeared a white and red flare on the horizon. It made him think of ground-level lightning and he felt an instant of almost detached curiosity. What could cause such a light? An instant later, the car was buffeted as the shock wave swept past. Only then did he hear the thunderclap from the explosion. Alarm gripped him. He stepped hard on the gas and the car leapt forward. Headlights approached and a car sped past, but he hardly noticed.

Sonny was still two miles away from Bonaparte Seafoods, but he could see that it was on fire. The dock was burning along its full length. He raced closer, horrified and unbelieving, and saw the superstructure of a shrimp trawler leaning toward the marsh, flames shooting higher than its mast. As he watched, its metal framework fell into the river.

It had to be the *Helen S.*, the only shrimp boat at the dock.

His tires were screaming as he braked at the shell driveway and turned off River Street. In front of him was a wall of orange flame. In the marsh and alongside the drive, jagged pieces of hot metal hissed in the tidewater, sending up plumes of steam. The headlights penciled into the billowing smoke as he stopped the car and jumped out. He rushed toward the fish house until the heat drove him back. The old building wore a crown of flames, but underneath there was no fire. He could see the pilings, black columns against the red-black shimmer of the river.

People were streaming from River Street and several were pushing his car. "Gotta clear this drive for the fire trucks," one man shouted, his hands on the hood of Sonny's car. Sonny quickly jumped in his car, released the brake and backed up closer to the water, jumped out, and again ran towards the fire.

Someone yelled, "It's Cap'n Stark's boat, done blowed sky high!"

Another hoarse voice screamed "Great Gawd Awmighty, it's Catfish! There's parts of him all over the place!"

Sonny leaned over the water and vomited. *Mel would be in the fire!* He started closer toward the flames when someone grabbed his shoulder. "Are you crazy? Git back!"

The fire truck was coming from Beaver City. Far up the highway their beacons were ruby pinpoints of light, even before the sirens were heard. People along the street pointed at the approaching headlights and backed away from the driveway. The first fire truck skidded as it left the pavement and plunged down the drive, sliding to a stop. A fireman was pulling a large black hose into the marsh.

Someone was calling to the fireman "You better get more'n two trucks in here!"

"They ain't got but them two trucks!" shouted another faceless voice.

Firemen from the lead fire truck, somber-faced men in helmets and rain capes, dragged a hose toward the burning walls. Soon, a great streaming arm of water arched over the flames. Fans of water streamed from the smoking column, running down into the fire as the whine of the pumper rose above the fire's noise. The flames rose no higher as the firemen crouched and inched forward, challenging the fire and the heat.

Only then did the crowd begin to relax, as if knowing that their side would win out over the flames.

Sonny found himself on the edge of River Street, numb, and dazed. He heard the woman before he saw her, then others pressed him in her direction as they tried to get closer.

She stood half a head taller than the rest, her coarse face working with emotion and reddened by the fire glow. Her lips were moving, but Sonny could not hear the words. He sensed the sudden panic extending out from the big woman as her hysteria communicated itself into the fear, and thrill flooded minds of the townspeople.

Then he began hearing her.

"I seen 'um a-creeping down the hall with that knife in his hand, long as yer arm, and..."

"Goddammit Belle, tell us what happened!"

"... there in the hospital, while he was a'sleepin', I seen 'um at Cap'n Stark's door and I throwed my bucket down the hall smack at 'um!"

"She shot 'um, Miz Rita did, right over her man's head, and I dragged 'um and his fancy red shirt from the Cap'ns room out in the hallway. He was dead 'fore he ever hit the floor!"

"Who, Belle, who did she shoot dead?"

"Musta been the guy 'bout the drugs who twas a tryn to kill our Cap'n." He musta been in cahoots with the mob guy what blowed up the cap'n's boat."

Sonny felt a hand on his arm. Turning, he almost fell to the ground. Standing there was Mel! Sonny put his arms around his big brother and cried. Mel was shouting to Sonny that the invention was safe, and so were Paul and Rita. It seemed to Sonny that everyone was yelling at once. Sonny just wanted to cry with relief that his big brother Mel was OK.

Belle's voice seemed to reach an even higher pitch. "And that knife, it jest missed Cap'n Stark. He was outta that bed quick as lightning, bending over Miz Stark on the floor!"

"Did she get hurt Belle?"

"No, praise the Lord! The pore little thing jest fainted dead away."

Sonny and Mel turned and walked away, as the big woman continued to tell the people of Bonaparte the latest about the shrimp captain and his woman.